MW01505684

# AFTER THE END

A NOVEL

# BARBARA ABEL

Translated from the French
by Natasha Lehrer

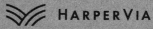

HarperVia

An Imprint of HarperCollinsPublishers

harpercollins.com

FIRST HARPERVIA PAPERBACK PUBLISHED IN 2025

Designed by Yvonne Chan
Illustration on page iii: © Nubefy/Shutterstock

Library of Congress Cataloging-in-Publication Data has been applied for.

ISBN 978-0-06-330635-6

25 26 27 28 29  LBC  5 4 3 2 1

# AFTER THE END

*Behind the respectable façades are secret gardens stretching from either side of the hedge, which conceal, beneath all the detritus of our tormented lives, the corpse of a past we want only to forget.*

# PROLOGUE

It is an ordinary Monday evening just like any other. Down at the police station in a small suburb of Paris, the duty officer Didier Parmentier is flicking through the newspaper. It's been a quiet evening so far: one complaint about a late-night disturbance, even though it's not even 10 p.m.; a report of a lost wallet; a fight at a nearby bar. It looks like it's going to be another long night with only the crackle from the scanner and the periodic comings and goings of colleagues on patrol for company. No matter: Didier has it all planned out. He folds up the newspaper, switches on his iPad, begins a game of solitaire. Just to warm up. Then he'll get down to business: Tetris, Max Awesome, and Angry Birds Friends. Later he'll log on to Facebook to check what's going on, maybe chat with a virtual contact or a real-life friend.

The sound of the phone ringing makes him jump. He looks up from his iPad and picks up.

"You've reached the police. How may I help?"

On the other end of the line, he hears a woman speaking very quietly, somewhere between a whisper and a gasp. Her voice is shaking. She sounds petrified.

1

"Please, you have to come quick! I heard a noise downstairs . . ." she begins the second Didier has finished his formulaic introduction.

She pauses, wary, as though listening out for something. She sounds genuinely afraid, her voice a whisper, choked with fear. A gulp of terror. It sounds like she's trying to be as discreet as possible for fear of being heard. Behind the icy timbre of dread, her breathing is ragged and panicky.

Didier can hear the urgency in her voice, how desperate she is to be heard, believed, and reassured.

"I'm right here, madame. I'm listening. What seems to be the problem?"

"You have to come, right away. I can hear a noise downstairs. Someone's broken in. I'm pretty sure it's my neighbor . . ."

"Your neighbor? Have you been having issues?"

"Please, I beg you, don't leave me here on my own! I think she's come through the yard. Through the back door. She hates me. She's threatened me a few times already. I think she might actually want to get rid of me."

"Try to stay calm, madame, we'll be there right away. I need your name and address."

The woman gives him her details, almost succumbing to full-blown panic when Didier asks her to spell out her surname. He tries to be reassuring, urges her to remain calm, promises a patrol car will be there in no time.

"Please, please hurry, I beg you! And if I don't open the front door, break it down!" she whispers, her voice hoarse with fear.

Didier is about to offer to stay on the line until his colleagues arrive, when the line is suddenly cut. Right away he radios all the necessary information with instructions to get there as quickly as possible.

"What was the reason for the call?" an officer asks over the radio.

"Some kind of neighbor dispute. Sounds serious."

# CHAPTER
# 1

**Several weeks earlier**

For the third time that morning, Tiphaine went into Milo's room, quietly and without knocking. She planted herself at the foot of his bed and, in an irritated tone of voice, addressed the pillow beneath which the teenager had buried his head.

"It's almost noon! It really is time to get up now. Fix yourself something to eat, and then get down to work. Your exams start tomorrow."

The total lack of response that followed this command drew an exasperated sigh from her.

"Now!" she said sharply.

An irritable grunt escaped from the bottom of the bed, beneath the quilt. Puzzled, Tiphaine picked up the pillow and saw, instead of a head, two feet. Rolling her eyes, she turned to address the other end of the bed.

"Can you hear me, Milo?"

"Mmmmh . . ."

"Listen to me, if you have to repeat the year for a second time . . ."

"Okay, okay, I'm getting up . . ."

Somewhat surprised he was giving in so easily, Tiphaine hesitated a moment then perched expectantly on the edge of the desk. After a few seconds, a head finally emerged from beneath the quilt and looked at her blearily.

"What are you doing?" Milo muttered.

"I'm waiting."

"Waiting for what?"

"For you to get up."

His face froze for a split second as if the neurons inside were struggling to make the connection.

"I told you I'm getting up."

"I heard you. Now I want you to do it."

More silence.

"Pain in the ass . . ." he muttered, slinking back under the covers.

"Don't speak to me like that, Milo!"

Tiphaine heaved a sigh; verbal confrontation was a direct line to a full-blown fight, and she didn't have the heart for another one right now. Milo was fifteen. The age of rebellion and for getting into all kinds of trouble. She couldn't possibly let him lounge around in bed any longer: his exams began the following day, and it was pretty clear his priorities were not the same as hers.

Tiphaine got to her feet, weighing up the pros and cons of the idea taking shape in her mind. Eventually she grabbed the quilt and yanked it toward her. Brutally deprived of his cozy, warm cocoon, the teenager sat up and bellowed:

"Hey! That's not right. You can't do that!"

"Get up!" she ordered, halfway out of the room already, dragging the comforter with her. She walked briskly down the corridor, aware of the shuffling sound of a body staggering out of bed.

"Give it back!" Milo yelled after her.

"Come and get it," she replied without turning around.

She could sense Milo behind her reaching for the quilt. The next moment she almost toppled backward as he pulled it toward him. Thrown off balance, she had no choice but to let go. Milo angrily snatched up the comforter and gave her a filthy look.

"Don't you ever do that again," he snarled.

"Calm down, Milo!" she retorted, trying to regain the upper hand.

"You're not my mother!" He'd already turned and was halfway back to his room.

"No, but I am your legal guardian. And, until you're eighteen, I'm—" Tiphaine didn't get a chance to finish her sentence. Milo slammed the door in her face.

"Responsible for you," she muttered under her breath.

She was indeed responsible. For a great many things. Many more than she could bear to admit.

Many more than Milo would ever be able to forgive her for.

It had been like this for eight years. Eight years of being imprisoned in the abject desolation of guilt. Worse than prison. She'd learned to live with—had forced herself, up to a point, to cope with—the secrecy, guilt, and lies. In a way, it had simply been a matter of getting used to it. A matter of survival. Some obscure instinct held her thoughts in check every single day, kept her from sinking completely into madness. Most important of all, it enabled her to save what could be saved. In other words, Milo.

For eight years, the boy had been her sole reason for getting out of bed in the morning. Without him, she'd have put an end to her life long ago. She had made choices and done terrible things, and nothing had turned out as she had thought it would, deluded as she was by a grief that never dimmed, despite the passing of time. And whenever Milo, in moments of anger that with adolescence were growing increasingly frequent and intense, reminded her that they had no blood ties, Tiphaine had to struggle with all her might against the temptation to give up.

"You're not my mother!"

And yet she had done everything to be that. Absolutely everything.

Including the worst thing of all.

# CHAPTER
# 2

A little later that same day—it was early afternoon, and Milo was munching his way through a bowl of cereal—Tiphaine caught sight of her new neighbors for the first time. Her attention was drawn by a moving van maneuvering in the street outside. She turned away from Milo and his breakfast to stand by the window and watch the comings and goings.

It wasn't hard to spot the only two women among the movers. One, despite her obvious efforts to look younger, must have been around forty, while the other couldn't have been more than fifteen, despite her obvious efforts to look older. Both were in T-shirt and jeans, although the girl's top was a good deal shorter and tighter than the woman's. There was no doubt of their relationship: mother and daughter, moving together in lockstep, picking up and carrying inside the boxes they were able to lift.

Instinctively, Tiphaine looked for a man who wasn't wearing overalls with the moving company's logo. There wasn't one that she could see.

"Cute ass!"

Tiphaine started in surprise. Milo was standing behind her.

"What are you doing?" she asked, turning away from the window.

"Same as you: checking them out."

"Have you finished your breakfast?"

Milo nodded.

"Then get down to some work."

The young man gave a sigh and ambled nonchalantly back upstairs. Tiphaine waited till he'd left the room before returning to her observation post.

The girl was cute. She had the poise of a teenager enjoying her body's metamorphosis, relieved that her interminable childhood was at last coming to an end. One of those girls who is delighted to discover the advantages of her budding curves. Who understands instinctively that real life is finally about to begin.

Apples don't fall far from the tree—the mother was also very pretty. She was tall, slim, and elegant, with all the assets of her North African heritage: olive skin; long, dark hair; and deep, black eyes. She exuded the self-confidence of an older woman aware that she had not yet reached her sell-by date. She walked back and forth between the truck and the house, never slowing her pace, telling the movers which rooms they were to store the boxes and furniture in, and encouraging her daughter to keep going. She looked nice, Tiphaine thought.

It wasn't a surprise that there were people moving in next door. It was five months since the owner, Madame Coustenoble, had died, and her heirs had immediately made it clear that they were going to rent out the property. Tiphaine knew the house like the back of her hand; she and Sylvain had lived in it for several years, until the tragedy that had destroyed their lives. The "events," as she and Sylvain had taken to calling that terrible period, which they'd agreed, quite openly, never to speak about again. After the "events," they had obtained custody of Milo, the son of their next-door neighbors, David and Laetitia. They had been good friends, who had shared everything: Friday-night drinks, barbecues, laughter, secrets.

And then horror.

Milo was seven when Tiphaine and Sylvain became his legal guardians. In this capacity, it was their duty to draw up a full inventory of the boy's assets, which included his parents' house. As his guardians, it was their responsibility to manage it, and within a few months they had made the decision to live there. This was, as they saw it, the obvious solution: moving out of the house in which they'd suffered the most appalling tragedy a parent can ever experience. The house where their little boy, the love of their lives, the quintessence of joy, had been born. Maxime. Every corner held some memory—a look, a smile, the smell of him. His voice, too, the way its echo resounded incessantly within walls that stood like informers—walls that ensure you never forget. Ever. Intolerable grief that borders on madness.

Maxime.

An angel who had not been allotted the time to spread his wings.

Their fallen angel.

They gave notice to their landlady, Madame Coustenoble, who, rather than trying to find new, reliable tenants, decided to move back in and end her days there. A project she successfully accomplished eight years later.

After her death, her heirs did some building work on the house: while she had been alive the old lady had always rejected every proposal that Sylvain, who was an architect, had ever put forward. There were builders onsite for over a month, and then Tiphaine had watched the round of visits of potential tenants. For the last couple of weeks things had gone quiet, and she'd begun to suspect they would soon be meeting their new neighbors.

The mystery of who they might be was a source of deep anxiety for her; it was the first time since the "events" that a new family was going to move in, take over her former home, and make it their own, relegating the history of the previous tenants definitively to the past. And, despite the suffering she had experienced every day for eight long years, there was nothing Tiphaine dreaded more.

Of course she was apprehensive about the kind of people they'd be. A couple of retirees who'd complain that the wind was blowing smoke over the hedge every time she and Sylvain had a cookout in the backyard? Or, worse, a young married couple like she and Sylvain had been when they'd moved into the house seventeen years earlier? This possibility terrified her: the thought of two young people, madly in love, turning up thinking the house would be the perfect place to start a family. She couldn't bear to have to listen to the wail of a baby or the chuckles of a toddler coming from their backyard. As long as Madame Coustenoble was alive, she'd been safe from this unbearable possibility. But now the old lady was gone.

Lost in thought, Tiphaine gave a brief, mirthless smile: so these were her famous new neighbors. Two women, assuming that the absence of a man wasn't due to a demanding job or a debilitating illness. It wasn't as bad as it could have been: a young, lovestruck couple with a beaming toddler, an insufferable picture of happiness whose cloying whiff would waft over the hedge and up her nose. And the cherry on the cake: the presence of a pretty young lady with a captivating smile seemed a good omen. Milo had noticed the teenager right away, and his spontaneous reaction, however indelicate, at least indicated curiosity on the part of a young man who was by nature withdrawn and solitary, and rarely inclined to seek out the company of people his own age.

All in all, the arrival of these two women was a pleasant surprise. Or at any rate the least bad eventuality. Which was about as much as Tiphaine dared hope for nowadays.

# CHAPTER
## 3

The move went smoothly, and by four o'clock that afternoon Nora had signed the movers' invoice and handed them a well-earned tip. She went inside and shut the front door behind her. She took a few deep breaths, then went from room to room checking the boxes and furniture stacked up in each one. There was still so much to do, but the hardest part was behind her: Gérard, her ex-husband, had kept his word and not shown up today. She'd been afraid he'd insist on being there, under the pretext of wanting to help—that really would have been the last straw—or to make sure she was taking only the furniture that was rightfully hers.

In fact, Nora had taken very few things with her from their marital home: a sideboard, a sofa bed, two bookshelves, an armchair, and her personal stuff. She hadn't overdone it. But given it was she who had left, she didn't feel entitled to clear out the house.

The last few weeks had been awful. Splitting up always is, especially after eighteen years together. But she'd made up her mind, and for all Gérard's remonstrations, wheedling, and intimidation he hadn't been able to get her to change it. She didn't love him anymore. The grinding routine of daily life and the constant squabbling had triumphed over love. Standard stuff.

Gérard had clung on, convinced he'd be able to rekindle their former intimacy. But her heart wasn't in it, and she couldn't keep up the charade, though she knew a lot about pretending. They had been the tight-knit couple that the years hadn't managed to unravel. She was the wife who understood her husband's regular absences—always on business, of course, but all the same!—and who was quite content with being a stay-at-home mother. But the reality was that Gérard and she had drifted apart, he absorbed by his work, she by all the things she did of which he managed to remain quite oblivious. Mutual lack of understanding set in, and they were arguing more and more about things that were both important and trivial. Even though he spent so little time at home, he still tried to control his wife's schedule and who she saw, and was constantly weighing in with opinions about what she'd gotten up to during the day. His distrust was pathological: as far as he was concerned, in this dangerous world there was trouble brewing on every street corner. His work was no doubt a big part of the reason he thought that way.

Eventually Nora, by nature more easygoing, grew tired of Gérard's endless admonitions. Every time she met up with someone, whether a parent of one of the kids' friends, a fellow willing torture victim at the gym, or just someone she hadn't seen in a while, she had to put up with her husband's paranoid suspicions. One person seemed ill-intentioned, another was after a piece of her ass, a third was dangerously stupid. People were pernicious. Not all people, of course. But most.

Eventually Nora grew so sick and tired of his comments, she stopped telling Gérard what she'd gotten up to during the day, thus avoiding his judgmental remarks and mean-minded takes on anything and everything.

On top of this was the latent violence. Gérard had it absolutely under control, but over the years Nora had learned to be wary. Not that he had ever raised his hand against her, but at certain moments during one of their bitter fights, when she sensed the valve about to burst, she grew afraid. A visceral fear alert to danger.

Gérard was an inch or so shorter than his wife, but he compensated for it with a brilliant mind and strong character. His lean physique seemed to suit his manipulative temperament. An iron fist in an exfoliating glove. Gérard preferred the power of words over physical strength, making speech a weapon more formidable than blows. He wielded cruel words the way other people threw punches, and the mental wounds he inflicted sometimes proved more painful than physical assault. But when even words were powerless to subdue his warlike instincts, Gérard was ready with a response. Early on in their relationship, Nora had seen him beat up a man who'd been foolish enough to push his luck after a few well-chosen verbal salvos. The result had been crushing for the unlucky guy, even though he was a whole head taller than Gérard. Nora recalled her ambivalence at the time, the way that on the one hand she'd admired and even been turned on by Gérard's virile show of strength, while finding herself totally thrown by an aptitude for physical violence about which she'd never had even an inkling until then.

Over the years, any admiration she'd had for him had evaporated. All that remained was a wariness that ended up warping the love she'd once had for him. It reached the point where their married life added up to little more than the dull daily routine of chores and family responsibilities, a lackluster kind of cohabitation, and Nora decided to end it.

Sensing that he was losing control of the situation, Gérard detonated the last of his ammunition.

"What about the children? Have you thought about them?"

Nora looked at her husband, unable to conceal her distress. Of course she'd thought about the children. For years they were all she'd thought about: the reason she hadn't already left was that she couldn't bear the idea of breaking their hearts, turning their young lives upside down, seeing them only every other week. That was even worse than the idea of living with a man she was no longer in love with.

"They're bigger now," she replied simply. "They're old enough to understand."

"Are they? Are they old enough to suffer, as well?" he replied, in the tone of someone who knew all there was to know about suffering. Nora fell silent, heartbroken to be inflicting such pain on her family. She had sacrificed her own happiness for that of her children for a long time, with no misgivings whatsoever. What did it matter that her life was as smooth as a highway, with no curves, no rough edges, no highs or lows; a path already marked out, on which it was impossible to lose one's way, leading straight toward a cloudless horizon. Wasn't that precisely what had attracted her to this young attorney who'd promised her a future that was safe, free from insecurity? Wasn't that what he had guaranteed her?

But safe from what exactly?

From surprises, or accidents? From living?

She needed air. A change. A fresh start.

She was hungry for adventure. She yearned for chance encounters. A different life. A second chance.

"How are you going to make a living?" he said, running low on arguments. "You don't have a job. If you think you're going to rely on alimony . . ."

"I'll find a job."

"At your age?"

His reply, though cruel, was not without a certain realism.

"Fine, I'll stay," she retorted, without skipping a beat. "But only for your money."

Her words were like an arrow to Gérard's heart, and their venom devastated him. It was impossible for him to accept that money was now his only allure for Nora. If that really was the case, he was prepared to let her go. Before she sullied the last shred of respect there was left between them.

So Nora left. At the age of forty-four she set out to find a job, after eighteen years of not working. She had a degree in French literature that hadn't gotten her very far when she'd applied for a teaching job after leaving university. She'd done casual jobs to pay the bills, and a bit of substitute teaching, but she'd never found anything she really enjoyed. For a couple of years in her twenties she'd tried and failed to write. Then she'd met Gérard.

As the man at the employment office skimmed her résumé,

he couldn't keep himself from shooting her a mirthless smirk that betrayed his doubt.

"We'll see what we can do."

Nora understood straightaway that he wouldn't be able to do very much. It was up to her to think about what skills and experience she had. In the gloom of her situation the answer was clear: she knew about taking care of children.

She made an appointment to meet with the principals of two local preschools to explain her situation and demonstrate her commitment and motivation.

The principal of the first school gave her short shrift, even though her son had been a student there. The principal of the second turned out to be looking for a pre-K classroom assistant, but Nora's lack of training was a drawback.

"Lack of training?" Nora replied in dismay. "I've been doing nothing else for thirteen years!"

"You've been taking care of your own children. You can't call that training. That's not to say that I doubt your competence."

"Would you be prepared to take me on for a trial period?"

"That's not the issue," the woman said. The conversation that ensued was strained, but by the time she left her office Nora had obtained a commitment that the principal would consider her application and get back to her within two weeks. If she kept her word, she'd know soon enough.

Getting the job became an obsession. Nora thought about it night and day. What a triumph it would be if she pulled it off—for herself, of course, but also for her relationship with

Gérard. She knew he was patiently waiting for her to fall at the first hurdle and beg him to take her back. She wasn't afraid that she'd be destitute, scrimping and saving, never sure she'd make it to the end of the month. What she was afraid of was the different lifestyle she was forcing on her children, compared to the luxury they were used to with Gérard. The alimony payments barely covered the rent: against all logic, she'd made it a point of honor to find a place large enough for each of the kids to have their own room. It was out of the question for them to enjoy the comfort of a 3,500-square-foot house one week and the next find themselves slumming it in a tiny apartment.

The small house she'd found in a residential neighborhood was nothing like where they'd grown up, but it was nice enough: light-filled and welcoming. And affordable. With her limited means she was determined to make it comfortable and cozy.

As she looked around at the piles of boxes and furniture scattered about the first floor, the cozy dream began to fade. She looked at her watch: she had two hours before Gérard was due to bring their son back. Two hours for her to set up a snug corner in his bedroom. She had no time to waste. She went into the entryway and called up to Inès.

"I'm in my room!"

She went upstairs and pushed open the door to the bedroom at the end of the hallway. It was lovely and bright, filled with boxes waiting to be unpacked.

"Maman?" came Inès's voice from the other end of the corridor.

"I'm in here, sweetheart." A moment later, Nora sensed her daughter's presence behind her. She turned and stepped aside to let the teenager pass.

"Do you think he'll be happy here?" Nora asked, biting the inside of her cheeks.

"Sure he will! This is a great room. And look." Inès walked over to the window and opened it. "He has this amazing view over the backyard, and it's right above the deck."

# CHAPTER
## 4

Sylvain arrived back at six. He went into the kitchen and put down his keys, wallet, and a thick file of work he had to finish for the following Monday on the table, then went straight out into the backyard, where he found Tiphaine crouched down among her plants, filling in the soil around the roots of a young shrub. The minute she saw him, she stood up and went over to him.

"Something's happened," she said in a low voice.

"Why are you whispering?"

By way of answer, Tiphaine nodded at the hedge that separated their backyard from that of the neighboring house. Sylvain raised his eyebrows in surprise and curiosity.

"And?" he asked, lowering his voice in turn.

"A mother and daughter. There doesn't seem to be a man, so she's either divorced or widowed. About my age. She looks nice."

"And the daughter?"

"Teenager. Standard model. Cute."

"Did you talk to them?"

"No."

They looked at each other in silence. Since Madame Coustenoble's death, they had never spoken about who might move into the house next door, but they both knew perfectly well the repercussions it would have on their lives. Sylvain nodded mutely several times, without taking his eyes off Tiphaine. He was about to say something, but then he seemed to change his mind.

"Where's Milo?" he asked finally.

"Upstairs in his room. He's meant to be studying, but it might not be a bad idea for you to check on him."

"I'll go up and take a look."

As he turned to the house, he glanced back at the hedge. Alone again, Tiphaine finished planting the shrub, adding some homemade compost to the soil and methodically tamping down the mixture around its base.

Tiphaine was a professional horticulturist, but plants were more than merely her job. She was fanatical about gardening and spent most of her time with her hands in soil, sowing, planting, watering, weeding, propagating cuttings, pruning, and harvesting. Plants, flowers, trees, and shrubs held no secrets for her; she knew all there was to know about every variety, not just when they blossomed and what their yields were, but their properties, health benefits, and dangers. Alongside her undoubted physical proficiency, she possessed fine observational skills, excellent scientific knowledge, and an artistic sensibility.

Being in contact with the earth was vital for her, therapeutic even.

Lost in what she was doing, at first she didn't hear the rustling of leaves a few yards away, just over the hedge in the neighboring garden. A few seconds later, she caught a glimpse of a vague movement beyond the foliage. Intrigued, she turned her head and, otherwise motionless, stared at the place that had just stirred. A moment later she spotted a small figure, then a face and eyes watching her in silence. Slowly, she straightened up and walked to the hedge, on the other side of which was a small boy of seven or eight. He stood stock-still, as if he was debating whether or not to run away.

"Who are you?" she asked.

"Maxime."

The shock was instant. Agonizing. Brutal.

Tiphaine felt the ground give way. Her legs, suddenly deprived of all vital substance, felt like they were liquifying. In a fraction of a second her pulse went from a normal rhythm to an uninterrupted hammering, and everything around her began to spin. She reached out an arm to try to grab hold of something, but her hands closed around nothing. She felt herself falling backward and tried to regain her balance by tipping the weight of her body forward. Through her raging inner confusion, she saw the child's curious stare, and then a woman's voice slammed into the silence of her panic.

"Nassim?"

In the next-door garden she saw her new neighbor making her way from the deck toward the boy.

"Nassim, what are you doing?"

She caught sight of Tiphaine behind the hedge. "Oh, I'm sorry, I didn't see you there."

"Hello," Tiphaine managed to utter through ragged breaths.

The woman came closer, then stood on tiptoe, as if trying to get past the obstacle of the hedge that separated them.

"I'm Nora, your new neighbor. And this is Nassim, my son. Did you say hello to the lady, Nassim?"

"Hello."

Tiphaine swallowed.

"Hello, Nassim," she stammered, slowly regaining her composure.

There was a brief, polite silence, which Nora soon filled. "We just moved in today. I hope the movers didn't disturb you too much."

"Absolutely not," Tiphaine assured her. Then she added, "My name's Tiphaine."

"I'm so pleased to meet you."

There was another, longer silence, now filled with a palpable awkwardness.

"How old is your little boy?" Tiphaine asked in a tone of polite curiosity.

"He's eight," Nora answered with that peculiar parental smugness that suggests the age of their offspring is a source of particular pride. "Do you have children?"

Tiphaine nodded. "I have a fifteen-year-old son. Milo."

"Oh!" exclaimed Nora. "My daughter's thirteen."

"What's her name?" asked Tiphaine, thinking that the girl had looked older than that.

"Inès."

"What a pretty name."

"Thank you."

Between polite compliments and neighborly courtesy, the two women rapidly exhausted all possible topics of conversation and, once more, silence fell between them.

"Well," said Nora with a little sigh, "I'm so happy to meet you. I hope you have a lovely evening."

"And you, too."

Nora turned and went back into the house with her son. Tiphaine watched them walk away, her heart still thumping from the shock she'd felt when she thought she heard the child say his name was Maxime. Even if Nassim wasn't the same age as Maxime had been when he died, his presence made her feel uneasy.

Just as Nora and Nassim reached the deck, Tiphaine called out, "Excuse me!"

Nora turned.

"Yes?"

"Which one is Nassim's bedroom?"

"I'm sorry?"

Tiphaine bit her lip. It was a strange question and she immediately regretted asking.

"I'm sorry to ask but the thing is our houses are adjoining and as we share a wall—"

"Oh!" Nora nodded in the direction of the window directly above the deck.

"That one."

Tiphaine shut her eyes. It was the thing she'd been dreading since the moment she'd discovered Nassim's existence: he was moving into Maxime's old bedroom. Another little boy was going to play, sleep, laugh, cry, live in that room.

An icy grip tightened inside her chest, and for a few seconds, she found it hard to breathe. When she opened her eyes again,

Nora had retraced her steps to the hedge and was looking at her curiously. She'd obviously mistaken the significance of the question as referring to the shared wall that separated the two houses.

"Is there a problem with the soundproofing?" she asked, not trying to hide her discomfiture.

"No!" exclaimed Tiphaine, surprised by Nora's interpretation. "That's not what I meant at all."

What an idiot! She hadn't been able to stop herself from asking one too many questions. Now she was going to have to extricate herself somehow from this awkward situation. If she nodded along with Nora and agreed that she was already thinking ahead to her son potentially disturbing them with his noise, the question bordered on rudeness. On the other hand, she couldn't see herself replying lightheartedly, "I just asked because eight years ago my husband and I were living in your house, and that room was our little boy's. He died falling from that very window. That's right, your son's bedroom. Welcome to your new home!"

"Don't worry," Nora said. "Nassim is very well behaved, and I'll make sure he doesn't disturb you."

"I'm so sorry, you misunderstood. I . . ."

"I" what? What reason could she possibly give for her question that wouldn't be either rude or awkward? She fumbled for the right words, but after a few seconds she sighed as though she were throwing in the towel.

"I'm sorry. My question was silly and completely uncalled for. Forget I said anything," she said, with her warmest smile.

"It's fine, I absolutely understand your concern."

"You don't understand at all! I love children. It never even crossed my mind that Nassim might disturb us."

"Don't worry, I get it."

"It's my fault."

"No, no, I understand completely."

Simultaneously, the two women cut short their litany of excuses and understanding. They both burst out laughing, one warmly, the other dolefully.

That's how Tiphaine and Nora first met, over a misunderstanding, on either side of a hedge.

# CHAPTER 5

Back in her own house, Tiphaine rushed to the bathroom, a helpless hostage to waves of nausea. She stuck two fingers down her throat but couldn't get rid of the feeling of disgust. She coughed and retched and expectorated, trying to vomit up her repulsion. It didn't work. A little boy had moved in next door, into the house where Maxime had lived and died, trapped inside the walls of a life extinguished forever. This child, filled with life, had just annexed her son's bedroom, his memory . . . his home.

"Tiphaine?"

Alerted by the sounds coming from the bathroom, Sylvain grew worried.

"Tiphaine! Are you okay?"

Instead of replying, Tiphaine came out, wiping her mouth with her sleeve. White as a sheet, she looked at Sylvain with an expression of sadness and despair.

"What the hell is going on?" he said in a voice filled with both concern and exasperation.

Tiphaine shook her head. "She has a son," she moaned.

"What are you talking about?"

"The new neighbor . . . She has a little boy. He's eight. He's called Nassim, but at the beginning I thought—" She stopped, unable to articulate Maxime's name.

She didn't have to. Sylvain understood.

"Did you see him?"

Tiphaine nodded.

"Damn it, Tiphaine!" he began through clenched teeth. "You can't let yourself get into a state like this . . . I—"

"He's in his bedroom." She cut him off, distraught.

"It is not his bedroom anymore!"

"It'll always be his bedroom to me."

"No! It hasn't been his bedroom for eight years. Do you hear me?"

"Eight years!" repeated Tiphaine, as if she had only just become aware of the passage of time. Then she added in a broken voice, "This child was born the year ours died."

Sylvain looked at her without a word, his heart shattered at the sight of his grief-stricken wife. Tiphaine was only a shadow of the woman he'd fallen so madly in love with seventeen years earlier: life, sorrow, the intolerable ordeal of having lost a child had slowly eaten away at her, gnawing at her soul, her heart, her mind. She wasn't crazy, at least not in the conventional sense; but since Maxime's death, she'd been living in a world without a bulwark to keep her from falling. And he, Sylvain, mired in his own suffering and grief, increasingly found himself losing his composure in the face of his wife's distress. Riddled with guilt, he had been struggling with his own demons every day for eight long years, tormented by memories and recurring nightmares. The arrival of this little boy in the house next door, or at least the turmoil it triggered in Tiphaine's mind, suddenly felt like the last straw, the hurdle that they would not be able to overcome.

"Tiphaine, I beg you . . ."

Instead of an answer, she hunched over and began heaving with sobs.

The appearance of a child in the house next door reopened wounds whose scars, despite all the years that had passed, still oozed with grief and pain. When they had taken Milo in after the "events," she had been convinced she would drown her heartache in her love for him and the love that she was confident he would have for her. Nothing, however, had turned out as she'd hoped. Milo had gradually shut himself off, as if he wanted to remove himself from the world. He rejected their expressions of affection and turned his back on any attempt at a loving gesture. He displayed no more than a vague fondness for them, a cruel contrast to his former devotion.

Tiphaine and Sylvain had known Milo since he was born. They'd watched him growing up and blossoming alongside their own son; they'd babysat him, comforted him when he was sad, consoled and encouraged him when things didn't go well, congratulated him on his achievements. They loved him almost as much as they loved Maxime, and he had always returned their love. But since the "events," Milo's attitude to them had gradually changed; he grew distant, almost distrustful. Whenever Tiphaine tried to give him a hug he would cringe from the embrace. When she was faster than he was and managed to draw him to her, he'd tense up, stiff as a board, and wait for it to be over.

"We have to give him time," said Sylvain, when Tiphaine, in tears, told him this. "He's traumatized. It's his way of telling us he doesn't want to forget his mom."

Tiphaine waited patiently, devastated by a rejection that felt like a betrayal, a punishment even.

Twice a week, the three of them went to see Justine Philippot, the therapist David and Laetitia, Milo's parents, had taken their son to see in the wake of Maxime's death, to try to help him cope with the dreadful loss. Tiphaine hoped that through these sessions she would manage to get closer to the boy, that he would gradually lower his defenses and allow himself to receive—and give—a little love. For a time she thought it looked like it was working: Milo seemed more relaxed, less defensive, and though he was still grudging when it came to physical affection, at least he was less evasive and more open.

But her hopes were soon dashed: one day the child simply refused to go to the appointment. She and Sylvain had no idea why. He sat on a chair in the kitchen, straight as an "I," refusing to stand up to put on his coat and get in the car. Tiphaine tried to talk him around, but to no avail: he simply repeated that he didn't want to go, but seemed unable—or unwilling—to give any explanation. Even under duress, the child didn't concede.

She tried promises, with no more success.

Eventually Sylvain, who'd been waiting in the entryway, lost patience: he came into the kitchen with a heavy, determined step, grabbed the boy by the waist, forced him into the cloakroom, and wrangled him into his coat. Half an hour later, the three of them were sitting in the therapist's office.

As soon as they sat down Tiphaine and Sylvain told Dr. Philippot what had just occurred. She turned to Milo and gently asked him the reason for his refusal. The child sat there, mute. After a long moment of silence, she repeated her question. Another failure: Milo again refused to answer. She asked him if he was angry; still nothing. The entire hour passed in the boy's obstinate silence, interspersed only by the therapist's questions and his guardians' attempts at encouragement.

Dr. Philippot did not want to overdramatize the situation; she reassured Tiphaine and Sylvain, explaining that Milo's silence was his way of expressing anger, and gave them another appointment in three days' time. The same scene was repeated. Milo went to see Justine Philippot only under duress and did not utter a single word for the entire hour. It was the same at the following appointments.

At the end of the fifth unsuccessful session, the therapist suggested a break, advocating a return to a more "normal" way of life. She told them to relax the pressure. Stop worrying. Maybe Milo just needed to get back to ordinary life—if that was possible—or at least a daily routine where he wouldn't be reminded twice a week that he had lost more than half the people he loved and cared about and who mattered the most to him; a life where he would no longer be seen as a strange beast on the verge of falling apart.

This was a slap in the face for Tiphaine, and she left the therapist's consulting room feeling forsaken. It was as if the last rope she was holding on to in order not to tumble into the pit of despair had been severed.

That evening she lay in bed staring at the ceiling as if trying to penetrate its mystery, and whispered to Sylvain, who she knew was awake beside her:

"He knows."

"Stop it," he said after a moment.

"I'm sure of it. He knows."

After a few more seconds of silence, Sylvain leaned up on his elbow and tried to look Tiphaine in the eye. She was still staring at the ceiling.

"It's absolutely impossible," he said. "Stop playing games."

"He might not know it consciously, but he senses it."

"Tiphaine, please. Milo's just . . ." He paused, unsure how to express his thoughts, then said, "He's lost both his parents. He's suffering. He's handling it in his own way. I know it's hard for you, but it's harder for him. You mustn't take it personally."

She didn't say anything for a moment, and Sylvain wasn't even sure she'd heard him. Then all of a sudden she stopped staring at the ceiling and turned to look at him.

What he saw in her expression didn't reassure him at all.

Since that day, Tiphaine hadn't been able to shake her slight wariness of Milo, even if, over time, the tension between them had eased. But Sylvain had the sense that his wife's sadness and frustration were eating away at her more and more each day. And now that another little boy had moved into the house next door, was going to live and grow older before their eyes, he knew that the casket of memories had opened up again and was going to take over her mind.

And now Tiphaine was realizing with horror that she simply was not going to be able to bear the presence of this child.

---

In the house next door, on the other side of the wall, Nora tapped out a number on her cell phone; she waited for someone to answer then placed an order for three pizzas, gave her name and address, and asked how long they would take to be delivered. Just as the call ended, Inès and Nassim burst into the kitchen.

"I've ordered pizza," announced Nora, with a big smile on her face.

The two children showed their delight by flinging their arms around their mother's neck.

"Did Nassim tell you?" she asked her daughter. "We just met the lady who lives next door."

"What pizza did you order for me?" Nassim asked.

"Four cheeses, your favorite."

"Tell me about the neighbor. What's she like?" asked Inès, stuffing two pieces of gum into her mouth.

"She was pretty nice. We had a laugh, actually. She seems like she could be fun," Nora said, smiling. "I think we're going to like it here."

# CHAPTER
## 6

Gradually the boxes were unpacked and Nora began to organize her life. Tidying, sorting, choosing which things to throw away, which to keep. Finding a place for every object, a nuance in every gesture, a motive behind every decision. She was furnishing both her house and her life, the life of a single mother with daily responsibilities that weren't the most straightforward. Her children gave her the motivation to deal with myriad things, but at the end of the first week her confidence took a knock when Inès and Nassim walked out the front door, their overnight bags slung over their shoulders, and climbed into their father's car. The door slammed shut with a week on her own ahead of her, during which she found herself beset by doubts. She missed them. What was she doing there, all alone in an empty house? Wasn't she supposed to be with her children, no matter the sacrifice? Had she really tried everything before making such a radical decision?

The relationship between her and Gérard remained strained. He was furious with her for leaving, for not having given their relationship another chance, and thus denying their family a future. And to make matters worse, she hadn't found a job yet.

Her financial situation was terrible, and every morning, when the mailbox spat out nothing but bills and flyers, she had to fight to keep panic at bay.

And then, one Tuesday, two weeks after she moved into the house on rue Edmond-Petit, a phone call shone the first ray of sunshine onto the gloom of her increasingly worrying situation.

It was the principal of the nursery school, Madame Stillet. When she realized who she was speaking to, Nora held her breath. Her heart began to race. After the usual preliminaries, Madame Stillet told her she was going to take her on part-time, for an initial three-month probationary period. Nora stifled a triumphant little cry. She would obviously have preferred a full-time job, but this half-positive answer was nonetheless excellent news. Madame Stillet said she'd like her to start the following week, and Nora found herself getting all tangled up in thanks.

At last, some good news. The proverbial light at the end of the tunnel. Even if it was still only a faint glimmer, Nora was determined to see in it a sign that things were going to get better. The children were with their father, which meant she'd have to wait until the following Sunday before she could tell them the news. Not that she couldn't phone them, on the contrary: she spoke to them briefly every evening, just to hear their voices, ask about their day, send them her love. But she didn't want Gérard to know yet. Not right away, not until she actually started working.

Instead, the newly minted kindergarten assistant called her lifelong friend Mathilde. She had to celebrate with someone. Mathilde answered on the second ring. She tried to understand through Nora's laughter and cries of joy what she was so happy about, and let out a shriek of delight when she eventually understood.

"Can you get away this evening?" asked Nora. "I don't want to celebrate on my own."

"I could be at yours around eight. That way I'll have time to put the little one to bed. Do you want to go out?"

"Not necessarily, we could have a bite to eat at my place."

"I'll bring the champagne!"

It was a wonderful evening. The two women sat on the deck enjoying the mild early summer evening that foreshadowed the gorgeous days and starry nights to come. For the first time in weeks, Nora felt renewed self-confidence. She wasn't out of the woods yet, but at least there was some hope that things were soon to get better.

"What you have to do is make yourself indispensable," Mathilde told her. "I bet you at the end of the three months she'll be begging you to work full-time."

"I goddamn hope so!"

Mathilde and Nora had known each other since their mildly reckless student days. They'd plotted their dazzling futures, shared the typical sorrows and joys of that age of promise, sworn to be friends forever. And then they'd lost touch. Mathilde met her first husband, who sent her into exile in the suburbs of Paris. There were rules to being in a couple: girls' nights out became more and more infrequent, and then Mathilde's pregnancy finished the friendship off entirely. They saw each other again five years later, quite by chance. Nora, by then pregnant with Inès, and Mathilde, divorced but about to remarry, fell into each other's arms, swore to see each other again soon. Another four years passed until they reconnected on Mathilde's initiative: she had just had her second child, and she wanted Nora to be godmother.

Nora was surprised and delighted to accept, and this time the friendship was truly rekindled. They introduced their respective families, and the two couples began inviting each other over regularly. Nora and Gérard succumbed to the charms of the affluent suburb where their friends lived, and a few months later they moved there too. That was where Nassim was born.

The two friends spoke to and saw each other all the time. Mathilde gave birth to her third child, a little girl named Justine, who was now four. Even though she was juggling work and marriage, she was very present during the painful period of her friend's separation, always there to listen to Nora's sorrows and anger. She was particularly good not only with supportive words, but also with healing silences.

For Mathilde, too, the evening was life-affirming: it had been too long since they spent such a joyful time together, and to see Nora getting tipsy for a reason other than her misfortunes was a delight.

"Okay, so you're a kindergarten assistant." Mathilde giggled as she refilled their glasses. "How about this: a three-year-old kid keeps smacking his little buddies. What do you do?"

"I crush his hand in the door to teach him a lesson," Nora answered as if it were obvious.

"Excellent!" Mathilde laughed. "How about this, then: a little girl asks you to go with her to the bathroom, except you're on your own, surrounded by kids, and you can't leave the classroom."

"That doesn't work. I'm the one who's meant to be helping the teacher with this kind of thing."

"Let's say she's had to leave the classroom for half an hour."

"Well then, I tell her she has to hold it in."

Mathilde burst out laughing.

"You're going to be great, babe. You're going to be a real hit."

"You said it."

"You know what, I'd kill for a joint."

"Are you kidding?"

"Nope. I haven't smoked in years. I have this urge suddenly."

Nora grinned at the memory of getting stoned with Mathilde when they were students; endless late nights filled with delirious laughter.

"Well, we don't have any weed, anyway," she said, lifting her shoulders in mock resignation.

"I do," said a voice from the other side of the hedge.

The two women started with surprise. For a moment they stared at each other, each trying to work out from the other's expression how to respond.

A figure appeared through the foliage, standing on next door's deck.

"Hi there!" said Nora, with insincere enthusiasm.

"Hi," answered Tiphaine.

"Hi!" said Mathilde in turn, suppressing an embarrassed giggle.

"So, will you join me?" asked Tiphaine.

Mathilde and Nora exchanged a glance. Hesitation quickly gave way to excitement, and they acknowledged their assent with perfectly synchronized nods.

"Do you want to come over here, Tiphaine?"

"Oh no! You should come over to my place."

"All right."

"Bring the champagne," said Tiphaine.

# CHAPTER
## 7

A few moments later, the two women stood outside the neighboring house and rang the bell. Tiphaine opened the front door and stepped aside to let them in.

The Geniots' house was more or less identical to Nora's, and she had no difficulty finding her way to the back door. She walked out onto the deck and let out an involuntary gasp of admiration, then began rhapsodizing about the glorious colors of her neighbor's delightful yard. Plants and flower beds were planted in perfect harmony, shrubs and bushes seemingly in dialogue with the wind, an enchanting concerto of color and scent. Nora had seen the beautiful backyard from her first-floor window, but looking at it up close, stretched out in front of her, she was able to appreciate it in all its glory, the perfect balance of order and creativity.

"It's stunning," she said, utterly beguiled.

"Thank you," said Tiphaine.

"How do you do it? You have a real gift."

"It's kind of my job, actually. Do you want me to show you around?"

Nora and Mathilde were happy to accept.

Tiphaine gave them a tour of the yard, with explanations about each flower or shrub, its properties, and why she had chosen to plant it there instead of somewhere else.

Two-thirds of the way down, the path split the terrain into two equal sections, which Tiphaine had transformed into a vegetable garden, where she grew different types of lettuce, carrots, tomatoes, potatoes, and zucchini.

When they reached the very end of the yard, she showed them behind the row of bushes that concealed the boundary wall. Here Tiphaine had created a space about three feet wide and ten feet long, where a compost bin filled with decomposing organic waste was concealed.

Tiphaine explained to Nora and Mathilde the composting process and its multiple benefits: its use as a fertilizer, the valuable and varied properties that improve soil structure and increase biodiversity, and, last but not least, the recycling of household waste.

Nora, whose gardening activities were limited to repotting, was impressed. And a little revolted by the off-putting stench of rotting organic matter.

"It's true it doesn't smell great," Tiphaine admitted. "Which is why I planted this row of bushes: they keep the smell of the compost on this side and hide the bin, too. So, are we going to smoke this joint?"

They walked back up to the deck and sat down. Tiphaine started to roll a joint. It was an odd moment; they made small talk, as if to make their illicit activity seem ordinary.

"I prefer staying outside," said Tiphaine. "My son's up in his room. If he caught me smoking a joint . . . He doesn't often come down after ten, but I'd rather not take the risk."

"It's funny to think we used to hide our smoking from our parents, and now we hide our smoking from our children," said Nora with a chuckle.

"How old's your son?" asked Mathilde.

"Fifteen."

"Oh god, I'm sorry," she said, making a face.

Tiphaine nodded and sighed deeply, and the other two women laughed.

"My eldest is eighteen," added Mathilde, sympathetically. "I won't pretend it's nirvana every day, but let's just say the turbulence is behind us. At least as far as that one's concerned."

"How many do you have?"

"Three," said Mathilde, eyeing the joint that Tiphaine had nearly finished rolling. "Eighteen, nine, and four. Two boys, one girl. And not a minute to myself."

"Such is our lot in life," said Nora with a pensive sigh. All three suddenly froze as they heard a noise from inside the house. They held their breath and waited, throwing nervous glances at one another, ready to hide the evidence of their crime in case of an untimely intrusion.

"It's probably Sylvain," Tiphaine said in a whisper, glancing at her watch. "He's normally back around now."

"Is that your husband?" asked Nora.

"Yeah, he has a lot of work on right now. He often gets back late."

"What does he do?"

"He's an architect. Designing projects, putting in planning applications and tenders, making maquettes. He's very busy." She said it in a tone that managed to be simultaneously proud and sardonic, but Nora thought she detected a hint of barely concealed resentment. She—long neglected by a husband whose professional activities left him no time for a mistress—couldn't help feeling sorry for Tiphaine. No one can fight a partner's passion for their vocation. She didn't think Gérard had ever cheated on her, but the upshot was much the same.

Nora was tempted to try to broach the subject with a conspiratorial remark or a knowing quip. But she refrained; she'd already had quite enough experience with her own marital problems to get involved with someone else's.

Tiphaine used a match to finish tamping down the mixture of tobacco and cannabis and lit the joint. She took a deep puff and then passed it to Mathilde, who grabbed it enthusiastically.

"To your new job, babe," she said to Nora as she inhaled the fragrant smoke.

"You've found a job?" asked Tiphaine.

"I'm starting as a kindergarten assistant next week at Colibris."

"Oh! That's where my son went. He liked it there, except for the beds at naptime. They were just metal posts with heavy canvas slung between them. He hated those," Tiphaine chuckled.

"Maybe I should ask him to tell me about everything that needs to be improved. I need to make myself indispensable."

Tiphaine froze, then threw Nora a horrified glance. As a newcomer to the neighborhood, Nora was unaware of the tragedy that had shattered their lives eight years earlier. This was the first time in a long while that Tiphaine was just a woman chatting away like any other, no longer a mother indelibly branded with the mark of calamity. For that was what she had become: when she walked down the street conversation died away, eyes were lowered, smiles tightened. She was the person whose life had fallen to pieces and could never be fixed. She was the person people snuck sidelong glances at and pitied behind her back. Tiphaine had grown accustomed to it, and in truth, she didn't care. After the horror she'd been through she had no time for petty grievances. But what broke her heart was that people didn't think of her as the entirely innocent victim of a fate as cruel as it was unjust. She was somehow responsible for her misfortune. Guilty of negligence. Involuntarily accountable.

It was a life sentence.

Disoriented, Tiphaine stared at Nora for a moment, then seemed to waken from a daze, as if she were shaking off a malevolent curse.

"Maybe," she said, sounding quite jaunty. "I am sure he'd have plenty of ideas for you."

And then suddenly, as if her defensive levee, under strain for so long, was cracking, because it was so lovely to be a mother like any other, to be allowed to enjoy the normality of a perfectly ordinary moment—and probably also because she was stoned—Tiphaine began to talk about her son.

Her boy.

Her little boy whom the awkward teen years were transforming into a man. A beanpole now, no more than a vague memory of the chubby baby, the cuddly toddler, the sunny child he'd once been.

# CHAPTER
## 8

When Gérard brought Inès and Nassim home the following Sunday, he seemed in better spirits than usual. He actually bothered to get out of the car and show up with the children on the doorstep, which demonstrated, if not a conciliatory intent, at least a willingness to communicate.

Nora was taken aback at first, but she quickly recovered and gave him a welcoming smile. She hugged her children to her, showered them with kisses, her face radiating joy at seeing them again. Then she turned to Gérard and suggested he come in for a few minutes. He hesitated briefly, before declining the invitation with long-suffering courtesy.

"Come on, don't make me beg," insisted Nora. "If you've gotten out of the car, it wasn't to stand here on the doorstep." Gérard gave a half smile, then eventually nodded. Nora took a step back to let him into the house.

Once inside, they had to contend with the awkwardness of being in each other's presence. It was the first time they had seen each other since Nora's move. Until now she had only glimpsed him through the windows of his car, and he had never given her so much as a nod or a smile.

"Would you like coffee?"

"A quick one."

"Are you in a hurry?"

"I don't want to disturb you."

"You're not disturbing me."

She led him to the kitchen, invited him to sit down, and began preparing the coffee.

"It's rather nice here," Gérard remarked, looking around.

"Thank you."

Silence. The kind that's broken only by some trite observation uttered in a deceptively upbeat tone of voice.

"What's the landlord like?" Gérard asked.

"Nice. I don't really know. Discreet, which is all I care about. You still take two sugars?"

"Yes. Some things never change."

Nora flinched imperceptibly. She knew by heart all Gérard's acerbic little comments and equivocal asides. This one wasn't malicious, but it betrayed a state of mind that was not hostile exactly, but undeniably bitter. Gérard was resentful by nature; he found it hard to forgive anyone who hurt him, and rarely failed, when the opportunity arose, to hold a grudge.

Nora didn't rise to the bait. She poured out two cups of coffee, handed one to Gérard, and sat down opposite him.

"I know this house," he declared, as if he had been waiting for her to sit down before making this revelation.

"You do?"

"Yes. This one or the one next door, I'm not sure. They all look the same."

"What are you talking about?"

"A couple of days before Nassim was born, I was summoned to the police station to represent a suspect. A murder disguised as a heart attack. Don't you remember?"

"Vaguely."

"Yes, you do! You were literally about to give birth, Nassim could have arrived at any moment, and you didn't like being home alone in the evening with Inès."

"It's coming back to me now. And?"

"The cops didn't really have any evidence against the guy, and he was released that evening. I drove him home. And it was here. The next day, they found him hanging in the stairwell."

Nora shuddered. "Thanks for the information," she said sarcastically, making no attempt to hide her displeasure.

"The dumbest thing," continued Gérard, as if he hadn't heard her, "was that the cops had nothing on him. He'd have been fine."

"Do you think he was guilty?"

"Honestly, I have no idea. The guy hanged himself, which everyone took as an admission of guilt, and the case was closed, bang. I must admit I didn't delve into it any further. To be honest, what with Nassim's birth, I had other things on my mind."

Though eight years had gone by, Gérard remembered the case pretty well. David Brunelle had a teenage history of petty crime, and a criminal record for drug possession, home invasion, and armed robbery. He'd spent four years in jail, but then seemed to have cleaned up his act and become a loving husband and exemplary father with a well-ordered life.

Until that Saturday afternoon when Ernest Wilmot, his sixty-five-year-old former probation officer and Milo's godfather, suffered a fatal cardiac arrest at the Brunelles' house. At the autopsy, the medical examiner detected in the man's body unusual quantities of digitoxin, a powerful cardiotonic extracted from the foxglove, whose diuretic action can seriously damage kidney function. The form of digitoxin found in Wilmot's urine after his death was so pure that the coroner was able to conclude that the plant itself had been ingested. When they searched the Brunelles' house, the police found a pot of beautiful purple foxgloves on the deck. That was all it took for him to be arrested. Of course, having flowers on one's deck is not in itself a crime, and Gérard Depardieu, his court-appointed attorney, took less than two hours to get his client released.

There was one thing that still played on the attorney's mind: he remembered the way Brunelle never stopped protesting his innocence. He was rambling a lot, and not always very coherent, but Gérard recognized the sincerity in his client's voice. The news of Brunelle's suicide two days later had unsettled Gérard, challenging his faith in his own instincts, but he had never quite managed to rally behind the police detectives' insistence that this desperate act amounted to an admission of guilt.

"What are you trying to tell me?" said Nora, losing her temper. "That I'm living in a murderer's house?"

Taken aback by Nora's anger, Gérard glanced at her with a look of surprise.

"Maybe not a murderer," he said with a nonchalant shrug. "But there's a fifty percent chance a man hanged himself here."

With that, he lifted the cup to his lips and emptied it in a single swallow. He stood up.

"Thanks for the coffee."

Nora glared at him.

"Seriously? You came in just to tell me that?"

"You're the one who invited me in."

"Next time you can stay in the car!" she retorted angrily.

She went into the entryway and opened the front door. Gérard, following behind her, seemed to regret the turn their meeting had taken.

"I'm sorry," he said. "I didn't mean to be rude."

"It's a shame that you were, then," she replied dryly.

"Can I make it up to you?"

"I doubt it."

"Nora . . ."

Standing very close to her, he looked at her pleadingly.

"Come back to me," he murmured.

She rolled her eyes in exasperation.

"Please, Gérard, don't do this."

"I won't work so hard. I'll spend more time with you and the children."

"Stop it!"

"Let's give it one more try."

"It's too late."

"Too late for what?" he said. "To save our family?"

"Oh, enough with your fancy phrases, we're not in the courtroom now."

Hurt, Gérard stopped. His features grew hard, and his manner changed. Now he looked at her with a contemptuous expression.

"You're making the biggest mistake of your life."

Nora's heart sank. She didn't like the look on his face, as if he were struggling to control a surfeit of violent anger. She was familiar with his explosive temperament, the barrage of reason that collapsed under a wave of fury if he didn't get what he wanted. She felt a ball of anxiety in her solar plexus, and with it the need to get away from him, to protect herself from the simmering cruelty that he exuded from his entire being. Instinctively, she stepped back. Gérard gave a brief, mirthless smile, a fusion of malice and mockery.

"Am I scaring you, Nora?" he said, going toward her.

Nora tensed.

"Get out of my house!"

Gérard didn't move. He stared at her in silence for a long moment, spurred on by tenacious resentment. She had dared. She had dared to leave him, to take him away from his children, to make him unhappy. To cast him into the darkest solitude. And all this for what? To live in this ridiculous little house on her own every other week, with barely enough money to survive? The poison of bitterness was slowly making its way into his veins, swelling the fury that he was increasingly unable to keep in check.

Nora sensed danger. She tried to stay calm and control the fear that gripped her, paralyzing her ability to think. Gérard had nothing to lose now. And she knew him sufficiently well to anticipate his reactions.

"Go and say goodbye to the children," she ordered in the firmest tone she could. "And then I would like you to leave."

Gérard, glaring, blurted out with a sardonic laugh, "You say goodbye to them from me."

He stormed out of the house, got into his car, slammed the door, and sped off.

Alone in the entryway, Nora, trembling, softly pushed the front door closed.

# CHAPTER
## 9

Gérard forced himself not to speed up as he drove home. He was enraged by Nora. He'd tried to reconnect with her and, as usual, she'd misconstrued his intent. And even if he couldn't deny it hadn't been particularly sensitive of him to tell her the story of the suspect who'd hanged himself in her house or the one next door, as always, she had assumed a negative ulterior motive on his part.

She'd thought—

What had she thought?

That he wanted to scare her? Or was trying to worm his way back into her life, into the very place she'd taken refuge to get away from him?

He gripped the steering wheel even harder, trying to shake off the rage that was choking him, the bitterness, pain, anger, sorrow, and grief at losing the woman he loved, despite the scant time and attention he'd spent on her when they were together.

But no, all that was before! Before she'd left him, before she'd shattered all that they'd built together during eighteen long years.

Why wouldn't she accept that he'd changed? And how could he communicate it without triggering a heap of accusations that would be bound to lead to another rift? Since she'd told him she was leaving, he'd sensed himself doing the exact opposite to what he needed to do to get her back: he was either clumsy or, as he'd been just now, downright insensitive; or he formulated his thoughts out loud in a way that came out sounding ambiguous. It was always when he was in the middle of saying something that he realized how it might be misconstrued. It was a bit like being under a spell. As if he'd been bewitched, like a cartoon character who suddenly loses control of what they're doing or saying.

He didn't recognize himself anymore.

The case of that guy who'd hanged himself had been nagging at him for days, ever since the last time he'd come to fetch the kids. It had come to him in a flash as he was waiting for them in the car. He thought he vaguely recognized the neighborhood. He had a feeling he'd been there before. And then out of the blue he remembered the strange case of the foxglove poisoning. David Brunelle. Some poor beleaguered guy overwhelmed by life. His criminal record wasn't in his favor, but there was no evidence against him. The cops had brought him in hoping he'd crack under pressure and they'd get a confession out of him.

Gérard had gotten him out of custody in no time and dropped him back at his house. Then two days later he heard he'd committed suicide. But Nassim had just been born, and his priorities had changed. For once, work had taken a back seat.

As soon as he got home, Gérard went straight into his office and stood there perusing the shelves where he filed his archives.

He found the year of the case—the year of his son's birth—took down the corresponding file folder, and began flicking through the pages. It took him a couple of minutes to find what he was looking for: two sheets of paper, one outlining the case, the other with the suspect's details.

28, rue Edmond-Petit.

Nora lived at number 26.

Yet another opportunity he'd missed to keep his mouth shut. And, for an attorney, that was no small matter.

# CHAPTER
# 10

Turn on the computer. Google. Facebook. Four notifications, one message, no friend requests. He began with the message. Arthur. For a change. *Hi Mil, lost my notes for the French assignment, LOL, can you scan them for me?* Lol? What was so funny about that?

Milo turned to his notifications. Two invitations to play online games, a "like" from Arthur, and a message from Arthur. Milo clicked on it. It was a photo of a dog with a stately bearing and a haughty look named Clint Eastwoof, next to a black cat with a squashed muzzle and eyes slightly too far apart, named Samuel L. Catson. Underneath Arthur had commented: *LOL. Plus they look like each other. Don't forget the French assignment.*

Milo was careful not to click "like" so as not to show he'd been on Facebook, then sighed when he realized Arthur would already know he'd read his message. He clicked "like," then swiveled forty-five degrees on his desk chair, located his backpack on the other side of the room, and stood up to get it.

As he walked by the window, a movement in the next-door yard caught his eye. He didn't stop moving until he was already past the window, as if the image he'd seen had only just reached his brain. Slowly he turned back to look.

His bedroom looked out onto both yards, so he had an unimpeded view of what was happening on both sides of the hedge. Inès was strolling across the grass toward a sun lounger, wearing a bikini and holding what appeared to be a BlackBerry attached to a pair of earphones whose cord reached up to her ears. She had her back to him. Instinctively, Milo went closer to the window to enjoy the view. She was very pretty, with black hair tied back in a ponytail, dark skin, long legs, and a nice ass.

Milo swallowed.

He watched her for a few seconds, and then nothing more happened—she was lying down now and not moving—so he went back to his desk, sat down, checked his Facebook page, remembered about the French assignment, and got up again to get his backpack.

Back at his computer, he thought for a moment. Then, briskly, he left the room and went down to the front door and out onto the street. He walked a few feet to the house next door, where he peered at the names on the mailbox: Nora Amrani, Inès and Nassim Depardieu.

Inès Depardieu.

He turned around and went back into the house, strode up the stairs two at a time, and sat back down at the computer. He typed Inès's name in the Facebook search box, consulted the first four suggestions, and clicked on the second. There she was, grinning mischievously at him. He dragged the arrow to the "add friend" icon. The arrow turned into a hand. He hesitated, briefly, then clicked.

That was it. He'd cast his hook. Well, an invitation, anyway. Social formalities in the third millennium. A virtual initial contact without risk of rejection. No stammering or blushing. The only drawback was that now he had to wait.

With nothing better to do, he stood up and went back to look out the window. The girl was still lying on the sun lounger, looking at her BlackBerry. Too late, he realized she must have just received a ping alerting her to his friend request: suddenly she turned her head to his window and caught sight of him spying on her. It was too late to conceal himself; Milo could think of nothing better than to hurriedly hide behind the curtains.

What an idiot! What did he look like now? How on earth was he going to fix this? But even in his discomfiture, a thought occurred to him that made him smile. His profile picture was a drawing of the hero of Assassin's Creed, which meant that if Inès had identified him, which she clearly had, she must know his name. And there was no way she could have known it if she hadn't made inquiries. Which meant she must have noticed him.

Milo cowered behind the curtain, not sure what to do next. His attention was drawn by a ping indicating he had a new Facebook notification. He went over to his desk and, with a click, saw that Inès had accepted his request.

Milo smiled in delight.

A few seconds later, he received a new message. His heart

began to beat a little faster. She'd clearly wasted no time in contacting him. He knew that when he read the message, she'd be notified immediately, so he forced himself to wait, so as not to betray his impatience. After ten minutes, which felt more like an hour, he opened his mailbox.

It was Arthur, reminding him about the French assignment.

# CHAPTER
## 11

Soon conventional introductions were made. Nora decided to invite the neighbors over. She mentioned it one morning to her daughter, who thought it was a cool idea, and then that same afternoon she happened to run into Tiphaine on the sidewalk as she was leaving the house. She went straight up to her and asked her to dinner on Friday evening. An opportunity to get to know each other.

Caught off guard, Tiphaine tried to hide her surprise by pretending to figure out if she and Sylvain were free on Friday. In truth, it wasn't an issue: their social life had long been as ruined as their relationship.

"How nice," she said. "I don't think we have anything planned, at least not that I know of . . . I'll check with Sylvain and let you know." And with that she let out a small laugh that was meant to be casual but betrayed her awkwardness. It was hard for her to be on familiar terms with people, at least anyone she didn't know well, whether her own age or younger. Over the last eight years, there had been no frivolity in her life: a kind of barrier, that she no longer tried to push away, had been established between her and other people.

She promised Nora she'd call that evening, once Sylvain was home from work. The two women exchanged cell phone numbers and said goodbye as they parted.

As Tiphaine closed the front door behind her, Nora's invitation sounded in her like a warning: the idea of returning to her old house made her feel nauseated, even though she knew the walls held no trace of their former life. Perhaps that was what she dreaded most, being confronted with the ruthless power of time passing, indifferent to her grief. Even before she told Sylvain about the invitation, she knew she could never set foot in the house again.

She had to find an excuse that allowed her to keep up appearances, hang on to the fragile thread that linked her to an ersatz normality, the pleasing image reflected back by Nora of an ordinary neighbor, an anonymous woman, a potential friend.

By the time Sylvain had gotten home, Nora's invitation had taken on a disproportionate magnitude in Tiphaine's mind. Sylvain sensed at once that something was wrong—how well he knew her—and tried to get her to talk. Tiphaine resisted for a few moments, saying, "Everything's fine, I promise," before giving in as though announcing a catastrophe.

"Nora, you know, the new neighbor next door, has invited us over on Friday evening."

Sylvain looked at her for a moment, waiting for her to continue. But Tiphaine said nothing more, just stared at him with a troubled expression in which he could read her fear.

Over the next hour, he used all the power of his imagination to find the right words, comforting images, effective arguments. He talked about it as if it were an opportunity to move forward, to chase away the ghosts without denying the past, to turn the page without forgetting Maxime. To give herself the chance to start enjoying life again. Not like before, not as if nothing had happened, but to find a way to get beyond the fear, deal with the pain. He promised her that if she couldn't cope, if the memories came flooding back too intensely, he'd find an excuse for them to leave.

Eventually Tiphaine agreed.

When Milo found out he was going to spend Friday evening at his pretty neighbor's house—Tiphaine and Sylvain offered him the option of coming too—he concealed his delight with a blasé shrug.

"I don't know. Yeah. Maybe."

"You have to tell us if you're coming, Milo," Tiphaine insisted. "Nora needs to know how many she's feeding."

Of course he was coming! He wouldn't miss it for the world. But he was paralyzed with anxiety at the prospect of spending an entire evening with Inès. What would they talk about? Would she make fun of him for cowering behind the curtains? What did she make of him? Was he worthy of a girl like that? What was he going to wear? Even though the invitation was like the fulfillment of his wildest dreams, Milo pretended to accept it without any particular enthusiasm.

It was all set, then. Tiphaine, reassured by Sylvain's promise, searched for Nora's number in her cell phone and made the call. Nora sounded delighted they were coming. They agreed on a time (8 p.m.), what to bring (a bottle of wine), and the tone of the evening (no fuss, it'll just be us).

On Friday evening, the three gathered on Nora's front step. As he rang the doorbell, Sylvain prayed the evening would go well. Tiphaine was trying to control the knot of anxiety in her stomach, and Milo was simply scared to death.

When Nora opened the front door the Geniots understood that "no fuss, it's just us" didn't mean the same thing to them as to her. Nora had pulled out all the stops: the food, the tableware, her outfit. She looked dazzling. Her Moroccan looks were the perfect complement to her European elegance. She welcomed her guests with a brilliant smile, inviting them in as if they were good friends she hadn't seen in a while. She did it all with artlessness and ease.

As she walked into the living room, Tiphaine took a deep breath, as if to give herself courage. What struck her immediately was that there was no lingering trace of their life there. The rooms were, of course, the same size, and the layout hadn't changed—the living room at the front of the house, the dining room at the back, the kitchen to the side. But everything had been redone: the paint, the floor tiles in the entryway, the parquet in the living room. The furnishings and decor reflected Nora's style. It was as if this were the first time Tiphaine had ever set foot there. The avalanche of memories she had been expecting, each more painful than the next, didn't materialize. Gradually, she relaxed.

Nora invited them to sit down, then asked what they'd like to drink. She went through what she had, and Sylvain cracked a joke that made everyone laugh. Milo sat there looking uncomfortable and said nothing. Nora noticed his awkwardness and called up the stairs, "Inès! Nassim! Our guests have arrived!"

Nassim was the first to appear. He hid behind his mother, pretending to be shy, peeking out curiously at the three guests with a timid smile on his face. Nora introduced him to Sylvain, since Tiphaine and he had already met, and told him to say hello. The boy complied with good grace. Tiphaine and Sylvain were so busy lauding the boy's manners and charm, it slightly spoiled Inès's entrance.

But not for everyone.

Milo was the first to see her. His heart gave a little leap at the sight of her, an unwelcome quickening that he tried to control. If he let himself be impressed, he was lost. As she walked into the room their eyes met, and Milo thought he detected a teasing glint in the teenager's eyes.

"Hey there, Connor Kenway," she said.

Connor Kenway! She knew Assassin's Creed, which, for a girl, was really something. Milo was so surprised he felt silly. What did he know about what she liked?

"Hi!" he replied.

"This is my daughter Inès," said Nora, pushing her forward.

Inès embraced first Tiphaine, then Sylvain, and then found herself in front of Milo.

"Shall we go upstairs?"

The way she asked was so natural that Milo thought he might faint. He felt his face grow longer, his eyes widen beyond his control, and he did the last thing he should have done: he looked at Tiphaine and Sylvain as if seeking their approval. As he did so, he felt an overwhelming desire for the ground to open and swallow him up.

"Yes, why don't you take Milo and show him your room?" Nora agreed. "I'll call you when dinner's ready."

Inès turned on her heel and Milo followed her.

Then it was Nassim's turn to take off, leaving the adults to themselves. Nora served drinks and began talking about the neighborhood, which was all they had in common. The conversation flowed; Tiphaine and Sylvain heard about Nora's recent separation, and how the relationship with her husband remained strained. Speaking candidly, but without going into detail, she told them that despite the upheaval, she had no regrets.

The evening went off wonderfully. By the time they sat down to dinner Tiphaine felt completely relaxed. She smiled and chatted throughout the meal. Sylvain, too, was in good form. He talked a little about himself, told a few anecdotes about his work, they discussed the political situation in France and discovered that they pretty much agreed on everything.

Meanwhile the teenagers were also getting to know each other. They did some gaming on the PlayStation, listened to music, smoked cigarettes out of Inès's bedroom window, and compared their interests.

Tiphaine was slightly worried that Milo would tell Inès about their family situation. The fact that he wasn't their biological son. She thought he might reveal the awful circumstances of the "events." It was so nice that Nora knew nothing about it, and she couldn't bear the thought of one day seeing the familiar sympathetic yet accusatory gleam in her neighbor's eye. When the two young people joined them at the table she looked to see if anything had changed in Inès's manner, but she couldn't spot anything. When they went back upstairs after dinner, she reassured herself that Milo would never reveal something so private to a girl the first time he met her. He, too, was hungry for normality.

Was it really the first time they'd met? And what was going on up there? Was it reasonable to leave them alone for so long?

"Are you aware that my son and your daughter are alone upstairs, unsupervised?" she said to Nora, affecting a mischievous tone.

"Does my daughter have anything to worry about?" Nora replied, imitating Tiphaine's tone of voice.

"Given your daughter's looks, I'd say it's more likely Milo who's in danger," said Sylvain.

Nora gave him a confused smile, as if she thought the compliment was for her.

"Anyway, this is the age of first love," he said with a fatalistic air. "No matter how much we watch them, if something's going to happen, nothing and nobody will be able to prevent it."

"Let's not get ahead of ourselves," Nora said. "They've only known each other for two hours and we're already marrying them off."

"Some things are unavoidable," Sylvain murmured pensively. Tiphaine turned to her husband with a confused expression on her face.

"What are you talking about?"

Sylvain didn't answer. He seemed lost in thought. For a few seconds, there was silence around the table.

Sylvain's comment disturbed Tiphaine, though she wasn't sure why. She had the uncomfortable feeling she hadn't quite grasped what he meant.

"Coffee?" Nora suggested, as she began to clear.

Tiphaine and Sylvain nodded, and Nora disappeared into the kitchen.

Tiphaine took advantage of being alone with Sylvain to take him to task.

"That really was going a bit far."

"What? She's very pretty."

"They're just kids . . . She's barely thirteen."

"You're being very naïve," said Sylvain.

Nora came back in, and the two fell silent. Sylvain stood up and began to clear the rest of the table, obliging Tiphaine to do the same so as not to appear rude.

"Leave it, I'll do it later," said Nora, which didn't stop them.

The evening drew to an end. They finished their coffee and Nora offered them a liqueur, which they politely declined. Tiphaine, eager to go home, threw Sylvain a pointed look that he registered, then continued chatting for a few minutes before giving a nod to indicate he was ready to go. It was time to gather the troops (it took Milo a good five minutes to come downstairs). In the entryway, everyone hugged goodbye and they all promised to get together again soon.

Back at home, the Geniots began getting ready for bed. Tiphaine was in the bathroom and Milo in his bedroom. Sylvain wandered around in circles in the living room for a few minutes, then went up and knocked on Milo's door. Milo responded with a grunt that Sylvain wasn't sure how to interpret. To be on the safe side, he pushed open the door and poked his head around.

"I was just wondering—did you have a good time tonight?"

"Yeah."

Milo was sitting in front of his computer. Clearly Sylvain was disturbing him.

"Okay . . . I'll leave you to it, then. Turn the lights off in fifteen minutes, okay?"

"Don't worry, I will."

"Okay, then. Sleep tight."

"Night."

As Sylvain was pulling the door closed, Milo added, almost as if he regretted his earlier lack of warmth, "How about you, did you enjoy the evening?"

"Yeah."

For a brief moment, the two men held each other's eye, and a glimmer of complicity passed between them.

# CHAPTER
## 12

As the door closed, Milo slumped back in his chair. It was true, he'd had a really nice evening. Surprisingly nice. He'd been expecting it to be much more awkward, a bit of an ordeal even, but Inès was lovely. And extremely pretty, he had to admit. After the first half hour, which they'd basically spent discreetly checking each other out, they found they had plenty to talk about. They started with Facebook, the way they used the sprawling network that nipped in the bud any sense of solitude. And even if their shared vocabulary didn't always have quite the same resonance—Inès thought she had a modest number of friends, only 173, while Milo took pride in his 32—they both agreed on how important it was not to think that what they saw on the computer screen bore the slightest resemblance to real life. They talked about a few particularly memorable or funny memes that had gone viral recently, and discovered they had a ton of stuff in common.

Milo was tall for his age; by the time he'd hit adolescence he'd already started to shoot up in a way that seemed almost tyrannical, completely arbitrary and out of control. Curiously, his features had retained a certain regularity, and the hormonal surge barely showed on his face: just a few pimples, if you looked closely. He was turning into a handsome young man. Inès was impressed by the light fuzz on his upper lip: Milo was fifteen, and when she told her friends she'd spent an evening up in her room with a guy that age (information she'd let drop in passing, as if it were a mere detail), they'd swoon with envy.

Léa and Emma. Her partners in crime. They'd been inseparable since kindergarten. The terrible threesome. Angels when they were on their own, devils when they were together. Even Nora sometimes disapproved of their behavior. Inès told Milo about them, her eyes shining with the confidence that true friendship bestows.

"What about you? Who are you friends with?" she asked after she'd recounted a few stories that exemplified the tight bond she had with her two best friends.

Milo didn't have many friends. Maybe Arthur could be considered a friend, though all they really had in common was that they were both frozen out by their fellow students. Milo liked it that way, Arthur did not. Arthur was heavy, both literally and metaphorically. He was overbearing in group situations, and systematically ostracized, despite his cheery, open manner. He and Milo were in the same grade and had a few classes together, one of which was French. Arthur hung around Milo at recess and in the cafeteria at lunch, boring him with endless risqué jokes whose punch lines were rarely funny. Every so often, Milo would release a torrent of criticism, drowning the poor kid in cruel words before telling him to get lost. Arthur would slink off and find another equally miserable companion until the evening, when a reconciliation would take place on Facebook. Milo let it happen, as much out of weariness as out of need: Arthur's friendship, however inadequate, filled a solitude that was at times oppressive.

Apart from Arthur, Milo sometimes hung out with a kid called Benoît, who was seventeen and went to the high school across the street from their middle school. They lived in the same neighborhood and often took the school bus together. Milo liked Benoît's reserve; he wasn't afraid of silence, unlike most kids their age. They didn't talk much but seemed to like each other's company.

Benoît also knew a bit about basketball, which Milo played every Monday evening. Sylvain was his most ardent supporter and, in what had become their weekly ritual, he would drive him to practice, then afterward they'd go to eat at the Ranch, a restaurant specializing in steak, a food that Tiphaine hated with a passion and never cooked. Ever since Milo had taken up basketball two years before, Monday night had become guys' night out.

Milo had a complicated relationship with the outside world. Life had not been kind to him—by the time he was seven, he'd lost most of the people he was close to in quick succession. The first was Maxime, his brother from another mother, his partner in crime, with whom he'd shared almost everything since early childhood. The next was his godfather, Ernest, an elderly man with a grumpy temperament, a boorish manner, and a florid vocabulary, but who melted every time the child asked him to play or to read him a story.

And then the ultimate tragedy, from which no one ever recovers. The nothingness that devours, the emptiness that engulfs, the dark abyss that sucks everything into it. First bewilderment, then anger, bitterness, and fear. Deep, relentless, unending grief.

Since the tragedy, Milo had become very withdrawn. Suffering had distilled its venom in the little boy's heart, and he developed the obsessive belief that everyone he loved was doomed to die. In his tormented mind any affection he had for others released a deadly poison that gave them no chance of survival. Without understanding how or why, he was cursed with a mysterious affliction that made his love fatal.

So he stopped letting himself get attached. He learned to bury all his emotion deep within him, leaving room only for polite indifference. He saw it as a matter of life or death.

Loving someone put that person in danger. From then on, withholding affection became proof of his love.

He quickly put this logic into practice: he began by detaching himself from Tiphaine and Sylvain, terrified at the idea that they might die. If he lost them, he'd be all alone in the world. Not only did he reject any gesture of affection from the two of them, he also forbade himself to acknowledge the slightest bond. The first months of their life together were hard: while the new parents lavished the child with all the love they had, Milo was determined to rebuff it. Tiphaine and Sylvain obviously attributed his withdrawal to the trauma he was suffering. With the help of a therapist, they armed themselves with patience and understanding. The early sessions went well, providing the child with the psychological support he so desperately needed, until one day Milo realized that he was growing fond of this attractive, friendly, supportive woman. From one day to the next, he refused to go back.

The next time he found himself in the therapist's office, having been dragged there by Tiphaine and Sylvain, who were bewildered by the child's rejection and thought he was merely being capricious, he sat there for the entire hour without uttering a word.

After several fruitless sessions, Justine Philippot decided to put an end to his therapy for a while. Milo breathed a sigh of relief: he had just saved Dr. Philippot's life. He was filled with a rather gratifying sense of pride.

The phenomenon occurred whenever he felt good in someone's company: a classmate; or a family member, such as Tiphaine's nephew, who was two years older than him and got a kick out of teaching him "grown-up stuff"; or one particular colleague of Sylvain's who, without fail, brought Milo chocolate or cookies whenever he came to visit. As soon as he realized that these people stood out from the crowd of acquaintances, that he was beginning to think of them with pleasure and looking forward to seeing them again, he felt a sense of unease. What if something happened to them? It was perfectly possible. It had already happened, multiple times. Why would the phenomenon suddenly come to an end?

With a heavy heart, but convinced that the only thing to be done was to tear out the evil by its roots, he turned his back on everyone he cared about. Evil was his twin. The child's only salvation would have been to communicate his fears to someone he trusted, but instead he turned away from everyone.

With time, the fear that he might cause the death of anyone to whom he was close began to subside. No one he knew had died recently, though according to his logic this proved nothing: he no longer had deep feelings for anyone.

But that evening in Inès's company, with her captivating face and the feelings she provoked in him, awakened his demons.

# CHAPTER
# 13

Nora was so stressed, she felt like she was preparing for a test. She decided not to wear a suit, which seemed a little too formal for the circumstances. Jeans and a sweatshirt felt too casual for her liking. Eventually she opted for a pair of taupe linen pants and a navy-blue cotton top, a subtle blend of comfort and style.

She arrived at the preschool fifteen minutes early, short of breath and very nervous. Madame Stillet greeted her warmly, then led her straight to the teachers' lounge, where she introduced her to Jeanine Lambinet. Though she was in her fifties, the woman looked like a schoolteacher from the 1970s, in her pleated skirt, opaque tights, lace-up ankle boots, and a checkered tunic, impeccably pressed and buttoned up to the neck.

"Madame Lambinet, this is Nora Amrani, our new kindergarten assistant."

"At last!" exclaimed the teacher. "I'd almost given up hope."

Despite her apparent relief at Nora's arrival, Madame Lambinet's handshake was cool. She looked her new colleague up and down with the kind of probing expression one might use to examine a new product.

"I hope hard work doesn't scare you," she said without preamble. "You'll need nerves of steel."

"I'll do my best," Nora replied simply.

"Your best isn't good enough, Madame Amrani. As you are about to find out!"

The principal bobbed her head and gave Nora a reassuring smile. "Well, I'll leave you to it. I'm sure everything will be just fine."

She moved closer to Nora, and added under her breath, "Don't worry. Beneath that surly exterior, Madame Lambinet is very kind."

"Flattery will get you nowhere, Martine," said Madame Lambinet in a loud voice.

Madame Stillet contented herself with a simple "Have a good day, Jeanine," as she left the lounge.

Left alone with Madame Lambinet, Nora gave her a shy smile, which was ignored. Madame Lambinet tugged sharply at the sides of her tunic and then, with a brisk toss of her head, indicated to Nora that she should follow. Nora hurried after her.

Madame Lambinet had not been lying: the next four hours were grueling. Their class of twenty-five raving maniacs didn't give them a moment's respite, despite the teacher's authority and experience. Nora spent the whole time running from one end of the classroom to the other, handing out saucers of paint, sheets of paper, and aprons to some of the children, building blocks and puzzles to others, explaining her presence, surveying, tidying, explaining, and accompanying them to the bathroom. When it was time to go for lunch, which meant that her work-day was coming to an end, it felt like her head was about to explode.

Madame Lambinet may not have been particularly warm to her, but Nora couldn't help admiring the efficiency with which she delivered a program that managed to be simultaneously creative, playful, and personalized. And despite her gruff exterior, Nora detected an undeniable affection for her little charges.

The rest of the week went by in the same way. From 8 a.m. till noon, Nora ran from one end of the classroom to the other, answering multiple questions at once, trying as hard as she could to combine efficiency and understanding, two qualities that can be tricky to reconcile.

When it was time to go home, she was too exhausted to do anything, but very thankful she hadn't gotten the full-time post she'd wanted.

Things grew still more complicated on Friday morning, when Madame Stillet stopped her in the hallway to discuss a little problem. Nora felt her heart clench. Was there a problem with her work? Had there been a complaint? She nodded gravely, all ears, and prepared herself for the worst. It turned out that Eloise Villant—whom Nora had never heard of—was sick and would be absent the whole of the following week. Nora tried to piece together what Madame Stillet was talking about. Eventually she realized that Eloise Villant was one of the two women in charge of the after-school daycare program. Would Nora be able to replace her and change her schedule to come in from three till seven until Eloise was better?

Relieved, Nora happily agreed. Madame Stillet thanked her warmly, assured her that she'd helped resolve a very thorny problem, and promised she wouldn't forget it. Then she disappeared into her office.

At that very moment, Nora remembered that she had the children the following week and would have to find someone to fetch Nassim from school. Inès wasn't really a problem, since she could be dropped at home by one or another of her friends' parents and stay home alone until her mother got back. But things were trickier with Nassim. He finished school at 4:30. Even if Nora could find someone to pick him up, they would have to stay with him until 7:20, or even 7:30.

As soon as she got home, Nora called Mathilde and told her about her predicament. Mathilde said she could fetch Nassim from school on Monday, Wednesday, and Friday. She said she'd rather take him back to her place and look after him alongside her own children there. Nora could swing by and get him on her way back from work. On Tuesday and Thursday her two eldest children had activities—one did music and one judo. Mathilde spent both afternoons ferrying them back and forth in the car.

"It's hell," she told Nora. "Nassim would be bored to death. I don't think it's right to impose that on him. It would be much better if you could find another solution."

"What do you do with Justine on those days?" asked Nora. Mathilde's youngest child was only four.

"My neighbor looks after her till Philippe gets back. But I can't ask her to take care of another child."

"I understand," said Nora resignedly. "It's great you can look after him for those three days. I'll figure something out."

Mathilde warmly wished her luck and said goodbye. She already knew about her friend's terrible mornings: Nora called her every afternoon to relate the multiple challenges of her working day.

Nora hung up, still not having figured out a solution for Tuesday and Thursday. There was no way she was going to ask Gérard to help out. Either he would use it to prove she couldn't cope without him, or he'd remind her at every turn that she owed him. Nora's parents lived in Paris, and she couldn't expect them to make the round trip twice a week. Plus it wouldn't be right to ask them to get back in the car at eight o'clock at night, so she'd have to put them up for the night. And in any case they were getting on in age, and had their routine. So that wasn't an option.

She could always leave Nassim at the after-school club, but he wouldn't be happy about that at all. He hated staying in school after class and would be bound to complain about it to his father, who'd then inundate Nora with an endless flow of criticism. In any case, the after-school club at Nassim's school closed at half-past six, so it wouldn't really solve the problem. Nora was disappointed that Mathilde hadn't at least asked her neighbor. She might have been able to persuade her.

Hang on, what if she asked *her* neighbor? She was on good terms with Tiphaine, and she'd noticed that she got home from work every afternoon around four. Tiphaine could pick Nassim up at the end of class, and Nora could fetch him from next door when she got back. That would be the ideal solution.

She realized it was a bit premature to ask such a favor of a woman she barely knew, and continued scrolling through her contacts for an alternative solution, but either her friends worked late, or they lived too far away, or they weren't close-enough friends to ask. Nor was Tiphaine, of course, but the advantage was that she got home early and lived right next door. With no other option, Nora decided to ask her if she'd be prepared to do her this favor.

To her enormous relief, Tiphaine agreed immediately. It was only for two days and Nassim didn't come across as a difficult child. They agreed she'd pick him up from school, bring him home, give him a snack, supervise his homework, and keep him occupied until Nora's return.

"What about Inès?" Tiphaine asked. "What will she do?"

"Inès is older, so I don't mind if she's home alone for a few hours."

"She can come over, too, if she wants company. I'm sure Milo would be more than happy to see her."

Nora couldn't find the words to adequately express her gratitude. Then the two women turned to the practical details. "I'll get you a key made," Nora said. "Just in case."

"In case what?"

"I don't know, in case you need something for Nassim, or if he wants to come and pick up a game, or a book, or whatever."

"Inès has a key, right?"

"Yes, but she might get back later, or spend the afternoon at a friend's house . . . It'll be simpler if you have your own."

"Okay. But I'll give it back to you at the end of the week."

"If you prefer."

The idea of having the key to her old house disturbed Tiphaine. Being able to go inside whenever she liked seemed like taking a gambler who'd been barred from the casino on a trip to Las Vegas. It felt like she was inexorably growing closer to Nora, and she wasn't at all sure she wanted to be friends with her. Still, the prospect of looking after Nassim gave her a thrill she couldn't quite put her finger on. A complicated mix of excitement and unease. She'd agreed to this favor without properly thinking through what it involved, but she didn't care. When Nora had asked her if she would pick up Nassim from school and babysit him until she got home, she'd felt something akin to consolation. Like a soothing balm on the open wound of her sorrow.

# CHAPTER
## 14

Inès woke up in an excellent mood on Saturday. No class. Not that she didn't like school, but she was looking forward to two days off. And to going back to her mother's house the next day. She missed Nora's kindness, attention, and the fact that she was always around. Her father was more distracted, as if he had a thousand things to do and think about. Which he did.

Anyway, the weekend was shaping up to be fun. Her father had told them he'd be gone for part of Saturday to tie up the loose ends of a case he was pleading first thing Monday morning. If he wasn't going to be around, she might as well make the most of it: when he was at home, not that it guaranteed that he was mentally present, he was always putting his foot down about the things she wanted to do.

So, given that he was going to be out of the house all day, Inès planned to ask Emma and Léa over. They'd surf the internet, take selfies making crazy faces, post them on Facebook, like them, comment, like the comments.

Saturday nights with their father were always fun: he'd order takeout, burgers or pizza usually, for the three of them to eat in front of a movie. They used to fight over which movie to watch;

everyone had their own idea of what they wanted to see, which usually didn't correspond to what the others wanted. So their father had ruled that to avoid ruining the evening with endless squabbling, they'd take turns picking the movie. That evening it was Inès who had the delicious task of imposing her choice. She hadn't yet made up her mind between *Harry Potter and the Goblet of Fire* and *Rebel*, which she'd missed seeing in the movie theater when it came out. She'd decide during the day.

Sundays were a day of transition, when they didn't do much, except pack their bags with whatever they needed to take to their mother's house, tidy their rooms, finish their homework assignments for Monday, and try to get a little ahead for the rest of the week.

Gérard always seemed to realize suddenly that the week was over, his kids were leaving for seven days, and he hadn't really made the most of them being there. They hung out in their pajamas until after lunch, enjoying the munificence of a father whose pangs of guilt made him indulgent.

On Sunday evenings they went back to Nora's. The rhythm there was different: slower, calmer, much less stressful. Inès found the house more comfortable somehow, smaller and cozier. And above all there was her mother, who understood her so much better, even if they did fight like cats and dogs. Nora was far from perfect, but she was so much easier to deal with than the quick-tempered Gérard, who could be in perfectly good spirits one minute, only for his mood to change dramatically in the face of some trivial annoyance.

Inès jumped out of bed and went straight down to the kitchen for breakfast, half-dressed in a T-shirt and panties. She found herself thinking about Milo and wondering if she was going to run into him during the week. She liked him living next door. They had very different personalities, but they'd hit it off the other evening at her mother's house. Milo was reserved while Inès was gregarious, he was shy and she was a chatterbox, she was sociable, he seemed quite introverted. And he hadn't appeared attracted to her, which was no doubt the reason he'd awakened her desire for him.

Inès's body had been changing for a while, and with it the way people looked at her. She was just beginning to develop a vague sense of her new power, unknown to her until recently, which was giving birth to a whole variety of sensations that she had to admit she found extremely pleasurable. The boys she hung around with (apart from her brother and father, of course) were endlessly eager to please. Their behavior betrayed their infatuation. But it was happening too often now; boys were getting crushes on her all the time. She was beginning to tire of it, or so she liked to think—and, more to the point, to say within earshot of her friends, who had no idea of all the excitement to come.

But with Milo, the promise of a new challenge was rather thrilling. And there was something about him: she liked that he was tall, his dark and concentrated gaze, his unhurried movements, his tact. She felt comfortable and confident when she was with him, without really understanding why. Whatever it was, she was looking forward to seeing him again.

In the kitchen, Nassim put two *pains au chocolat* to heat up in the oven and sat down at the breakfast table opposite his father, who was tapping away on his iPad, a steaming cup of coffee within reach.

"Good morning, princess!" he said, then looked up and noticed her state of undress. "You could put on some clothes before you come down for breakfast, you know."

Inès didn't rise to the bait.

"Did you hear what I just said?" Gérard asked.

"Whatever," she replied with a shrug.

"You're not eight anymore, Inès. It's a question of respect. Do I come down for breakfast in my boxer shorts?" Nassim giggled at the thought of his father sitting at the table in his underwear. Inès didn't react.

"Go upstairs and make yourself decent!" said Gérard, in a tone that didn't brook any dissent. Inès sighed, as if she were dealing with a complete idiot. She stood up and walked out of the kitchen.

Up in her bedroom, she switched on her computer and while she waited for it to start up picked through her wardrobe for something to wear. Once she was dressed, she returned to the computer, opened Facebook, quickly scanned her notifications, and clicked on Milo's profile. She hovered the mouse over the message icon and thought for a moment. She didn't have a lot of time. She began to type.

**Hi. I'll be at my mom's this week. It would be fun to see each other.**

She reread the message, hesitated, then deleted the last sentence, which she immediately rewrote. **We could get together if you like xxx**

She hesitated again, deleted **xxx**, then dragged the cursor to click "send."

# CHAPTER
# 15

Sunday, late afternoon. The kids would be back soon. Nora was putting the last touches on tidying the house: the bedrooms had been vacuumed, the beds made up with clean sheets, there was a meal simmering on the stove, tonight was going to be a celebration! She glanced at her watch. They'd be back any minute. She hastened to sort out the final detail—little gifts she'd bought the previous day to place on Inès's and Nassim's pillows, symbolic really, her way of welcoming them home. Three packs of Pokémon cards for Nassim and a pair of earrings for Inès. She went back downstairs, looked around to check that everything was perfect. The doorbell rang.

She opened the front door with a radiant smile, spreading her arms wide to take the children in her arms, her heart full of joy . . . and saw Sylvain standing on the doorstep.

"Hi, Nora," he said, hopping from one foot to the other. "Am I disturbing you?"

"No," she said, more curious than surprised.

"It's stupid, I'm making dinner and I'm clean out of eggs. You don't have one I could borrow, do you?"

"I think I do."

She moved aside to let him past and shut the front door behind her. Then she disappeared into the kitchen.

"Do you need one or two?" she called, peering in the refrigerator.

"One'll be perfect."

She came back holding an egg and handed it to Sylvain.

"Thank you so much."

Nora nodded her head, indicating it wasn't a problem. There was a brief pause, then Sylvain said with a smile, "Well, I'd best be going. I owe you one."

"Yes indeed, and you'd better give it back soon or I'll start totting up the interest," she answered, returning the smile.

"How do you calculate it?"

"Well, if you take too long, you'll owe me a cow."

"Okay then. Better check you have room for a side of beef in your refrigerator!" They both laughed.

Sylvain headed to the front door, followed by Nora. Just as Sylvain was leaving the house Gérard pulled up in the car. The children jumped out and ran toward their mother, who welcomed them with open arms. It was so good to have them back. Nora dropped into the embrace, holding her two beloved children against her, smelling their heads and squeezing their bodies. Gérard got out of the car and walked around it to join the small group on the sidewalk. As he approached, he stared at Sylvain with open curiosity: the sight of a stranger coming out of his wife's house—they were still married, after all—elicited some questions. And, seemingly, some animosity too.

Nora introduced the two men. "Sylvain, my neighbor . . . Gérard, Inès and Nassim's father."

The two men acknowledged each other with a nod, jovial on the part of Sylvain, suspicious on that of Gérard. Sylvain turned to Nora with what seemed to Gérard a conspiratorial smile.

"Thank you again," he said, holding up the egg. Nora smiled back. Then he took his leave and disappeared into the house next door. As he watched him go, Gérard noticed the number 28 painted in white on the wall by the front door. He recalled the case of the man who had hanged himself, and his getting the two houses mixed up.

The children had already gone inside. Standing there on the sidewalk, Nora clearly had no intention of inviting him in. Despite that, he went up to her.

"I owe you an apology."

She lifted her eyebrows in surprise.

"It really wasn't very tactful of me to tell you about the man who committed suicide. Particularly given that he didn't hang himself in your house." Gérard paused for a moment, as though for effect.

"It was in that house," he said, indicating next door with a tilt of the chin.

"What are you talking about now?" She sighed wearily.

"I checked. My client lived at number twenty-eight, not number twenty-six as I first thought. That's the house where he hanged himself."

"Great," Nora said coldly. "Thanks for letting me know."

Gérard ignored his wife's chilly tone and turned his head to the house next door with a smirk.

"Poor guy . . . if only he'd known."

# CHAPTER
# 16

Once again, Gérard felt very dispirited on the journey home. Nora had been distant and cold, deliberately showing her antipathy to him while being gracious to her neighbor. And when that idiot had gone home and the children had run into the house—in other words, when he'd found himself alone with her for two minutes—she'd dismissed him unceremoniously, indifferent to his obvious desire to reestablish a cordial relationship with her. He'd apologized, hadn't he? What more did she want?

Feeling bruised by his wife's obduracy, his self-esteem wounded, Gérard clenched his jaw as he recalled the conspiratorial smile Nora had exchanged with her neighbor. Who was that guy? He looked like your standard-issue suburban liberal, a schmuck who'd scented a potential lay when he saw a single woman with two kids show up next door. An asshole who clearly hadn't wasted any time before getting friendly with her. And she, of course, was completely oblivious, always convinced that people were only motivated by good intentions. She was so naïve.

Or maybe he was the one being naïve. Maybe Nora was completely aware of the lecherous motivation of her bastard of a neighbor and actually liked it. He pictured Nora's body in her neighbor's arms and let out a cry of sheer rage. The very idea of another man touching her, or even just going near her—merely laying eyes on her—was unbearable. His chest tightened with fury. It felt like he'd been stabbed with a white-hot dagger to the heart.

It hadn't taken her long to flaunt her availability in front of the first person who came along, and that guy was certainly making the most of it. It was so obvious they were having fun—you just had to see the way they smirked at each other in front of him, in front of everyone, not even thinking about whether it might upset the children. Gérard felt so alone, betrayed, scorned to the depths of his being, his love for her sullied. He was such a fool. The elevated image he had of his wife, the esteem in which he'd held her, the way he'd been so sure she was not like other women, that this kind of thing would never happen to them.

But she'd left him, after all they'd built together, all their memories, intimacy, affection, contentment. Eighteen years. Eighteen years together, swept away in a few days, packed up in boxes and pitched into a moving truck. The things she'd left behind in the house—his home!—had lost all depth, shape, color, smell. There was nothing left. Everything was now a kind of transparent gray, glassy and flat.

Impersonal.

She'd gone, leaving behind nothing but a void.

Clutching the steering wheel, Gérard stifled a sob of despair, overwhelmed by the urge to burst into tears. What was stopping him from crying? He was alone now, alone in his body, his heart, his soul, cut off from the watchful eye and soothing presence of the woman he still adored. Her absence racked his body every hour of the day and night. There was no respite. Every moment was torture.

The whole thing had come out of the blue, with absolutely no warning—no revealing details or clues that might have allowed him to parry the mortal blow she was about to deal him. Maybe he'd have been able to reason with her, talk her out of it. He might have persuaded her to give up this insane project by reminding her of her priorities—the children, the family. *Their* family. But no, she hadn't given him a chance. When she left, she proved that everything they had built up together over so many years had lost all meaning for her.

It was beyond belief.

She had to wake up. She had to realize her mistake, recognize the appalling stupidity of what she'd done. She was going to come to her senses and return to their house. It might take a little time, but it would happen, he was sure of it. Hell couldn't last forever. It would all come to an end one day. Sure, not right away, it would take time for her to overcome the shame and deal with her wounded pride, but the day would come, it had to. And when it did, he'd welcome her with open arms, make a thousand promises, forgive her for everything, and pretend it had never happened. He was tired of living like a hermit, being on his own when she was just a few miles away. So near and yet so far. She and the children. His engine, his motivation, the reason he needed to get up in the morning to go to work, to play the role of father, lover, citizen.

That was why he had to do everything he could to see her, to spend time with her, to make her understand he wasn't angry with her, she could come back whenever she wanted, he wouldn't talk about any of it, or ask any questions. To make her understand how he'd changed.

How much better things would be from now on.

But for that to happen, for him to be able to show her he wasn't the same man anymore, they had to see each other! How was he going to make her realize the immensity of her error if not in person, in flesh and blood, palpable? He had to find the words to convince her. Words were his forte; he knew how to use them better than anyone. He didn't doubt for a moment that, given the chance, he'd be able to make her see everything differently.

What he had to do now was assess the situation, weigh up the enemy threat, and get organized. He needed to know who exactly he was dealing with. He pulled over to the side of the road, switched on his blinkers, and checked to see if there was any oncoming traffic. Then he swung the car around and drove back to the end of Nora's street. He parked the car far enough away that she wouldn't spot it, and walked the rest of the way, taking long strides, his eyes fixed on Nora's house, ready to duck behind the hedge in case she suddenly appeared. There was no reason for her to be going out at this time of day, but it was better to be cautious and prepared for any eventuality. He mustn't be seen. What he wanted to do would take only a few seconds; it would be extremely dumb to mess it up.

He didn't slow his step when he reached number 26, but hunched down so he couldn't be seen from the living room window, and kept going till he reached number 28. When he arrived at the front door he stood up straight and read the names on the doorbell.

What he saw left him speechless.

Tiphaine and Sylvain Geniot—Milo Brunelle.

Brunelle. The same surname as David Brunelle. The man who'd hanged himself. The foxglove poisoning. Could this Brunelle be his son? Yes, he remembered now David Brunelle mentioning he had a seven-year-old son.

The memories came back in waves: the atmosphere in his client's cell that night, the man's extreme agitation, his palpable anxiety, how desperate he'd been to go home and pick up his son, who was being looked after by a neighbor while he accompanied the police down to the station. Gérard frowned as he tried to remember. David had become increasingly distressed as he realized what he was being accused of and heard the circumstances of Ernest Wilmot's death. That was when he'd mentioned a neighbor who had gifted them the pot of purple foxgloves the police had found on the deck. A neighbor who was, he said, the only person he knew capable of transforming a simple plant into a dangerous weapon.

The same neighbor who was looking after his son. Who was none other than Milo Brunelle.

It was all coming back to him now.

Eight years after the affair, David Brunelle's son was still living in the house where his father had hanged himself. The horror.

Baffled, Gérard tapped the names of Tiphaine and Sylvain Geniot and Milo Brunelle into the Notes application on his iPhone. The most pressing question that needed answering was the nature of the relationship between the Geniots and Milo and, ultimately, David Brunelle.

# CHAPTER
## 17

On Tuesday, Tiphaine left work early. She stopped by the minimart to stock up on cookies, cereal, and fruit juice, then drove to Nassim's elementary school, the same one Maxime and Milo had gone to—not surprising, since there were only two elementary schools in the town, one of which was Catholic. Tiphaine, an avowed atheist, had never even briefly contemplated sending her son there, but Laetitia, Milo's mother, had considered it. Eventually she'd reached the same decision as Tiphaine, partly so as not to separate the two boys, who had been like brothers since their birth, and partly for the sake of convenience: back then, the Brunelles and the Geniots always helped each other out, particularly when it came to the children.

When she arrived at the school gate, Tiphaine felt herself gripped by a feeling that was simultaneously heartwarming and gut-wrenching. It had been three years since she'd last set foot in the building where Milo had once been a pupil. Coming back to this familiar place filled her with a mixture of pleasure and apprehension. The noises, the lights, the smells, the particular atmosphere that had once been part of her daily life took her back for a moment to a confused time when pure joy had rubbed shoulders with utter horror.

Tiphaine followed the corridors that led to the playground, passing a few familiar faces on her way, who either didn't notice her, or—

"Madame Geniot! How lovely of you to come and see us! How are you?"

Coming out of her classroom, Madame Dufrêne, Milo's teacher in his last year of elementary school, gave her an open but curious smile. Her expression betrayed the question that was clearly on the tip of her tongue: *What are you doing here?*

"Hello, Madame Dufrêne. I'm well. How about you?"

"I'm very well indeed, thank you. To what do we owe the honor?"

"I'm picking up my neighbor's little boy. His mom's working late tonight."

"Oh! That's so kind of you . . . How's Milo doing?"

"He's fine."

"What grade is he in now? Twelfth?"

"No, eleventh."

Madame Dufrêne looked surprised.

"He had to repeat eleventh grade," Tiphaine was forced to admit.

The question mark in the teacher's eyes turned into an exclamation mark.

"Oh, what a shame. Such a smart little boy!"

Tiphaine was tempted to respond that it had nothing to do

with how smart he was, but managed to check herself. Instead, before the teacher had time to fire off another question, she asked where she might find Nassim Depardieu.

"At this time of day, they'll be in the cafeteria having a snack."

"Thank you." She hurriedly said goodbye to the teacher and went off in the direction the woman had pointed.

"Say hi to Milo from me!" Madame Dufrêne just had time to call after her. Tiphaine turned and waved in assent before turning left down the next corridor. She found Nassim exactly where Madame Dufrêne had said he would be, eating a snack with some friends. When he saw her, he obediently rose to his feet. He was obviously well brought up, but his slightly peeved expression nevertheless betrayed a certain irritation with the woman who had come to fetch him instead of his mother. Tiphaine told herself she had a few hours to win him over. Wasting no time, even before they'd left the building, she began to list all the things she'd bought him to eat, and various TV programs they could watch, depending on the young man's preferences. At last Nassim hazarded a smile.

In the car, Tiphaine bombarded the child with questions, to which Nassim responded in polite monosyllables. She asked what he was learning, what his friends were called, what he liked doing best, if he had any hobbies, what his favorite cartoons were. But instead of answering, the child had a real gift for unearthing the most vague and neutral words in the French language. And when she tried to ask him something indirectly, as a way of teasing out some more detail, he just shrugged and came out with the ultimate platitude, "I don't know."

As they drove up the street to their respective houses, Tiphaine asked Nassim where he'd rather wait for his mother.

"Your mother gave me the key to your house in case you need anything. If you like, we can go there instead of my house." This time, Nassim pondered the question. The idea tempted him, except that it wasn't what his mother had planned, and he didn't know what the consequences of a change of program might be.

After a few moments of reflection, having decided he couldn't really see what difference it would make, he assented with a vigorous nod of his head.

"So you'd rather we waited in your house?" Tiphaine asked, to be sure.

"Yeah."

Tiphaine gave a gratified smile and ruffled the child's hair.

"As you wish. You're the boss."

As they got out of the car, Nassim saw an old lady sitting on a folding chair outside one of the houses opposite. She wore a beige overcoat and a pair of ugly but presumably comfortable walking shoes. On the sidewalk alongside her stood an old-fashioned suitcase whose clasp was half eaten away by rust. Nassim had seen her before. In fact, he saw her every time he left the house.

Noticing the boy's interest, Tiphaine told him, "That's Madame Appleblossom. She sits there every day, from morning to night."

"What's she doing?" asked the little boy.

"Waiting."

"Waiting for what?"

"No one knows. Least of all her, I imagine."

Nassim looked at the elderly lady with an expression that was both curious and pitying. Tiphaine told him that Madame Appleblossom had come to live there five years before, and ever since, weather permitting, she would sit outside the front door with her suitcase, as if she were about to leave on vacation. In the beginning various neighborhood acquaintances came by to ask what she was doing, if she was waiting for someone. She never answered, merely assuring all those who were concerned about her well-being that she was in great shape and in need of nothing. She didn't seem to have any children, and the few visitors she received were always other elderly people. When the neighbors tried to find out more about the old lady and what she was waiting for, they ended up lifting their arms in a gesture of defeat. Some tried to make her see reason, but one day Madame Appleblossom flew into an astonishing rage, yelling that if even at her age she was being pestered by a bunch of idiots, the world really had hit a new low.

"Is that really her name? Madame Appleblossom?"

"No. Her name is Adèle Malenbreux. We call her Madame Appleblossom because she stays inside all winter long, and no one sees her except when she goes out to do her shopping. Then, as soon as the weather warms up at the beginning of spring, out she comes, like an apple blossom."

Nassim took one last look at the strange woman, wondering how she could spend all day, every day sitting outside her house on a folding chair. Then he turned and followed Tiphaine up the path to his front door. She rang the doorbell, not knowing if

Inès was already home, and when no one answered she put the key Nora had given her into the lock and went inside.

The first hour went by quickly. She poured Nassim a glass of orange juice and offered him some cookies, then helped him with his homework. When that was done, the boy asked if he was allowed to use the PlayStation. Tiphaine said he could, and while he played she browsed the shelves in the living room. She looked at the titles on the spines of the books, amusing herself by searching for some meaning related to her life, maybe even her future, like a coded prediction that only she was able to decipher. *The Unbearable Lightness of Being,* by Milan Kundera. *Life Is Elsewhere* by the same author. *Dangerous Liaisons,* by Choderlos de Laclos. *The Flowers of Evil,* by Charles Baudelaire. *After the Funeral,* by Agatha Christie. A lot of classic French novels. Some North African writers, and quite a few British and American ones too. Nora was clearly a very sophisticated woman.

Tiphaine walked from the living room into the dining room. It was simply furnished, with a table, chairs, and a dresser, but otherwise the room was empty, evidence of the fact that the tenants had only recently moved in. Now that she was alone in the house, or at least Nora wasn't there, Tiphaine let her mind fill with bittersweet memories. She went slowly over to the corner where she used to sit and read or engage in endless bouts of tickling with Maxime in the old rocking chair that had once belonged to her grandmother. The corner was empty now, and all that remained of that blissful happiness was a gaping wound in the dark abyss of her memory. She stood there for several long seconds, fighting the impulse to give in completely to the siren song of the past.

"Can I have another cookie?"

In the room next door Nassim was fighting a ruthless battle against strange creatures from outer space, and this relentless combat had made him hungry. Tiphaine shook herself, landed back in the present with a thud, and hurried to comply with the boy's request.

Mission accomplished, she resumed her tour of the house. She opened the back door and went out onto the deck.

She stood there motionless for a moment, her eyes sweeping across her old yard. Over the years she'd watched from the other side of the hedge as all the things she'd planted, sown, and grown from cuttings withered and died. A few flowers had somehow managed to withstand the lack of care. The vegetable garden hadn't survived, and the lilac was completely blanketed by the Virginia creeper. From the living room came the repetitive sounds of Nassim's video game, bringing back once more a volley of memories. Tiphaine shut her eyes, almost reconciled to giving in to the delicious vertigo brought on by this assault from the past: standing on the deck, sensing the presence of a little boy playing a video game, going back in time, allowing herself to be lulled by the spell of irrational longing. Then, slowly, as if propelled by an outside force, with her eyes still closed, she raised her head to the upstairs windows and let herself be overwhelmed by the poison of her obsessive delusion.

"Hi, Tiphaine!"

Tiphaine flinched and let out a startled little cry, as if caught in the act of committing a shameful crime. She opened her eyes and saw Inès standing in the doorway, still wearing her jacket, gripping her backpack in one hand. She looked very annoyed.

"I didn't know you were babysitting Nassim here," she said. "I stopped by your place, I thought—"

"Nassim said he'd prefer it." Tiphaine justified herself, like a child accusing her best friend of being responsible for the thing she'd just been accused of. Surprised by the gratuitous vehemence of her response, Inès simply slowly nodded her head up and down. "Okay," she said. "I'm going up to my room." With that, she turned on her heel and disappeared.

The spell was broken.

Tiphaine shivered, despite the mildness of the summer's day, and went back inside.

# CHAPTER
## 18

Inès ran upstairs and opened the door to her room as if she were being chased by the devil himself, then pulled it shut behind her. Furiously, she flung her bag to the other side of the room and collapsed onto her bed in despair. What was wrong with that boy? Was he crazy, blind, or what? She couldn't understand it. There had definitely been a spark between them the other night. What was going on?

When she'd found out Tiphaine would be looking after Nassim until their mother returned, she'd realized it was the perfect excuse to see Milo again. A sign, even. Milo hadn't replied to her Facebook message, at least not yet, but maybe messaging wasn't his strong suit. When she'd gotten back from school, she'd gone straight over and rung the neighbors' doorbell, supposedly to make sure that everything was going well with her little brother.

Milo answered the door. When he saw Inès on the doorstep, his face darkened.

"Hi!" said Inès with a radiant smile.

"Hi," he responded without enthusiasm.

Thrown off by the frosty reception, she lost some of her self-assurance.

"I . . . I just came by to see if everything was okay with Nassim."

Milo looked at her in surprise, maintaining an expression that combined boredom and annoyance.

"Nassim's not here."

"Really?" said Inès, increasingly disconcerted. "But your mom was meant to be getting him from school."

"I don't know anything about that."

Inès felt the ground swaying beneath her feet. No boy had ever treated her with such indifference. Worse than indifference—contempt. The silence between them persisted, like torture.

"Well . . . sorry . . . I didn't mean to disturb you," she managed to say, her heart pounding in her chest under the assault of this stinging humiliation.

"No worries," he said brusquely as he closed the front door.

Inès found herself alone on the sidewalk, with the intolerable sensation of having just received a slap in the face. It took her a few seconds to realize what had happened: a boy had spoken to her as though she were boring and unattractive. She'd never felt so spurned and humiliated. How had it happened? What had she done? What had gone wrong?

It took almost a minute for shock to give way to anger. That was how he treated her? Okay, then. The moron would soon realize the error of his ways. She couldn't just let it go, not without reacting, not without showing him what she was made of.

This was not going to be the end of it.

# CHAPTER 19

It was 7:30 p.m. when Nora rang Tiphaine and Sylvain's door-bell. Sylvain answered, and if he was surprised to see her stand-ing on the doorstep, he didn't look disappointed. He invited her in and, even before asking the reason for her visit, offered her a drink.

"That's very kind, but no thank you," said Nora. "I've just come by to fetch Nassim and I'm going home. It's late."

"Nassim?"

Sylvain's blunt response took Nora aback. She frowned, then smiled very faintly in disbelief.

"Yes. Tiphaine was supposed to be getting him from school today."

Sylvain's expression made it clear that he knew nothing about it. Her heart clenched in her chest. Was it possible that Tiphaine had forgotten?

"Is Tiphaine here?" she said, her voice choked with anxiety.

"I've only just gotten home. Milo's up in his room. I was about to call to find out where she was."

As if to prove it, he took out his cell phone and called his wife's number. Nora had turned pale. During the few interminable seconds it took Sylvain to reach Tiphaine, she tried to remember their conversation and to figure out why things hadn't gone as planned. Had she gotten the day wrong? Had Tiphaine not realized it was this week? But surely the school would have called her to come and fetch Nassim. Someone had picked him up. Who could it have been if it wasn't Tiphaine?

A terrible thought crossed her mind. Maybe the school *had* called to say that Nassim was waiting to be picked up, but instead of calling her they'd called Gérard. He was bound to make the most of such a golden opportunity to prove to her she couldn't manage on her own. He'd pull out the big guns, for sure, use all his fancy phrases as if it were his big day in court. "It's the children's well-being that's at stake. You have no right to make them pay for your idiocy!"

Nora shuddered at the thought.

Fortunately, the suspense was short-lived. Tiphaine answered at the third ring, and from what Nora could make out of the conversation, she and Nassim were next door. She felt the viselike grip of anxiety loosen instantly, breathed a sigh of relief, and found she could smile again.

"They're at your place," confirmed Sylvain as he ended the call. "Tiphaine says she sent you a text."

"Really?"

She fumbled in her bag, took out her phone, and switched it on. She saw she had a new message.

"My bad. I didn't even think to check my messages."

Nora, turning to leave, noticed the look of annoyance on Sylvain's face; his lips were pursed, and the expression in his eyes was troubled. She could tell something was wrong.

"I'm so sorry to have disturbed you . . . Tiphaine and I agreed she'd babysit Nassim here and I'd pick him up after work. I should have checked my messages."

Sylvain's expression grew conciliatory. "You don't have to apologize, Nora." He paused, apparently at a loss for words, and looked at her with a benevolent expression tinged with discomfiture. She looked back at him, perplexed, waiting for him to go on. Words rattled around Sylvain's mind as he tried to find a formulaic expression to rationalize the absurd situation, to keep up appearances. And then the strange, thrilling giddiness of not saying anything, not trying to explain or deny. Not lying. Spinning out the moment, as pretense collapsed into the authenticity of emotion, the desire to be himself, to be true.

"Tiphaine didn't tell you she was picking up Nassim from school today and Thursday, did she?" Nora asked, sounding both sympathetic and apologetic.

At the mention of Thursday, Sylvain's expression clouded over almost imperceptibly: it was clear he was discovering what was going on in a drip feed of information. He took a few moments to answer, still torn between propriety and the intoxicating thrill of sharing a confidence.

"Things aren't . . . like they were between us."

Nora nodded. "I know all about that."

They both fell silent.

# CHAPTER
## 20

When Tiphaine arrived home fifteen minutes later, she found Sylvain waiting for her. He stood in the kitchen as she took off her jacket, put down her purse, and poured herself a glass of wine.

"You didn't tell me you were picking Nassim up from school today?"

"No."

Sylvain waited for her to go on, but she said nothing more.

"According to Nora, he was meant to be coming here."

"Nassim wanted to wait for his mother at home. All his games and toys are there, it's where he feels safe. There didn't seem any point forcing him to come and be bored at our place."

"But you don't go around to someone else's house when they're not home without checking it's okay with them first."

"I sent her a text," said Tiphaine, taking a sip of wine.

"Oh, that's fine, then! You knew she wouldn't say no, you were doing her a favor."

"Exactly."

They looked at each other cagily, as if sizing each other up.

"Look, where's the harm?" Tiphaine said. "What's the problem with picking up the neighbor's son?"

"You know very well what the problem is," he retorted, trying to stay calm.

"No!" she said vehemently. "I don't see what the problem is. I did Nora a favor because she asked me to. Remember, she's the one who called me."

"You jumped at the chance!"

"Damn it, no!" she cried.

"All right, then, explain to me why you went over there. To that house! Ten days ago, she invited us over and you swore you couldn't imagine ever setting foot in there again. And now . . . It's not just any old house and you know that perfectly well."

"Shut up, Sylvain," she hissed. "I don't answer to you."

"You don't? Since when?"

Tiphaine was about to spit a biting retort at him, when suddenly she stopped and seemed to hold her breath. When the air left her lungs, her tone changed strangely.

"Everything is fine, Sylvain, I promise you. I don't know what you're worrying about."

She spoke with a surprising softness, a sharp contrast to the hostility in her voice a few moments before. Sylvain took a moment to catch up.

"Of course I'm worried," he said, still sounding exasperated. "I'm just not sure it's a good idea."

Tiphaine burst into laughter that sounded not entirely natural, but had the advantage of relaxing the atmosphere a little.

"What's not a good idea? Damn it, Sylvain! Can you hear yourself? All I did was fetch Nassim from school and wait in

Nora's house until she came home. That's it! A perfectly normal favor to do for a neighbor."

Sylvain couldn't help but let out an ironic chuckle. "To do for a neighbor."

Tiphaine threw him an icy look. "You asshole."

She walked out of the kitchen and up the stairs. The sound of her angry footsteps echoed around the house. If Milo didn't already know they'd been fighting, he would now. Sylvain heard a door slam, then silence.

Wearily, he opened the china cabinet, took out a glass, and tipped the rest of the wine into it from Tiphaine's glass. Then he walked pensively over to the dining room window and looked out onto the yard.

It was still light outside. The backyard was resplendent with colors, scents, and patterns. Tiphaine had reproduced almost identically their yard next door, with ornamental plants at the top end and the vegetable garden at the other, even down to the row of shrubs at the back concealing the compost bin. During the first years they had lived in this house it had been a bit like the communicating vase phenomenon: as their former yard withered, their new one grew lush with new flower beds and more climbing plants.

In fact, the whole house looked like the house next door when they lived there. They'd made the decision to move for several reasons. First, because they had become Milo's guardians and the house belonged to him. This had meant they had three options.

They could have rented it out, but they were put off by the work that would have involved.

They could have sold it, but it was Milo's decision whether to hang on to it or get rid of it, since it had belonged to his parents and was now his. When the family court ruled that he could make the decision only once he reached the age of legal majority, this was no longer a possibility.

The final option was for them to move in. Again, there were pros and cons. It was quite difficult to make the case for this option given the "events" that had happened there. But what had happened in their own house was even harder to bear. They had redecorated Maxime's old room for Milo, but it remained unoccupied for many months. When they had brought the child home with them after the "events," there were all sorts of reasons not to have him move into that bedroom. He was having terrible nightmares, which Tiphaine used as an excuse to have him sleep with them. To begin with, this was fine with Sylvain. Their priority was to support and protect the child and make him feel as secure as possible.

But as the situation dragged on, Sylvain tried to initiate a return to "normality," repeatedly bringing up the idea of moving Milo into the vacant bedroom. But Tiphaine's vehement response left him no hope. He understood then that it wasn't the child who needed Tiphaine, but she who needed him. She wasn't having him sleep in the conjugal bed for his sake; she was holding on to him with the force of despair, as though clinging to a life buoy to keep herself from drowning.

Their sex life, already on its last legs, didn't survive.

Once they officially became Milo's legal guardians, it fell to them to deal with the boy's possessions, which included the house. For weeks Sylvain had been thinking that moving away from the area was the only way out of the grief and sadness in which they had been festering for so long. But Tiphaine categorically refused to consider it, arguing that uprooting the child, causing yet more upheaval in his life, would be damaging for him. It was essential that he keep his points of reference and his routines, and that could be achieved only in a familiar setting. Sylvain capitulated.

But when the question of the house next door came up, he refused to drop it. What could be more familiar than that? For Sylvain, it was becoming increasingly urgent to leave the house where their son had died, even if it was only to move next door. It was Maxime's bedroom that he wanted to get away from. Tiphaine maintained it like a mausoleum, implicitly forbidding Milo access to it. In desperation, Sylvain gave her an ultimatum: either they move next door, or he would leave her. Terrified by the idea of finding herself alone with her shame and torment, Tiphaine resigned herself to the move. And so Milo found himself back in his own home, his own room, his own surroundings.

At first, Sylvain was optimistic that the situation would at last improve. Not that things would go back to how they were before; he didn't even fantasize about that possibility. Nothing would ever be the same again. But perhaps they were at last entering a new period in their lives, leaving behind their grief, self-loathing, and guilt.

But it wasn't to be.

Their relationship continued inexorably to deteriorate. The wall that separated the two houses was clearly not solid enough to contain the hell he had hoped they would leave behind. And now they didn't have Maxime's old room to remind them anymore of their lost Eden, they were pushing each other away, never to find each other again.

This time, Sylvain gave up and accepted his fate, like a guilty man relieved to receive the sentence that would, at last, allow him to atone for his crime.

# CHAPTER
# 21

It was agreed that Tiphaine would babysit Nassim at Nora's house on Thursday. Tiphaine left work at four o'clock sharp, drove to the school to pick the child up, and brought him home. She rang the doorbell as she had on Tuesday, to let Inès know they were there, in case she was already home. And, just like on Tuesday, there was no answer. She put the key in the lock, opened the door, and followed Nassim into the house.

A strange sensation came over her as she walked into the kitchen. A feeling of absence, almost physical, like the gnawing ache of hunger. Uneasy, Tiphaine tried to get ahold of herself.

"Would you like something to eat?" she asked Nassim as she opened the refrigerator to inspect the contents.

He did. She prepared a snack for him. He ate it, hungrily, at the kitchen table, with her sitting opposite him. How many times had she shared this moment with her son, sitting in this very room, asking him how he was, how his day had been. The only difference was that Nassim sat facing the window, while Maxime always used to have his back to it.

"Did you have a good day at school?" she asked Nassim.

The child nodded. He really wasn't talkative, not like Maxime, who'd tell her in detail about every noteworthy episode of his day.

"Tell me what you got up to!" she insisted.

"I did some work."

"I'm sure you did. But apart from that? How was recess? Lunch?"

"I don't know. Nothing special. Just like usual."

"So how is it usually?"

"Um . . . I don't know."

End of the discussion. The child's refusal to engage irritated Tiphaine, who was feeling increasingly on edge. She watched him sitting up straight as he munched his cereal, his eyes lowered—he was too perfect, too well behaved. Tiphaine gave a sad little smile and offered him a glass of orange juice, which the child politely declined.

Once he'd finished eating, they went into the living room and began on his homework. When it was done, Nassim sat down at the PlayStation. Tiphaine went back into the kitchen, put the cereal away in the cabinet, the milk in the refrigerator, and the bowl and spoon in the sink. There were a few other dirty dishes in there and so, almost instinctively, she washed them and put them to dry on the rack. She didn't know what to do after that.

Although in fact she did. There was something she wanted to do. To see, really. A place she could never stop thinking about that exerted an irresistible pull on her. On Tuesday, when she'd babysat Nassim for the first time, she'd not been able to keep from thinking about the room upstairs. But she'd had to look

116

after the boy and, on top of that, exploring the first floor had kept her from rifling through other memories. Now, though she didn't know why, the obsessive thought manifested itself almost the moment she entered the house. Perhaps Sylvain hadn't been entirely wrong in thinking that coming back here was a bad idea.

Tiphaine went into the living room, as if the kitchen and its proximity to the entryway that led to the stairs were no longer safe. She stood for a few minutes behind Nassim, watching with a distracted eye as he destroyed unlikely aliens with equally improbable weapons. Then she randomly took a book off a shelf and settled down in an armchair.

She didn't read a word, but the very fact that someone might come upon her and see nothing unusual made her feel more relaxed. She felt in control of her emotions and allowed her thoughts to wander freely. Her eyes skimmed the walls, floor, and ceiling. Everything was so different. Even the way the house smelled wasn't the same anymore.

She stood up from the armchair, walked around it, and began pushing it toward the dining room, all the way to the corner where her grandmother's old rocking chair had once stood.

"What are you doing?"

Nassim was standing in the opening between the two rooms, holding his joystick in one hand and looking at her, wide-eyed. Startled, Tiphaine stared back at the boy, then at the armchair, then back at Nassim.

"Well, as you can see, I'm moving the armchair."

A beat of silence.

"Why?" asked Nassim.

Tiphaine took a moment to answer.

"Because . . . because it's better here . . . Right?" Faced with the child's doubtful silence, she added, "Don't worry. I'll put it back before your mom gets home. What do you think?"

The child pouted, an expression of aversion more than approval, and went back to his game without another word. Tiphaine watched him walk away with a sense of dismay. This kid didn't seem driven by any emotion. It was like trying to grab hold of a bar of soap that kept slipping from her hands.

She braced herself and walked back to the living room, where she planted herself in front of Nassim.

"What do you like to read?"

The child looked up at her, startled.

"Stop gawking at me like an idiot every time I say something to you! We can talk, can't we? Do you read books? Stories, comics?"

"Yes, I like comic books."

"What are you reading at the moment?"

"Titeuf."

"I know Titeuf!" she exclaimed with exaggerated enthusiasm. "Milo used to read them all the time. Have you got some at home?"

"Yes. Up in my room."

Tiphaine's heart sank.

"Will you . . . will you go and get one?"

"Which one?"

"Your favorite."

Nassim hesitated for a moment, torn between wanting to

continue his game and being obliging and polite; then he stood up, dropped the joystick on the floor, and walked out of the room.

He came back a few minutes later and handed a book to Tiphaine, who took it and thanked him. He went back to his video game and Tiphaine sat down in the armchair she'd moved and opened the book. This time, she was really reading. From time to time, she let out an exclamation, followed by a giggle. After a moment, intrigued, Nassim went over to where she sat, leaving his avatar to be obliterated by extraterrestrials.

"Why are you laughing?" he asked. Tiphaine noticed the warm curiosity in his voice.

"Because it's funny. Have you read this one?"

He leaned down to see which story it was.

"Oh yes! That one's really funny!"

"And this one made me laugh too," she said, flicking back a few pages.

She angled the book slightly toward Nassim so he could read it too. The child burst out laughing.

"Yeah, that's a good one! It's one of my favorites."

"Which one is your absolute favorite?"

"This one!"

He grabbed the book and leafed through it until he found the story he was looking for. Tiphaine watched him out of the corner of her eye, delighted to see him loosening up. He pointed to a page and she read it, then laughed heartily.

"That's very good! Have you finished reading it?"

"Almost."

"Do you want me to read you the rest?"

"Yes, please."

Tiphaine made room beside her for Nassim. She put an arm around him and began to read.

Sitting there, Tiphaine felt suffused with a happiness she hadn't felt in a long time.

# CHAPTER
## 22

As soon as she walked through the front door, Nora's senses were assailed by something unexpected. There was a delicious smell coming from the kitchen. Something simmering on the stove. A cozy, liquid, welcoming warmth. She hung her jacket on the coatrack and turned to the kitchen to see what was going on.

Through the half-open door she saw Tiphaine, an apron wrapped around her waist and her hands protected by oven mitts, taking a pot off the stove. It smelled like soup. Surprised, Nora pushed open the door and went in.

"Tiphaine?"

Her neighbor turned, placed the pot on the table, and greeted Nora cheerfully. "Hey there! How was your day?"

"It was good, thanks!"

"Maman!" Nassim emerged from the dining room, rushed up to his mother, and gave her a hug.

"I took the liberty of making some soup," said Tiphaine, taking off the oven mitts. "I found some vegetables in the fridge and potatoes under the sink. Is that what you had planned for tonight?"

"No . . . Yes . . ."

Nora seemed to snap out of her astonishment and looked at Tiphaine with an expression of contrite gratitude.

"Tiphaine. You really shouldn't have. You're already helping me out so much."

"Don't be silly! It keeps me from getting bored."

"No, honestly, it bothers me! I won't dare ask you for another favor."

"Don't be silly."

Tiphaine took off the apron and looked around to see where to put it. Nora took it from her.

"Thank you," said Tiphaine with a smile. Then, after a brief pause, she added, "Okey dokey! I can't hang around, my men are waiting for me."

Then she threw an embarrassed glance at Nora. "Oh, I'm so sorry."

Nora didn't get it for a moment. She looked at Tiphaine in surprise, wondering what had triggered such a reaction. Tiphaine's words echoed in her head.

"My men are waiting for me . . ."

Suddenly she realized. And while Tiphaine's words weren't hurtful, her excuses were. Tiphaine realized it at the same moment. The two women stood in silence, each trying to find a way out of the awkwardness.

Nora tried, but somehow managed to make it worse. "No worries, Tiphaine. One more hassle I'm delighted to be done with." Even as she said it, Nora realized she was making Tiphaine's blunder worse. The fact that she knew about her and Sylvain's marital difficulties added to the confusion, as if she were pitying her neighbor for struggling in a foundering relationship. "Don't listen to me, Tiphaine. I'm talking nonsense."

"No, no, it's my fault, it was very rude of me."

They brushed it off with understanding smiles. Tiphaine began getting ready to go.

"I hope the soup's good. Let me know if you need me to pick up Nassim again."

"That's kind of you. I'm okay for tomorrow, Mathilde's fetching him."

"Mathilde? She doesn't live nearby, does she?"

"Oh, it's not very far. She's in Mésanges."

"That's crazy. It's miles away. I'm very happy to do it."

Taken by surprise, Nora hesitated.

"It makes no sense," insisted Tiphaine. "If I get him, he'll be here, and you can just come straight home. I'm very happy to do it."

"Are you sure?"

"Listen, I'm the one suggesting it."

Nora thought about it a moment before accepting her neighbor's offer. She walked her to the front door and then, as Tiphaine walked the three yards that separated the two houses, she said again, "Are you sure you don't mind?"

"On the contrary," Tiphaine said firmly as she put her key in the lock, "it'll be a pleasure."

# CHAPTER
## 23

Gérard Depardieu had already done a bit of searching online, and his investigations had turned up some interesting information. He found out that Sylvain Geniot was an architect; he consulted the firm's website and read some articles in various trade magazines. Nothing of any real consequence. When he searched for Tiphaine's name, he found only one site that mentioned her, but it caught his attention: it was that of the local plant nursery. He discovered she was a horticulturist, from which he deduced she must have a good knowledge of plants. He pondered the information thoughtfully.

In the course of his searches, he came across one startling news item. It was an article in the local newspaper from eight years earlier, relating a horrifying domestic accident: Maxime Geniot, age six, had fallen from his bedroom window on the second floor of the family home. The article gave few details, beyond the fact that, despite the swift arrival of the paramedics, nothing could be done to save the child.

Looking over these various pieces of information gleaned from the internet, Gérard noted a puzzling coincidence: the Geniots had lost a child just a few weeks before Milo Brunelle had lost his father.

But he was unable to find any link between the two families. He spent the week pondering the mystery of the relationship between the Brunelles and the Geniots. His deliberations led him to consider two possibilities. The first was as simple as it was logical: Tiphaine was Milo Brunelle's mother. After the death of David Brunelle, her first husband, she'd married Sylvain Geniot and taken his name, while her son had kept that of his father. Gérard decided he had to see if this hypothesis checked out; if it did, it would put an end to the matter. If, on the other hand, Tiphaine was not Milo's mother, that meant she and Sylvain were his guardians; it was unlikely that the Geniot family had adopted the child, otherwise he would bear their surname.

The only way to find out what linked the Geniots and the Brunelles was to consult the records of the family court that would have met at the time when the couple were formally appointed the boy's guardians.

This raised further questions: if Tiphaine wasn't Milo's mother, why had the boy not gone to live with his mother? And where was she now? At the time, Gérard had been told that his client had committed suicide, and the case had been closed. Preoccupied with the birth of his own son, Gérard had not delved any further and he, too, had closed the case.

But now the case had risen from the ashes, triggering his interest again. If only because he needed to find out who this asshole was who was hanging around his wife.

The immediate problem he had was time.

Since Nora had left, Gérard had been obliged to reorganize his life. Having custody of the children every other week was a real challenge for him, on top of shopping, cooking, and keeping the house in some semblance of order, despite the maid who came in twice a week. The weeks he had the children he had to adjust his work schedule, leaving work much earlier than he would have liked, and being frustrated by not being able to complete a fraction of what he had to do. The weeks he didn't have them he doubled the number of hours in the office and worked ten times as hard, spending almost all his waking hours going over his cases and drafting pleas.

He arranged as many of his appointments as he could for that week, to avoid finishing late when the children were with him. Inès didn't like to stay home alone, or at least that was the pretext she used to hang out in the street with girlfriends or—worse!—with boys when he told her he wouldn't be back until the end of the afternoon. Nassim didn't like staying behind in the after-school program, as he had let his father know in no uncertain terms the one time he was late to pick him up after class. Not to mention that he would rather be at his mother's house anyway than at Gérard's. That was out of the question. And the thing Gérard feared most of all.

Almost without noticing, he had begun to realize how much he missed the children when they weren't there. Terribly. It was true that even back when they were still a real family, he'd never spent much time with them. But at least he saw them every day. Enough to know they were happy and doing well at school. He talked to them and gave them hugs. And when he got home too late in the evening to see them, or at least too late to see Nassim, he'd slip into his son's bedroom to watch him for a few minutes, filled with quiet happiness as he observed the serene expression on the face of the sleeping child.

Now everything had changed. When Inès and Nassim weren't there, the silence that filled the house, Nora's absence, the darkness that greeted him when he came home gave him a feeling of being stifled that he couldn't shake off. Ironically, solitude is like being caught in a vise, when it's meant to give you space and freedom.

And meanwhile when he had the kids, every day was a race against time that began at dawn and ended only when he went to bed. Inès was fairly independent—although he did have to make sure she'd completed her homework assignments and didn't go to school dressed like a prostitute—but Nassim still needed a lot of attention and affection. It seemed to his father that it was Nassim who was suffering the most from the separation. Apart from Gérard himself, of course.

Nassim had a tendency to sink into a state of listless gloom at occasional moments, which worried Gérard. Every time it happened he blamed Nora for having left a family that he had believed was solid and strong.

Then he'd be struck by a pang of conscience. Didn't he have things to be ashamed of, too? According to Nora there was no doubt, leaving aside the passage of time and the waning of desire, that he was almost entirely responsible for the breakdown of their marriage. Her principal argument was that she didn't see a problem with the separation since he was never around anyway. In other words, he never appeared to need to see her and the children, and therefore wouldn't miss them. Such a cruel assertion, for she knew full well that when things slip from our grasp, they become even more desirable. And even more so when it comes to people.

How had she moved from desire and the need to see more of him to disinterest and rejection?

But honestly, what could he have done about it? His work was demanding, and he was passionate about it, that was a fact. And where was the harm in it? Isn't that what everyone dreams of: a career that's not only fulfilling but that fills up the bank account with a welcome succession of figures every month? When a golden opportunity presents itself, why would you turn it down? Gérard loved his work. But more important, over the years, he had seen an increasing number of innocent people being wrongly accused. He had won a number of cases, and success brought in more and more interesting work. As a result he had begun to make a name for himself in the legal world. Everything was turning out how he and Nora had hoped it would back in the early days of their marriage, when they had barely been able to make ends meet. And now the goal had been reached, she blamed him for the consequences! That was a little too much. It was true that he sometimes found himself in a spiral of activity that he couldn't control, but wasn't that what made life exciting?

What would she have preferred? A boring civil servant? A husband who was always on time, whose constant presence would have ended up driving her crazy?

He couldn't imagine giving up his work. It would have been

like amputating a limb, falling into a black hole, depriving himself of air. His work was what gave him worth. It was who he was. It wasn't the kind of work that could be done by half measures, from eight in the morning till four in the afternoon. It demanded that he immerse himself in it utterly, sparing neither his strength nor his time. It was a vocation.

Gérard Depardieu prided himself on his cunning. On several occasions he had won cases by putting forth tortuous arguments and bamboozling his adversaries in court. With his quick intelligence and capacity for empathy he had the ability to consider a situation from multiple angles and put himself in other people's shoes. This made him particularly effective at anticipating the other side's reactions. But above all he had a kind of sixth sense that set off an internal alarm when something seemed anomalous. And he was rarely wrong.

Now his intuition was telling him there was something off about the David Brunelle affair.

He had only Friday to spend any time on his little personal investigation. He popped into the town hall between two appointments to request a birth certificate for Milo Brunelle. With the file folder tucked under his arm, he went into the register office, praying to all the saints that Amélie, the little redhead who was always so helpful, would be there. He had no right to ask for a copy of the document, except in his position as Milo's father's attorney. The problem was that he didn't know the child's date of birth. All he had was the boy's name and address and his father's name and date of birth.

When he got to the counter he breathed a sigh of relief:

ever-faithful Amélie was there. She saw him and gave a little wave. When it was his turn, he opened the file folder and
showed Amélie a few official documents concerning his client.

"Eight years ago, I was appointed defense attorney for a man
named David Brunelle, who was, I believe, wrongly accused of
a fatal poisoning. I won't go into detail, because my client died
shortly afterward, and the case was closed. But recently I discovered something that's been niggling at me and I'd like . . ."

"Niggling!" Amélie exclaimed with a little giggle. "You must
be the only person left on earth who still uses that word."

Gérard gave a faint laugh, trying to sound friendly despite
his irritation at the young woman's interruption.

"Let's say it's been playing on my mind."

"You're curious?"

"Yes, that's exactly it. I'm curious. I'd like to be sure, and for
that I need to see his son's birth certificate. Do you think that
might be possible?"

"Monsieur Depardieu, you know that if you're not the person concerned or a relative, even if you were his lawyer, I can't
give you the document."

"I know that, Amélie. The truth is . . ." He paused and gave
her a shrewd smile. "I don't really need his birth certificate. I
just need his mother's name."

"Your client's wife's name, in other words?"

"That would make sense. If she's the child's biological
mother."

"I see."

She looked at Gérard with a doubtful expression. She looked
like she was wavering. Merely giving him a piece of informa-

tion wouldn't put her in an awkward position. And she liked him. She was just a lowly city hall employee, and he always treated her with kindness and respect, aware of the value of her work and her worth. Not like some other people who, with a look, a comment, or a tone of voice, displayed the contempt or straightforward indifference they felt for her.

"All right!" she said decisively. "I'll see what I can do. What's his name?"

"Milo Brunelle."

Gérard spelled out the boy's first and last names, then his father's. Amélie noted them down on a Post-it note.

"Date of birth?"

"That's just it . . . I don't know."

She threw him a disappointed glance but made no comment.

"Wait here."

She disappeared into an adjoining room. The minutes dragged on. Finally, she reappeared, wearing the victorious smile of someone who has successfully completed a challenging mission.

"Here you are, the information you're looking for. Milo Brunelle's mother. Laetitia Marlot. Wife of David Brunelle."

Gérard scribbled down the information on a piece of paper in his folder. He smiled at the young woman in gratitude.

"Thank you, Amélie. You've been hugely helpful."

"What are you going to do with the information?" she asked, curious.

"Not much . . . I just wanted to check a detail."

"No, what I mean is, if you're trying to find her, there's no point."

Gérard looked up from filing the sheet of paper away in his folder. "Really? Why not?"

Amélie gave him a broad smile that betrayed her pride in her efficiency.

"Because she died. Eight years ago. Suicide."

# CHAPTER
# 24

Inès had more or less recovered from her humiliation, and over the past three days she'd been trying to put the insult into perspective. Maybe she'd shown up at a bad time and Milo, taken by surprise, hadn't known how to react. Boys could be awkward, she'd noticed, and they didn't necessarily feel the way their behavior suggested. After she'd gotten over her anger she decided, with her great goodness of heart, to give him a second chance. At least that was how she liked to think of it.

She left school on Friday afternoon determined to try a different tack. She headed straight home and, as she expected, found Nassim in front of his PlayStation and Tiphaine sitting at the kitchen table reading the newspaper. Tiphaine greeted her warmly, folded up the paper, and offered her something to eat, which Inès gladly accepted. Tiphaine made them each a cup of tea and brought out a plate of cookies, and they sat and chattered about school, life, the neighborhood, and the weather. Then Inès turned the conversation to the topic she was really interested in.

"And Milo? He's doing okay?"

"I think so," Tiphaine replied, taking a sip of tea. "You know, he's at the age where you don't tell anyone much about what's going on in your life, let alone your mother."

"I don't really know him, but he doesn't strike me as the type to talk about himself much to anyone."

"Why do you say that?" Tiphaine asked with curiosity.

"I don't know. It's just the impression I get."

They sat in silence for a few moments, then Inès said, "Will he be home by now, d'you think?"

Tiphaine looked at her watch. "He should be, yes. Why?"

"No reason." Inès bit her lower lip. She could feel she was getting it all wrong, and it was obvious Tiphaine wouldn't be any help.

"Why don't you go and ring the doorbell?" Tiphaine suggested. "I'm sure he'd be delighted to see you."

"Do you think so?" said Inès, surprised to hear Tiphaine finally telling her what she wanted to hear. "Wouldn't I be disturbing him?"

"Of course not! I'll call him, if you like."

"No, don't worry. Do you have a message you want me to give him?" Inès had already stood up from the table and was heading for the entryway.

"You could ask him to empty the dishwasher."

The girl winced: it wasn't exactly the kind of message she wanted to give Milo, but she'd settle for it. She bolted out of the house and into the street. She took a deep breath before smashing her finger against the doorbell of the house next door. On the sidewalk across the street, Madame Appleblossom was sitting on her folding chair with her suitcase beside her. Inès looked at her with a mixture of compassion and repulsion. Who was that crazy woman? What was she waiting for?

Milo opened the front door.

"Hi!" she said, before he had time to react. "Your mom's over at my place, she told me I could swing by. Can I come in?"

An indefinable expression appeared on the boy's face, a mixture of pleasure and irritation. He mumbled something and then, as if resigned, stepped aside to let her in.

"Who is that crazy old woman?" asked Inès, gesturing to the old woman.

"Madame Appleblossom," replied Milo.

"Yes, I know, my brother told me her name. But what does she do there all day?"

"I've no idea."

"Have you ever spoken to her?"

"Nope."

"Don't you want to know?"

Milo shrugged. "What difference would it make?"

Inès looked at him. "You're so weird."

The young man didn't reply and pushed the front door shut behind them. They stood there in the entryway, ill at ease. Milo shoved his hands into his pockets to give himself a sense of composure. Inès seemed to be waiting for something to happen. After a few moments of awkward silence, she took the lead.

"Can I see your room?"

"Yes . . . No!"

"You don't want me to see it?" Inès exclaimed, alarmed by this unexpected rejoinder.

"It's not that," Milo stammered. "It's just . . . it's a mess."

Inès laughed. "Who cares if it's a mess? You should see mine." Without waiting, she walked to the stairwell and up the stairs. Discomfited, Milo followed.

Both houses having been built according to the same plans, she saw immediately that Milo's room was exactly the same size and configuration as hers. But that was the only thing the two rooms had in common. The young man's bedroom was furnished in a no-frills, functional way, with a few ungainly decorative touches: some posters pinned haphazardly to the walls; his childhood curtains, with their jarringly naïve design; a cluttered shelf displaying a few books and a jumble of disparate objects; a large, unspeakably untidy desk; and the obligatory unmade bed. Inès was careful to make no comment. She glanced around the room and then went to look at the books on the shelf.

"*Viper in the Fist.* Have you read it?"

"Yeah, I had to."

They both laughed. Gradually, lulled by Inès's easy manner, Milo let himself be won over. Inès had a knack for talking about anything and everything without sounding frivolous or inappropriate. He cast shy glances at her, touched by her gracious chatter, the enthusiasm she put into everything she talked about, the questions she asked, the way his brief responses didn't seem to irritate her. She seemed to like him as he was, without judgment, and Milo felt his defenses melt away like snow in the sun. God, he liked this girl! How gratifying it was to give in to the thrill of flirting, even more so when it was without any insincerity or pretentiousness. For the first time in a long time, Milo was enjoying hanging out with a young person who seemed also to like his company. Being weird was his hallmark, and yet now here he was enjoying a normal conversation, relishing the surprising pleasure of what was, for most young people his age, completely ordinary. His unremitting preoccupation with death was diluted by the buoyancy of the exchange, and all of a sudden life seemed strangely uncomplicated.

An hour or so later Inès decided it was time to go home.

She told Milo and he nodded, though his heart sank at the thought of her leaving. They went back downstairs. She was about to leave and he wanted to stop her, or at least tell her how much he'd enjoyed spending time with her.

"Well, bye then!" she said, rising slightly on tiptoes to kiss him goodbye. He felt her lips, too fleetingly, graze his cheek. It was one of those moments when the seconds flee like thieves in the night, when it's obvious an opportunity is presenting itself, but by the time you realize and try to grab hold of it, it's already too late.

"Bye," he replied awkwardly. She had already turned away. Then she stopped and looked back at the young man with a touch of reproach in her eyes.

"Do I have to do everything myself, then?"

"What do you mean?" Milo asked in bewilderment.

She sighed loudly, retraced her steps and, rising on her tiptoes again, placed a kiss on his lips as if leaving an offering on an altar that she feared might be unsound.

Milo's heart exploded in his chest.

He couldn't breathe, was paralyzed with emotion. He felt like he'd been turned to stone, even though neurons were firing in his brain, telling him to react. This was his chance, and if he missed it he'd have no choice but to disappear off the face of the earth. The fear of regret was stronger than panic and so, his body inflamed with desire, he leaned toward Inès, who lowered herself back onto her heels. He took her face between his hands and returned the kiss, in an embrace whose awkwardness was equaled only by its passion. The sensations going through him were so intense they seemed to destroy any possibility of conscious thought. Of this first kiss, Milo would remember an explosion of emotion that contained as much joy as terror.

When their faces separated, it felt like his lungs, deprived of air for too long, were at last able to take in life-saving oxygen. He looked at Inès, who was smiling at him mischievously, a bit like in her Facebook profile picture: she looked like she'd enjoyed the embrace, and Milo would have given anything for it to be true.

"I was worried there," she murmured, giving him an impish look.

"Worried about what?" asked Milo, bewilderment inscribing itself on his features once more.

She laughed and shrugged. "That you weren't making a move."

It took him a moment to understand, but she turned away, this time for good, and went to the front door. A moment later, she left the house and ran the few steps along the sidewalk to her own house, while Milo stood and watched her go.

Just as she was about to reach her front door, a moped driving on the sidewalk sped around the corner. Surprised by the sudden ear-splitting appearance of the two-wheeled vehicle, Inès froze, as if paralyzed by the choice she had to make: run back toward Milo, or ahead to her front door. Her hesitation made her lose precious seconds and the moped was heading straight for her. Milo had just enough time to leap up and spring at her to pull her back as the driver of the moped swerved away. An accident had been avoided. Just. The moped sped off as quickly as it had appeared, leaving no time for the young people to express their indignation.

"Are you okay?" asked Milo, discovering Inès in his arms.

Instead of an answer, she kissed him. Disconcerted, the teenager let himself be carried away by the intoxication of the embrace. But a cold shiver ran down his spine. A retrospective fear. What if he hadn't intervened? Might Inès have been hurt? Had she been in real danger? In his mind, the irony of such a twist of fate shot through him like an electric current, triggering an alarm. A dull anxiety thudded in his chest. It had been a close call.

Was this some kind of a warning from the depths of the curse that had imprisoned him since he was a child? Was this destiny refreshing his memory about the terms and conditions of an agreement, made with whom and for what reasons he didn't know, condemning him to endangering anyone to whom he became attached? He felt a lump in his throat, and a sense of bleak inevitability. He clutched Inès by the waist and held her tightly against him, folding her into an embrace that he made last as long as possible.

He knew it would be the last time.

# CHAPTER
## 25

On the other side of the shared wall, Tiphaine was vainly trying to reestablish the nebulous bond she had managed to establish the previous day with Nassim. To her disappointment, today the child was withdrawn, lacking all enthusiasm and warmth. One step forward, two steps back. She really didn't like the kid. Too polite and well behaved. Always in control. He was cute, but the lack of spontaneity made him seem cold, almost unpleasant. She tried to reach out to him, find subjects that might interest him, but he responded with infuriating indifference. When she suggested they carry on reading the book they had begun together the day before, he declined with a look of undisguised boredom.

The boy's rejection was like a slap in the face. Tiphaine felt a wave of dislike come over her, and the profound injustice of having to endure the presence of this kid in this house, this unwelcome stranger, was like a torment. Her own son was no longer there. Her sweet, funny, happy-go-lucky, bright-eyed child. Alive! The grief she had managed to suppress the last few years began growling in her guts, rising into her chest and exploding in her throat, ripping into it with poisonous fangs, torturing her. A feeling of oppression. Suffocation.

She went out onto the deck. She needed air. She took a deep breath to control the violence raging within her, a destructive storm, like a tornado of dislike. Feeling a little calmer, she glanced up and noticed an open window. It was Nassim's bedroom window.

Maxime's bedroom window.

A dagger. Straight through her heart, a blade laying waste to everything, sinking into her flesh and releasing the venom of guilt, perhaps the worst poison of all. The one that never leaves you. Whose fire slowly consumes you.

How she had tried. Tried to make it an ally. An obstacle to the destiny that taunted her, reopening old wounds and mocking her distress. She had done everything to defeat her demons, to keep going. To reconcile the past with the present.

She turned, went back into the house, and collared the little boy.

"Nassim, will you go and fetch a comic book from your bedroom?"

The boy was sitting at the dining room table drawing. He looked up unenthusiastically.

"You can go if you like."

Tiphaine let out a deep sigh of irritation.

"Nassim, the reason I've asked you to go is precisely so I don't have to."

Her tone was cold, verging on mean. With a hint of malice. Nassim sensed menace. He put down his pencil and went upstairs.

Tiphaine calmly went back out onto the deck. She hesitated a moment, then stood on her toes, looked up, and called, "Nassim! Nassim!"

She waited a few seconds, then called up again, "Nassim!"

The boy's head appeared at the open window.

"Yes?"

"Can you bring down the same comic book as yesterday?"

"What?"

Tiphaine was speaking too quietly for the boy to be able to hear. He leaned out a bit farther.

"Can you bring the Titeuf that we were reading yesterday?"

Tiphaine didn't raise her voice and Nassim frowned, embarrassed that he couldn't understand what she was asking.

"I can't hear you," he said, leaning out even farther.

Tiphaine lowered her voice even more.

"Come on, Nassim, it's not exactly complicated. Titeuf, the same comic book we were reading yesterday—can you bring it down?"

"Bring what down?"

Time stopped. The little boy leaned a little farther out, on tiptoes now, his hands gripping the window ledge.

Suddenly Tiphaine screamed and lifted her arms in a panic.

"Nassim! Be careful, you're going to fall!"

Her fear took the boy by surprise; startled, he tipped forward. He was leaning a little more out into the void. His feet left the ground for a long-drawn-out split second, during which it was as if he were weightless, horizontal, so light and fragile . . .

He looked like an angel about to take flight.

The next moment, stunned and in shock, he leaned back and, in a survival reflex, pushed hard with his hands against the window ledge and fell heavily back onto his bedroom floor.

Down in the garden, Tiphaine looked up at the sky and uttered a sigh of frustration.

# CHAPTER
## 26

That weekend, Nora decided she was going to make the most of her time with her children. It had been a frustrating week, because of the shifts she had worked. Nassim had been very grumpy since Wednesday, complaining multiple times about his mother's absence. His reproaches hit home.

"You said you left Papa because he worked too hard. And now you're doing exactly the same."

"I'm not doing the same," Nora defended herself despondently. "I don't work long hours at all. It's only that I've been starting just as you finish your school day. But it was only for this week: I'll be picking you up next time."

Nassim smiled when he heard this, but Nora's expression darkened. The child wasn't wrong: she was making them go through exactly what she had always criticized Gérard for. She was going to do everything she could to make up for it. She was dreading the thought of Sunday night and wanted to fill every second spent with her children with fun activities. It was only two in the afternoon and they had already been to the market, prepared the batter to make crepes in the afternoon, and had the roast chicken for lunch that they'd bought that morning.

Then Nora had given Inès and Nassim permission to spend an hour (which had morphed into an hour and a half) in front of the screen of their choice. Nassim had rushed to the PlayStation while his sister went online, and Nora had spent the time reading. What joy!

Now she and Nassim were in the garden bickering over the game they were playing, halfway between soccer and rugby, with only the vaguest of rules. The objective was basically for each player to run both after the ball and after each other, tackle the other person, make them fall, then tickle them. Which they did unsparingly.

When the ball went over the hedge—Nora had terrible aim—their fun was abruptly interrupted. Nassim couldn't decide whether to mock Nora or be annoyed. Nora stood on tiptoes to survey the next-door yard: if Tiphaine, Sylvain, or Milo were outside, the incident would be no more than a brief break in the game. But there was no one in the yard. She craned her neck to try to see through the French doors whether there was any movement inside the house. She thought she spotted a figure in the dining room.

"Wait here, I'll be back in a second," she said to Nassim.

She walked through the house and out the front door into the street, and rang the bell next door. A few seconds later she heard footsteps, then the sound of a key turning in the lock. Sylvain opened the door.

He seemed surprised to see her on the doorstep, and once again was visibly delighted by her impromptu visit.

"You're not going to tell me you've come to pick up Nassim again!"

Nora burst out laughing.

"No, he's at home. I've come to fetch the ball that's landed in your yard."

Sylvain rolled his eyes, making it clear that he knew what it was to have once—long ago—had a child that age.

"I'll go get it for you. Come on in."

Nora gave him a grateful smile. She came inside and Sylvain closed the door behind her, before disappearing into the dining room. There was no sign of either Tiphaine or Milo. Barely thirty seconds later Sylvain returned holding the ball.

"Can I make you coffee?"

Nora felt her throat tighten. The way he was looking at her, the tone of his voice, warm, soft, and deep; the way he offered her coffee, with an intonation that blended confidence and hope . . .

"That's so kind, but no. Nassim's waiting for me to carry on our match."

"Got it. An herbal tea, maybe?"

Nora burst out laughing. The hope in Sylvain's voice had become a plea, as if he were begging her not to leave.

She felt the same warmth inside that she had felt in his presence a few days earlier, but this time it was much more pronounced. As were the signals he was sending out, which no longer left room for doubt.

Nora looked at him with an ardent expression, almost imploring, that said, "Please, don't insist, I'm not sure—" Not sure of what? If she wanted it, or would be able to resist? The previous Tuesday—the day she'd come by to pick up Nassim when he was actually at her house—when Sylvain had mentioned that he and Tiphaine were having problems, and she'd told him she knew what that was like, they had both fallen silent and their eyes had locked . . . those few seconds of quiet had felt surreal, outside time. She had seen in Sylvain's expression all the desire she provoked in him, and she felt a desire that was just as powerful. That feeling of time standing still, of everything else being meaningless, pointless . . .

She hadn't stopped thinking about that moment for three days, those few seconds of eternity that had set her icy heart beating once more, after so many years.

And the implacable guilt of desiring a married man, only to have to face Tiphaine's smile and her kindness; she had picked up Nassim from school and brought him back home, looked after him all afternoon, helped him with his homework, and even made soup for supper . . . how she had hated herself for her guilty thoughts, despised herself for the forbidden desire filling her throat, her breast, and her gut with corrosive, almost painful confusion.

But the truth was she didn't care at all.

Standing there in front of Sylvain, she was filled with an overwhelming urge to embrace him. She could have tried to resist, like the decent person she was, but she knew it wasn't worth trying. If she managed to avoid the inevitable, she knew she would regret it her whole life. Whatever the consequences, what was about to happen would be worth all the soul searching in the world.

She didn't have to do anything. Before she even realized what was happening, Sylvain was leaning toward her, then he brushed her lips with a shy kiss. Nora held her breath. Because she didn't draw back, Sylvain moved closer, and the next kiss was more palpable, more confident. She closed her eyes and tilted her head up to his, so that she could look at him and relish his presence. She felt his warm breath. Shivers ran up and down her body. They kissed, very gently and unhurriedly, and both knew that this moment would remain engraved on their memories for a long time to come. It awakened in both of them emotions whose existence they had forgotten. It was an extraordinary, tender kiss that conveyed both sadness and a mutual thirst for joy; a kiss that lasted for a long time; a kiss to which both gave as much as they received. And when at last their lips parted, because it had to end at some point, they looked at each other and recognized in each other's eyes that tiny gleam of trust that each was feeling.

# CHAPTER
## 27

It was a turbulent night for certain inhabitants of the two row houses in rue Edmond-Petit. Nora, in a confused state of euphoria, took a long time to get to sleep, playing that stolen kiss over again and again in her mind, all the while brooding ruefully over her guilty desire.

In the next bedroom, Inès was sleeping peacefully, a happy teenager's beatific smile on her lips.

But on the other side of the wall Sylvain lay, eyes wide, a feeble onlooker to the pitiless struggle between his heart and his mind, his complicated feelings for Nora filling his thoughts. He couldn't find a way out of the maze of his tangled emotions, the sour tang of guilt, the sweet delight of these new feelings; he was engulfed by a desperate desire to see his neighbor again, and distraught about what he knew would be the inevitable consequence. Tiphaine was not only the woman with whom he had shared his life for seventeen years, and to whom he had bound his destiny for better or for worse . . . she was also his accomplice, the two of them keepers of a terrible secret.

For years now they had not been able to count on anyone but

each other to take the edge, even faintly, off their grief and their guilt. He knew their marriage was the only reliable guarantee of their mutual security: they had to trust each other blindly, and the slightest betrayal would put them both in danger.

And more important than anything else, in the middle of all this there was Milo, the child to whom life had been so cruel. Sometimes Sylvain could barely look him in the eye as they sat opposite each other at the Ranch restaurant on a Monday evening after basketball practice, when the boy nodded at him in gratitude or gave him an affectionate smile. What would happen should he ever find out the truth? At the very thought of it, Sylvain felt a shudder of distress. Not for himself, of course. The guilt and remorse that had eaten him up for the last eight years was worse than any punishment the human system of justice could mete out. But if Milo ever were to find out what had really happened . . .

Sylvain shut his eyes, preferring to ignore the dark void into which the boy would collapse once and for all were he to find out the truth. If Sylvain were to leave Tiphaine for a new life, it would be tantamount to shattering the fragile equilibrium that kept them all safe.

However he looked at the situation, the one thing Sylvain knew for sure was that leaving Tiphaine wasn't an option. And yet it was the thing he wanted to do most in the world. To leave behind all the guilt of a sin that no amount of atonement would ever undo. To forget the shame, the suffering, the past. Knowing that a better future might once have been possible made the present even more unbearable.

Eventually he fell into a troubled sleep, tormented by dreams and nightmares, vain hopes, and certain despair.

Tiphaine was woken by the sound of whimpering. She rushed into Milo's bedroom. The boy was bathed in sweat, and seemed to be battling invisible demons beneath the sheets. She sat on the bed and tried to calm him, but she realized, despite his jerky movements, that he was still asleep.

At a loss, she thought she might try to wake him, but the moment she touched him his movements intensified, and she couldn't get close to him in case he hit her in the face. And then, amid the confusion, the young man began to speak in scattered words and broken sentences.

"No! Not that . . . Inès . . . Stop . . . Leave me alone! You shouldn't. Get out!"

Horrified, Tiphaine abandoned her attempts to calm him so she could listen. Milo was thrashing about, his confused speech alternating with moans and gasps, his features twitching with dark thoughts. He kept begging Inès to leave him alone, telling her to get out, saying her name over and over in a voice that betrayed his desperation. And then, for no apparent reason, he calmed down and fell into a peaceful sleep.

Tiphaine stayed in the room for several more minutes, listening as Milo's breath grew relaxed and regular. The ferocity of his distress disturbed her, and she wondered what could have happened between the two teenagers to provoke such a reaction. She recalled the words she had exchanged with Inès the previous day in Nora's kitchen, wondering suddenly if it might have been a scheme to go over to see Milo. She wondered if the girl's angelic face concealed a more complicated personality.

She tiptoed quietly back to her bedroom and slipped under the covers. In the darkness she tried to suppress the maelstrom of questions whirling around in her head, wondering what she was going to do to get some answers. She knew there was no point in trying to talk to Milo directly: the boy was not forthcoming at the best of times, and he might not even remember having had a nightmare. She would need to find another angle of attack.

The next day Milo came down to the kitchen at noon, his face crumpled from lack of sleep. Tiphaine made him some breakfast and murmured a few reassuring words. Then she sat down across from him at the table.

"Did you sleep okay?" she asked, trying to sound detached.

"Uh-uh . . ." he mumbled, almost as though in assent, while managing simultaneously to indicate that he didn't want to expand on the subject, which hardly surprised Tiphaine. She didn't push it, thinking it better to find an alternative approach.

# CHAPTER 28

Nora spent the rest of the weekend in a daze, consumed by the memory of her kiss with Sylvain, vacillating between euphoria and apprehension as she contemplated the future. How on earth was she going to deal with such an absurd situation? And how would she ever be able to look Tiphaine in the eye again? Or Sylvain, come to think of it. He was the first man apart from Gérard she had kissed in eighteen years.

Even if she survived a confrontation with Tiphaine, or Sylvain, or even Tiphaine and Sylvain together, she couldn't imagine getting into any kind of conflict with Milo. How would she be able to face the strange, withdrawn teenager, who had better things to do than deal with a major conflict between his parents?

How could she have done such a thing! She shuddered, as much with disgust as with elation.

She didn't see Sylvain on Sunday. She didn't seek him out, either. She certainly didn't want to talk to him. Like a little girl dreaming of her Prince Charming, she would have liked simply to catch a glimpse of him.

During the day, doubt intruded on her wistful contempla-tions. What if he was actually the local womanizer? A guy who collected women like other men collect stamps? A Casanova with a super-sophisticated radar for detecting a woman whose sad past made her vulnerable and fragile? She found herself contemplating Sylvain from a different angle, and then reflect-ing on Tiphaine's excessive generosity, how thoughtful and kind she was. Was it possible that Tiphaine was in the know? What if the whole thing was a setup to gratify the fantasies of a couple of perverts?

Even when the memory of their kiss came flooding back, she berated herself as an idiot with a foolish desperation to believe in a love affair that, for all she knew, was never going to happen.

It was he who got in touch with her on Monday morning, around ten. He rang her cell phone. When she saw the un-known number come up on the screen, she knew it had to be him. With her heart in her mouth, she grabbed the phone, glancing instinctively at her face in the mirror, rearranging a lock of hair, and using her finger to rub away a smudge of mascara; she answered only once she had decided she looked presentable. When she heard Sylvain's voice she thought her heart would burst.

He asked politely how she was. She tried to make her re-sponse sound neutral, allowing him to set the tone of the con-versation. Her mind filled with muddled thoughts, and she decided it was a bad sign that he'd called. It's true that people usually call because it's a more personal way of communicating than by email or text message, thus giving the exchange more significance, but—particularly when the person lives right next door—calling could also be a way of avoiding having to spend too long talking to someone. In other words, it could be significant, but not very. Nora was suddenly aware that there were not only Prince Charmings and bastards in the world, there were also penitents who asked you to forget everything that had happened: *It's my fault, I loved it but I can't do it, it's not you, it's me, I could kick myself, it's not my style at all, do you understand?*

"I was just calling to say," said Sylvain, "that I haven't stopped thinking about what happened on Saturday. I didn't want to bother you over the weekend when you were with the children. But I'd like to see you again. Alone. Soon."

Nora's apprehensive expression relaxed, then her face lit up.

"Me too," she murmured, as if she were whispering in his ear.

"I . . . We could have lunch today, if you have nothing else planned."

"Sure!" Nora answered, a little too promptly.

They settled on a time and a place, then exchanged a few banalities, as if to give the illusion they were doing nothing wrong. They ended the conversation with mumbled words that were both affectionate and awkward.

By tacit agreement, they had chosen a public spot, which gave their first illicit rendezvous a veneer of acceptability. It offered, apart from anything else, an efficient shield against the desire they felt for each other. Torn between the euphoria of their budding passion and its dizzying consequences, they wanted to keep their feet on the ground, even as their eyes betrayed what their words were trying, in vain, to cover up. They didn't allude to the past, the future, Tiphaine, or the children. In fact, they didn't talk about anything much, both carefully avoiding mention of anything sensitive. Nora wasn't sure she could cope with intimacy, even though events had thrown her headlong into it. She wanted to hold on to the mystery of discovery, prolong the intoxication of fantasy, give the dream a whiff of possibility. They looked hungrily into each other's eyes, drinking up each other's words, reveling in the other one's presence. They barely touched their food. When they said goodbye, briefly stealing a little extra forbidden time, their kiss seemed to go on forever, like a promise.

After this first rendezvous, all at once their daily lives changed. The unavoidable proximity of forbidden fruit altered the most insignificant aspects of their activities. Whenever Nora left the house, whether into the street or into the yard, her heart began to beat fit to burst, just like a teenager's. Before she left she would check her appearance multiple times in the mirror. She never went out without makeup, even if it was only around the corner to pick up a baguette. She stopped paying attention to anything else, focusing entirely on her neighbors' front door, or checking to see if Sylvain's car was parked in the street. If the front door wasn't open and she couldn't see the car, she would look out for cars coming down the street, hoping to bump into him. It was entirely possible, probably inevitable.

Whenever she went out into the yard, she always made an

effort to look her best, walking with a light, graceful step and pulling in her stomach.

The codes and rules of their relationship were established from the start, almost naturally. It was always Sylvain who contacted her, never the other way around. A few sweet nothings by text throughout the day, which she always responded to straightaway, heart fluttering, a blissed-out smile on her face. And whenever he could slip away to see her, he called.

That week, the children were with their father, which meant Nora had plenty of time to herself and so, in a burst of reckless enthusiasm, she overstretched her bank account and went first to the aesthetician, then the hairdresser, and finally for a manicure. Mathilde was let in on the secret, and played her role to perfection: she briefly brought up the morals of the affair, vaguely warned Nora of the inevitable disappointment, and then spent rather longer demanding all the details and expressing excited delight for her friend.

On Wednesday Nora came home after an exhausting morning with twenty-five overexcited jack-in-the-boxes at kindergarten. She made herself a sandwich and ate it as she flicked through a magazine, then hesitated between whether to take a nap or a bath. A bath, she decided. She went up to the bathroom, put in the plug, turned on the hot tap, took off her clothes . . . only for the chime of the doorbell to interrupt her as she was about to climb in. With a sigh she pulled on her robe, went downstairs, and, half hiding behind it, answered the door.

Sylvain didn't wait for her to invite him in. She watched, too taken aback to speak, as he stepped inside, briskly pushed the door closed, and drew her to him. She didn't resist as he took her face between his hands and embraced her with ardor. She felt herself dissolve in the warmth of the kiss, yielding to pure pleasure, as powerful, irresistible desire overwhelmed her, responding to the caresses of his hands traversing her body, feeling beneath the fabric of her robe to find her soft curves, lingering whenever her sighs grew deeper and more intense. He picked her up and she clung to him as he carried her to the living room and laid her on the sofa where, languid, she offered herself to him.

They spent the entire afternoon making love, irresistibly attracted to each other, skin against skin, arms and legs entwined in a vortex of sensation, unable to imagine ever drawing apart. And when the clock chimed the end of this stolen interlude and summoned them back to their ordinary lives, it was a genuine wrench for them to part.

As soon as she was alone, Nora collapsed against the wall in the entryway, exhausted, dissipated, replete, between ecstasy and despair. She battled to calm the emotions raging within her—she missed him already—and her heightened desire. How was she going to survive until they saw each other again? Knowing he was so near, barely a few meters away, and yet unreachable, was a torture that only memories of their lovemaking could assuage.

But by the end of the following day, the little cloud she'd been floating on blew apart in a flash, heralding a thunderclap.

Someone at the door.

Nora was sitting at the dining table surfing the internet on her laptop. Her heart leaped when she heard the doorbell, for she wasn't expecting anyone. It was him! Who else could it be?

Excited, she stood up from the table and hurried into the entryway. She stopped in front of the mirror, unclipped her hair, and shook it out. The doorbell sounded again. Nora opened the door with a smile, to find Tiphaine standing on the step.

# CHAPTER
## 29

"Nora. I hope I'm not disturbing you," said Tiphaine.

Nora's throat felt dry. She swallowed, then gave a flustered smile by way of welcome.

"Not at all," she said in a voice that seemed to emerge from the depths of her guilty conscience.

Tiphaine waited for her neighbor to invite her in, but Nora stood there, plainly terrified, staring at her with wide, questioning eyes.

"May I come in?" asked Tiphaine. "I need to talk to you." All manner of thoughts were running through Nora's mind as she tried to figure out from Tiphaine's tone and expression the extent of her anger, bitterness, and loathing.

"Nora! Can I speak to you for five minutes? It really won't take long." Tiphaine's voice was sharp now, even a little imperious. Nora shook herself.

"Of course. Come right in."

"Thank you."

All her senses were on alert. In the absence of any sign of animosity, she tried to pull herself together. Tiphaine sat down at the kitchen table and Nora offered her a cup of coffee, which she accepted with a distracted air. While Nora was pouring water into the machine, her neighbor began to talk.

"Something's happened that I'd like to talk to you about. Woman to woman," she said, emphasizing the words. "Or rather, mother to mother."

Nora thought she might pass out. Tiphaine's accusatory expression seemed to unmask her with agonizing intensity.

"I'm listening," she said, swallowing.

"You know that Inès and Milo hung out together last Friday, while I was babysitting Nassim."

It was a statement, not a question. As if Tiphaine were letting her know she had no desire to beat about the bush but intended to get straight to the heart of the matter. Nora was so surprised—and relieved!—by what her neighbor wanted to talk about that she almost burst out laughing. She managed not to, but she visibly relaxed.

"No, I had no idea," she said, her voice much steadier now.

"When Inès got back from school on Friday she asked if she could go over to see Milo," Tiphaine said. "She was there for, I don't know, an hour or so. There was no one else in the house. I mean, no one to keep an eye on them, even from a distance."

"I see."

"And then two nights later Milo had a nightmare. He was begging Inès to leave him alone." She stopped and looked at Nora as if expecting an explanation.

"And?" said Nora.

"Has Inès said anything about Milo?"

"No."

Tiphaine sighed with disappointment. She sat for a moment,

pensive, and then, as if she had been struck by an idea, gave Nora an odd look.

"What kind of girl is your daughter?"

"I'm sorry?"

"Inès. What's she like? Is she an introvert, extrovert, controlling, empathetic, selfish? A victim, a tease, a slut—"

Nora interrupted her. "Tiphaine, please!" She didn't like the turn the conversation was taking one bit. "What are you trying to get at?"

"My son spent half the night tossing and turning because of your daughter and I would like to know why!"

"How would I know?" said Nora indignantly.

"That's why I'm asking what kind of person Inès is. You must have some idea."

"I don't like what you're insinuating."

"I'm not insinuating anything, Nora," said Tiphaine wearily. "I'm saying something happened between Inès and Milo and it seems it didn't have a fairy-tale ending. Did your daughter sleep well last night?"

"Perfectly fine!"

"Well, it was like *Guernica* at our place. I'd like to help my son, so I need to know what happened."

"Why don't you ask him?"

Tiphaine flashed Nora a brief, cold smile. "Could you find out, please?" she asked.

"Find out what?"

"About our children. Could you find out?"

"Find out what, for goodness' sake?" said Nora angrily.

"Why my son spent half the night begging your daughter to

leave him alone." It was strange, but something about the way she said this gave Nora the feeling that Tiphaine was really asking Nora to leave her husband and family alone. To stick to her own problems. Get out of their lives.

"Okay," she murmured, feeling the grip of despair, fed by her guilty conscience, tightening in the pit of her stomach.

Tiphaine's tone softened when her neighbor assented.

"Thank you. You must understand, I'm not accusing your daughter, it's just that Milo isn't in great shape at the moment, and I'm worried. As any mother would be, right?"

"Of course," Nora agreed heartily, not wanting to upset her neighbor any further.

"I must go," said Tiphaine, getting up.

"You're not staying for coffee?"

"I don't have time. Milo will be back soon and I want to be there when he gets in."

Nora didn't insist. She saw Tiphaine out, relieved to see the back of her.

"Will you let me know if you hear anything?" asked Tiphaine as she left.

"I promise I'll do what I can," replied Nora with a lump in her throat, ashamed of her duplicitous pledge.

Tiphaine seemed grateful. "Thanks," she said by way of acknowledgment.

Nora felt a stab of guilt in her belly.

# CHAPTER
# 30

That Friday, Gérard Depardieu managed to free up some time to go over to the courthouse to see what he could find out about Milo Brunelle in the archives of the family court. The archives were classified in chronological order, but since he didn't know the date, he had to use the registry's various research tools, alphabetical and chronological almanacs, and different lists. It took him fifteen minutes to find what he was looking for.

He found out that the family court for the Brunelles had been composed of a representative of the general council, Émile Trudert, someone Gérard had never heard of whose name was put forward by the council president; and two board members of a charity that worked with families, whom he did know, having dealt with them both several times: twenty-six-year-old Judith Bertrix and fifty-five-year-old Mélinda Hernandez. Of the two, the younger was the more unyielding. There was also Madame Lenoix, Milo's teacher at the time he'd lost his parents, who belonged to an association of caregivers for young children, a key element of the family court. And then there were two other women: Milo's therapist, Justine Philippot, and Tiphaine Geniot, his godmother.

So Tiphaine Geniot was the boy's godmother!

The boy's godmother's husband was hitting on his wife!

Depardieu's knuckles were white from the pressure of his fingers gripping the file as he agitatedly made his way through it. There was mention of Milo's assets, which included the house at 28, rue Edmond-Petit. Everything that had belonged to his parents was now rightfully his. Gérard assumed that it was the godmother who had made the decision that they should move in, although the idea of living in the house where his father had hanged himself and his mother had died from a barbiturate overdose did not strike him as being in the best possible taste.

He turned the page to find confirmation that the boy's godmother, Tiphaine Geniot, was also his legal guardian, along with her partner, Sylvain Geniot. The report concluded with details about each of the committee members present: profession, marital status, and address. That was when he discovered something he hadn't even known he was looking for. When he saw where Tiphaine Geniot had been living at the time of the events, his face froze, his body flooded with adrenaline, and he swallowed an expletive, which he eventually released, relishing the clack of the consonants.

"What the actual fucking fuck."

Tiphaine Geniot. 26, rue Edmond-Petit.

Nora's house.

So Tiphaine must be the neighbor whom his client had accused of murdering Ernest Wilmot, his probation officer. And she was the person David Brunelle had been afraid might hurt Milo. How on earth was it possible that the woman who, according to Brunelle, was the source of all his misfortunes and a danger to his family had gone on to be entrusted with bringing up his son?

Gérard lifted his head, lost in thought. Perhaps it was time to put into practice one of the precepts that had secured him numerous victories in court: attack is the best defense. He decided to stop vacillating and go to interview the interested parties about what exactly had taken place the night he'd dropped his client back at his house. In other words, he decided to investigate Milo's parents' double suicide.

Aside from his intuition, the lawyer didn't have anything much to go on, except for one memory that remained crystal clear even after eight years: when he had dropped David Brunelle at his house, the man had not seemed remotely suicidal. This was what was bothering Gérard, besides of course his extreme prejudice against one of the two people implicated in the affair. Not to mention that the Geniots had, if David Brunelle was right, gotten away with murder once already.

Never underestimate your enemy. If David Brunelle's accusation turned out to be true, the Geniots had already slipped through the net of the justice system.

Gérard was well placed to know that conjecture does not amount to proof, and while he had more than a few theories, hard evidence was conspicuous by its absence. His professional integrity told him to consult the police report for more details. He was seething with impatience at the prospect of pushing this foolish dandy off his pedestal. A fair amount of time had passed since the Brunelles' joint suicide, and evidently the Geniots, whether they had been directly or indirectly involved in the drama, had in the meantime gotten on with their lives. Gérard knew he could learn a lot from their reactions by marshaling his not inconsiderable interrogation skills. He figured that exploiting the surprise effect would be key.

He looked at his watch and tried to remember what he had scheduled, firmly intending to find the time to pay a visit to the Geniots later that day. He had to strike while the iron was hot. And boy, was he ready to strike.

On the way back to the car he called his secretary and asked her to push his last meeting of the day back by an hour. She told him that would be impossible. He'd suspected as much. She began a lengthy catalog of justifications, but he cut her short.

"Tell Martel I'll pop over to see him tonight."

"Impossible."

"Why?"

"You have the children this week."

"Damn."

He slowed his step. "Tell Martel," he said with a sigh, "I'm on my way."

He ended the call as he got to his car, muttering an expletive under his breath. He drove off in the direction of the office. He would have preferred to collar Sylvain Geniot at work, but perhaps the option of cornering him at home wasn't such a bad idea. The possibility that Milo Brunelle would be there would create an additional pressure that he would be a fool not to exploit.

As he drove, Gérard tried to figure out a strategy for tackling the subject on his mind: how to introduce himself to the Geniots. Should he act naïve or suspicious? Should he pretend to know nothing about the ins and outs of the tragedy or, on the contrary, make them think he knew all about it? He went through the various options, anticipating their potential reactions, elaborating theories that he thought interesting. Eventually he decided to trust his instincts.

The meeting with Martel seemed to go on forever. It took Gérard two hours to get rid of the man. At last, he told his secretary he was off. She asked where he was going.

"It's a private matter," he said. Then, glancing at his watch, his tone became more courteous.

"Mélanie, would you mind fetching Nassim from school and taking him back to my place? Inès should already be on her way home. I'll be an hour at most."

"The thing is, well, I have plans for this evening, and I was hoping . . ."

"What time do you need to leave?"

"No later than seven."

"I'll be back by six thirty, six forty-five at the absolute latest."

Mélanie knew her boss well enough to know there was no point arguing. She nodded her assent.

"Thank you so much, Mélanie. I owe you!"

She tried to hold him back with a brief rundown of various work matters to which he listened distractedly, before at last setting off for rue Edmond-Petit.

Just like the previous time, he didn't want to take the risk of being spotted in the neighborhood: he couldn't think of a solid excuse if Nora saw him and asked what he was doing there. Much better to avoid an embarrassing encounter. He parked his car in a nearby street and walked the rest of the way, crouching down as he passed Nora's house, until he arrived at number 28. Taking a deep breath, he pressed his finger to the bell.

Tiphaine opened the door.

"Madame Geniot?"

"Yes?"

"Is Monsieur Geniot at home?"

"What's this about?"

"My name is Gérard Depardieu, I'm an attorney. I'd like to talk to your husband."

Tiphaine frowned and regarded Depardieu with a penetrating expression that was both curious and skeptical. She looked at her watch.

"He's not home yet, but he shouldn't be long."

"Would you mind if I came in to wait?" Depardieu asked in an ingratiating tone that irritated Tiphaine. She took a moment to reply, clearly not very keen to let him in.

"First you can tell me what this is all about. How do I know you're really an attorney?"

Gérard gave a broad smile that indicated the obviousness of her request, giving Tiphaine the unpleasant feeling that this was exactly what he had wanted her to ask. She had no need to beg: he drew his wallet from the inside pocket of his jacket and, as he showed Tiphaine the card that indicated he was a member of the French bar, remarked in a tone that was coolly polite, "Eight years ago I was appointed to represent a certain"—he pretended to search for the name in the file folder he was clutching under his arm—"Monsieur David Brunelle while he was in police custody.

He committed suicide not long afterward. As Monsieur Geniot and you are now the legal guardians of my former client's son, Milo Brunelle, I have a few questions for you."

Tiphaine felt the ground opening beneath her feet, engulfing her in a vast wave of panic.

# CHAPTER
## 31

From the look on Tiphaine's face, Gérard knew he hadn't come for nothing. She turned pale, and her eyes flickered with unease. But then, in no more than a second or two, he witnessed an extraordinary metamorphosis. Barely had he time to enjoy the effect he'd anticipated than Tiphaine grew stony-faced: her expression became entirely blank apart, perhaps, from a vague hint of physical awkwardness.

"Sure, come on in," she said in a measured tone. "But just so you know, I don't have a great deal of time. It's already late and I haven't even started on dinner."

Her mind was racing, but despite her impulse to slam the door in his face, she knew that refusing to let him in would only raise his suspicions.

"Don't you worry, Madame Geniot. I'll be the soul of discretion."

She looked at him as if trying to figure out if what he'd said held some kind of double meaning. By way of an answer, Gérard walked past her into the house, flashing a disingenuous grin whose sole purpose was to erase any other facial expression. Taking advantage of the fact that he had his back to her,

Tiphaine let out her alarm with a horrified glance at the ceiling and then pulled herself together and once more put on her expressionless mask.

She showed him into the dining room, gestured for him to take a seat at the table, apologized that she couldn't keep him company, and offered him something to drink. Gérard asked for a glass of water.

Alone in the kitchen, she tried to gather her thoughts and figure out how to deal with this cataclysm. First things first. She thought she'd managed to pull off the ghastly few minutes of conversation with the attorney, but she wasn't sure she would be able to control her nerves if she and Sylvain weren't prepared. Buying time had to be her priority now. They would have to go back over the scenario they had come up with eight years earlier, just after the "events."

But first she had to warn Sylvain.

Where was her phone? Time seemed to expand as she desperately scoured her memory: where had she seen it last? In her purse. Where was her purse? Her ability to concentrate seemed to be running out like sand through an hourglass. She usually left it in the entryway; she looked through the doorway from the kitchen and there it was, beneath the coatrack. She went to get it, but rather than taking the purse with her into the kitchen she stuck her hand inside to find what she was looking for. She felt its cold, hard form and drew it out.

She tiptoed back into the kitchen like a thief and ran straight into the attorney. She let out a shrill little cry and hurriedly pushed the phone into the sleeve of her sweater.

"Did I scare you?" Gérard said, overplaying his concern. Tiphaine looked daggers at him: he was clearly playing mind games with her and taking great pleasure from it.

"You took me by surprise. I didn't realize you were in here."

"I was wondering if Milo Brunelle is home."

Tiphaine looked at him cagily.

"No, he's not back yet."

"That's a shame."

A pregnant silence hung over them for a few moments, which the attorney eventually broke. "May I use the bathroom?" he asked, with a polite smile.

"It's upstairs. Facing you when you get to the top of the stairs."

He nodded his head in thanks and went up the stairs. Tiphaine shut the door of the kitchen and pulled out her phone to call Sylvain, praying he'd answer quickly. She cursed as it went to voice mail.

"Sylvain, it's me!" she whispered into the phone, not even trying to hide the panic in her voice. "There's trouble here. Don't come home, some attorney's showed up to talk to you. Stay at the office till you hear from me. I don't know what he wants, but you mustn't come home. I'll call you when he's gone."

She heard Gérard coming down the stairs and slipped the phone into her pocket. As he reappeared in the kitchen, she heard the sound of a key in the lock.

She held her breath.

From where she stood, she could see the front door opening.

Gérard was about to go back into the dining room when he saw her standing there, frozen. Curious, he turned to see the door swing open and Sylvain appear in the entryway. Sylvain went straight over to the coatrack, dropping two file folders and his keys on the bench. As he began taking off his jacket he saw them both staring at him, one with a look of dismay, one of satisfaction.

The man looked vaguely familiar—something about his face triggered an alarm, which corresponded to Tiphaine's expression. Yes, he had seen this man before. He didn't know why, but his heart began to beat faster. He had the feeling something dreadful was happening, and he was about to find out what it was. A defense mechanism made him root around in his memory. He absolutely had to remember the circumstances in which he had last seen the man who was now standing in the doorway of his kitchen.

When he finally recognized Gérard Depardieu, the blood drained from his face, and he thought he might be about to have a heart attack. His face grew ashen, and in a fog of incomprehension he turned and looked at Tiphaine. Seeing her appalled expression, his last particle of composure melted away.

"Tiphaine!" he cried out urgently. "I can explain." He rushed to her, and as he brushed past the attorney, he caught the man's eye and felt a burst of fury in his chest that compressed his rib cage so hard it hurt.

"You bastard!" he muttered through clenched teeth as he grabbed Gérard by the collar and pushed him against the wall. "What have you been telling my wife?"

Surprised by this ambush, Gérard's only thought was how to get out of Sylvain's grasp. He didn't understand the question. The words went around in his mind. What *had* he told Tiphaine? Sylvain let go of him as suddenly as he had grabbed him and turned to Tiphaine.

"Tiphaine, it's not what you think. We need to talk. It was a mistake."

Tiphaine witnessed this strange scene with a mix of alarm and incomprehension. First there was the horror of witnessing skeletons emerging from the closet, armed with shovels and pickaxes to dig up sensitive stories about Sylvain and her. And now Sylvain was talking about a mistake that wasn't what she thought it was. Was that what the attorney had come to tell her about? She didn't understand what was going on.

Before she had time to ask Sylvain what he was talking about, and what on earth had made him manhandle this guy who had come to talk to them about David Brunelle, Gérard threw himself at Sylvain, grabbed him by the shirt collar, and yelled, "What should I not have told your wife? That you've been sleeping with mine? Is that it? Is that what you don't want her to know?" He was behaving like a madman. Sylvain's instinctive reaction had furnished him with the proof of what he had dearly been wishing wasn't true. The asshole had betrayed himself all on his own. He must have realized Gérard was Nora's husband, and when he'd come in and seen the two of them in his house, thought that Gérard had shown up as the jealous husband seeking revenge against the guilty party, who was, of course, Sylvain.

Gérard glared at Sylvain, his eyes gleaming with sadistic pleasure.

"Well, the funny thing is, I haven't told your wife anything, you goddamn fool," he said, his tone softened by vindictive pleasure. "You just told her yourself. All on your own. What a clever boy you are."

# CHAPTER
## 32

Tiphaine stood there rooted to the spot in the middle of the kitchen, ramrod straight, eyes bulging, staring at Sylvain with a mixture of disgust and disbelief, as her shattered heart, already wrecked by everything she had already been through, began weeping blood again. She turned to the attorney and, her voice cracking, asked, "Who . . . who is your wife?"

Gérard let Sylvain go. He looked him up and down with disdain, a cruel smile on his face. "Your neighbor, Nora Amrani," he said.

That was the final blow. Tiphaine looked at her husband, and the attorney thought for a moment she was going to throw herself at him and tear out his eyes.

Sylvain was only now gauging the extent of his mistake. He looked from his wife to the attorney, confounded, his throat blocked by an excess of words, none of which could get past the obstacle of his distress. Excuses, justifications, explanations, anything to try to salvage what he had just destroyed. Nora, who had until then embodied the fantasy of unattainable bliss, appeared to him suddenly as the emblem of misfortune. The weight of the consequences of his misdemeanor tipped the balance in terms of everything he stood to lose, wiping out forever the brief moments of pleasure he had enjoyed with his lovely neighbor.

Time froze. They stood there in deafening silence. Open wounds and scabbed-over scars split open. All three threw wounded looks at one another like squirts of acid; they watched one another, savage, hurt, and angry, waiting to see who would be the first to resume hostilities.

It was Gérard who, in his fury, drew on his venomous need to destroy, exterminate, reduce to ashes.

"Okay! Enough with the good manners. On to the serious stuff. I'm afraid you're about to find out your dumbass love affair is the least of your worries."

Still talking, he went into the dining room to fetch the apple-green file folder containing his documents. He came back brandishing it like a battle flag.

"David Brunelle was my client. Not for very long, though, it was while he was in police custody, which barely lasted two hours. Frankly, just between us, the cops had nothing on him. Do you know why?"

Tiphaine and Sylvain, frozen in horror, had eyes only for him, waiting for the words they knew must be coming.

"They had nothing against him because the guy was innocent. I can always spot an innocent man. And a guilty one as well."

He turned to Tiphaine and fixed her with a cold stare.

"One thing I remember very clearly is the purple foxglove. The deadly weapon was a flower! Which suggests the murderer was something of a botanical expert. I don't know why, but I can't quite see David Brunelle being an avid gardener. On the other hand, unless I'm mistaken, I believe you have a job at the local plant nursery?"

He paused, keeping his gaze focused intently on Tiphaine. She didn't reply.

"And then another thing struck me," he went on without relinquishing his prey. "It was a couple of days later when I heard he'd hung himself in the stairwell."

Gérard was using his oratorical gifts and years of experience in court to weave assumptions into certainties. Things had not gone quite as he'd thought they would, and he'd had to change his strategy. His original plan had been to put pressure on Sylvain by threatening to reveal to Tiphaine her husband's affair with Nora. Now that Tiphaine knew about it, any thought of blackmailing Sylvain had bit the dust. He was going to have to transform the gaps in what he knew into assets to maintain his advantage: he'd choose words whose ambiguity would conceal what he didn't know, hoping they would push Tiphaine and Sylvain to interpret his meaning. Insinuations are like laser beams, able to locate a guilty conscience and flush it out more surely than waving a carrot outside a rabbit hole.

"The entire time he was in custody, and the whole time I was driving him home, the poor guy seemed anxious, nervous, panicky even. But not *desperate*. What I'm trying to say is, at no point did he come across as someone who was contemplating doing himself in."

Tiphaine and Sylvain were hanging on Gérard's every word, jaws clenched, expressions inscrutable. Both looked like they could see what was coming, and already knew there was no point trying to avoid it. Still, Tiphaine drew on all her resources to come out with a final spurt of venom. The desire to finish Sylvain off probably wasn't altogether foreign to her.

"When he got home, David found his wife lying on the sofa. Dead," she said in a quiet voice. "They'd been fighting. And she killed herself."

"Do you know what, I don't believe that for a second. Since when has anyone taken an overdose because of a domestic spat? Funny how my client was so much more concerned about his son than his wife when I was driving him home. The son *you* were babysitting, if I recall correctly. He didn't think his son was safe with you. Have you come across a lot of fathers who'd hang themselves, yet are concerned for their children's safety in the house next door?"

"Then why did he ask me to babysit?" Tiphaine said with a mocking little laugh.

"He didn't know. It was only after he found out he'd been taken into custody for being in possession of a pot of foxgloves that he lost his temper and implicated you."

"You have no proof of anything."

That is always the clincher: when the accused doesn't bother to even try to prove their innocence but proceeds directly to the next level of defense: *you have no proof*—four words that sweep away any lingering doubts about their guilt.

Gérard clicked his tongue, as though weighing up whether or not he did have any proof. He waved the file folder at them as if it were bait.

"Maybe I do, maybe I don't!" he said, not even trying to hide his pleasure at seeing Tiphaine dig herself in deeper. "How would you know?" He smiled teasingly, then went on, "So, this is the way I see it: whatever the evidence, there are enough elements here to reopen the case, and I promise that I will not let you out of my sight. But understand this: getting you put behind bars is not the aim of the game, even though I can't deny it would give me immense pleasure."

"What is it you want?" asked Tiphaine, looking at him with undisguised hatred.

So there it was! A tacit acknowledgment. Better than a confession. Gérard didn't know if Tiphaine was conceding Ernest Wilmot's murder or the Brunelles' double suicide. He turned to Sylvain, who stood there, pale as a ghost.

"First off, I'd like Don Juan here to stop dunking his cookie in my wife's coffee. Got that, asshole? Forget she ever existed. You don't even look at her anymore. Her or my kids. Hands off. Got that?"

"You really think the police are going to reopen a case on the basis of a few conjectures?" said Tiphaine, desperate to get the upper hand. "If you have no proof, you have nothing."

"What's gotten into you?" Gérard gave her an ironic half smile. "Does it make you hot to think of your husband getting it on with another woman on the other side of that wall?"

"You have no evidence against us," said Tiphaine, ignoring the attorney's sarcasm. "The police will laugh in your face with your pathetic, empty file." Gérard gave her a dark look. The woman was unstoppable—further evidence that she was capable of just about anything.

"The police, maybe," he conceded with a wolfish grin. "But I don't think any of this will amuse Milo one bit."

# CHAPTER
## 33

At the mention of Milo, Tiphaine reacted like a tigress sensing a threat to her cubs. Though she was appalled by Sylvain's betrayal, it was the absolute necessity of protecting the boy from the attorney's meddling that brought out her aggression. Gérard realized it immediately. The moment he uttered the boy's name, Tiphaine was transformed; her eyes shone with a belligerent gleam, and she gave him a venomous look.

That was when he knew for sure she was capable of murder.

Gérard was a veteran of the terrible things of which the human soul is capable, and he was undisturbed by Tiphaine's suppressed violence. But he felt an instinctive quiver in his solar plexus that told him to be careful, the woman's dam of reason could, ceding to intense pressure, burst at any moment. He knew from experience that it is vital to leave the door open for the enemy to escape, or rather to give the illusion that there is the possibility of escape: someone who has nothing to lose . . . has nothing to lose.

"It's very simple," he said after a moment's pause. "You leave my family alone, and I'll leave yours alone. Everyone goes back to how things were. And we're all happy." He watched Tiphaine closely to be sure she had understood. The hostility in her expression was no less intense, but he detected something in her eyes that unnerved him. Was she determined to hold her course?

He had to get out of there. If Tiphaine and Sylvain wanted to get rid of him, there was nothing to stop them doing so there and then. Any lingering doubts he might have had about their guilt dissipated in the barely disguised hostility of the encounter. They may not have confessed, but their demeanor made their guilt obvious.

He made his way to the front door, his mind teeming with thoughts. He was going to have to watch his back now. The confrontation with Tiphaine troubled him; she had a malevolent energy that made him very uneasy. He had taken no precautions prior to his visit, beyond the plan to blackmail Sylvain, which had been rendered null by the man's idiocy almost as soon as he arrived and was now no more than a vial emptied of its poison. Even his secretary had no idea where he was.

"By the way, I must inform you I had a full medical check just recently, and I'm in excellent health," he said, looking meaningfully at Tiphaine. "Heart, blood pressure, cholesterol levels. Tip-top!"

"I'm very happy for you," she said, holding his gaze.

"I'm just saying that should anything untoward happen to me—a heart attack, say—my doctor would ask questions. And furthermore, my secretary has a list of documents to forward to various people concerning files I'm currently working on. Just a precaution I put in place for certain cases . . ." He stopped for a moment, before concluding his spiel. "So should anything happen to me, all the documents concerning you will be sent to Milo."

It occurred to him that covering himself like this made a great deal of sense. He would tell Mélanie when he was back in the office that if anything untoward were to befall him, she must send everything on to Milo. And he would warn Nora too. Put her on her guard. Maybe even convince her to come back home for a few days until things calmed down. Now that Tiphaine knew she'd been having an affair with her husband, their neighborly relationship was unlikely to remain cordial.

Just as he was leaving, a young man turned up at the house. He didn't need Sherlock Holmes's gifts to deduce that the young man must be Milo. Gérard gave him a warm smile, then reached into the inside pocket of his jacket for his wallet and drew out a business card.

"Milo! Delighted to make your acquaintance." Surprised, Milo barely had time to stammer out a greeting before the attorney went on, "Allow me to introduce myself: my name is Gérard Depardieu. I was your father's defense attorney eight years ago, the night he was in custody, which was in fact the same night that . . . Right, well, you know what I mean. This is my card, and if you'd like to talk about it, if you have any questions at all, please feel free to call."

More and more puzzled, Milo took the card and gave it a perfunctory glance.

"Depardieu. Any relationship to Inès?"

"Yes, indeed, young man. I'm her father. The world certainly does work in mysterious ways." Behind him, Tiphaine stifled a cry of rage. He glanced back and saw the anger in her eyes, a ferocious look of sheer hatred. They glared at each other with mutual hostility for a few seconds that felt like a lifetime. They both knew it now: war had been declared.

# CHAPTER 34

The door closed behind Gérard like the door of a vault slamming shut for eternity on the corpses of its tenants.

Milo stood in the entryway with the attorney's card in his hand, completely thrown by the unexpected encounter. Lost in thought, he didn't notice the strange silence, or Tiphaine and Sylvain standing there, stunned and dumbfounded with shock.

After a long moment he looked up and realized something was very wrong. They were staring at him with dread and trepidation.

"What's going on? What have I done?"

"Nothing," said Tiphaine bleakly.

"Who was that guy?"

Tiphaine felt a shiver run down her spine. Milo's words resounded in her head, their distorted syllables clanging inside her skull.

Who was that guy?

That guy?

A macabre obsession flushed out from the nightmare of the past.

The ghost of a grief that bordered on madness.

"Who was he? Is it true he was my father's defense attorney?"

Incapable of a response, Tiphaine turned instinctively to Sylvain—out of habit, and also because half an hour earlier he had still been an ally.

The specter she saw standing before her made her skin crawl.

"Hey," she heard Milo say. "Is anybody there?"

She forced herself to ignore her feeling of utter revulsion and looked at Milo with a pathetic attempt at a smile.

"Yes, apparently, when he was in custody," she said. She had the excruciating sensation that each word was gouging her throat. "I mean, he saw him for two hours in all. I don't see how he could tell you anything you don't know already."

"You're kidding!" Milo exclaimed eagerly. "He must be the last person who saw him alive." Tiphaine closed her eyes. She felt nauseated, disgusted, and she had to concentrate with all her being to keep herself from slumping to the ground. The boy's excitement finished her off, cast her into the depths of a nightmare from which she knew she would never awaken.

She had nothing left to lose now.

# CHAPTER
## 35

Gérard would have done anything to exorcize his rage after he left the Geniots. He wanted to howl with anger, to dislodge, destroy, flush out the misery eating away at his soul. The interview with the Geniots had been highly dramatic and full of revelations, but it had not gone according to plan. He had the unpleasant feeling that things had gotten out of hand, and he was no longer in control of what might happen next. He had pulled the pin out of a grenade that might still blow up in his face.

And then there was the confirmation of his suspicions, the intolerable fact that his wife, his Nora, had been wrapped in someone else's arms; her skin, her face, her mouth had been caressed by another's hands. Stomach churning, he darted past number 26, ignoring the urge to kick down the door and smash up everything inside.

He had to get away. Without delay. Get his emotions under control, fight the impulse to do harm. His mind was ablaze in a turmoil of resentment, a chaos of words and images, Nora's body, her moans, her mouth twisted in pleasure, and the poison of jealousy that was flowing in his veins, tensing his muscles, clenching his jaw.

He picked up his pace; he had to get out of this street, away from the neighborhood. Far enough away so he wouldn't give in to the urge. Calm down, somehow. He shouldn't act on a whim.

He glanced at his watch and let out an expletive under his breath. Mélanie was going to be furious. He had promised to be back by quarter to seven at the latest so she could leave. He had his children to take care of. How was he going to make it through the evening? Manage not to think about Nora alone at home, only a few steps from her lover?

He began to walk more slowly. Words and images flooded his mind, and his limbs felt as though they were struggling through thick molasses that kept him from moving forward. He thought of Tiphaine, the murderous gleam in her eye, the hatred she must feel now toward Nora. He stopped, his heart thudding with fear. Nora didn't stand a chance against Tiphaine, especially since she had no idea what had just happened. If Tiphaine went around that evening with the idea of settling the score, Nora would open the front door and invite her in, without suspecting for a moment she was welcoming a spurned wife rather than a considerate neighbor.

He took out his phone and called Mélanie. While it was ringing, he tried to figure out a convincing excuse. He was still scrambling for what to say when he heard the secretary's voice, so he said the first thing that came into his head: he was on his way, he just had one tiny thing to deal with, he wouldn't be long.

BARBARA ABEL

Mélanie, well acquainted with her boss's manipulative way with language, accurately assessed the situation. "Okay, I'll feed the kids. But if you're not back in an hour this is the last time I help you out." She hung up.

The attorney grimaced shamefacedly and slipped his phone back into his pocket. A few seconds later, slightly out of breath, he was standing outside Nora's house. He rang the bell and waited for her to answer.

When she opened the door he didn't leave her time to invite him in. Wedging the file folder under one arm, he grabbed her by the shoulders and pushed her inside, trying to explain as succinctly as possible what had just happened.

"Listen. There's no time to be lost: a nuclear bomb has just exploded next door and you're about to feel the shock waves."

"What are you talking about?" said Nora, pulling away from his grasp. "Where are the children?"

"Listen to me. Your neighbor knows you've been sleeping with her husband, and let me tell you she won't be bringing you homemade cookies anytime soon. Get your stuff, you're coming home with me."

"I hope you're joking."

Gérard suppressed a gesture of irritation.

"No, I'm not," he said, trying to contain his fury. "It took you no time at all, eh? You know, you didn't need to leave me if all you wanted was to jump into bed with the first asshole who came along. You could have just done it behind my back, it would have been easy, it's not like I was ever home."

The slap came like a lightning bolt streaking across a stormy sky. Stunned, Gérard dropped the folder; it fell to the floor and slipped beneath the chest of drawers.

"What have you been telling Tiphaine?" Nora yelled, her eyes wide with fury.

"That's exactly what your boyfriend said not even half an hour ago," smirked Gérard, rubbing his cheek. "What is there to tell, I wonder?"

"Get out!" Nora shot him a furious look. She tried to slip past him to the open front door so she could stand there and tell him to leave, but as she tried to pass he blocked her way.

"Jesus, Nora, stop being such a fool! You don't know what these people are capable of."

"Oh yes, I forgot," she said, with a contemptuous laugh. "So many potential psychopaths, isn't that so?"

Gérard grabbed her wrists and forced her to look at him.

"That's not what I'm talking about, Nora. This is serious. You have to trust me."

"Let go!"

Gérard was losing patience. He couldn't find the words to convince her of the gravity of the situation. His impotence, on top of his anger and resentment, were driving him crazy. He had to make her understand that the two of them were in way over their heads, and that despite his jealousy he was doing this to protect her.

"Let go!" she shrieked. "Let go or I'll scream!" This was a little absurd, given she was already screaming. She began to struggle, desperate to get away from him. He held on, trying to get her to calm down and listen, but it had the opposite effect: the tighter his grip, the harder she fought to break free.

Realizing that he would get nowhere if he carried on like this, Gérard let go, hoping that way he could make her listen. Free now, Nora tried once again to reach the front door, not to force her unwanted guest to leave, but to get away from him, to put as much distance between them as possible. Again, Gérard blocked her way.

Nora felt a jolt of panic as she realized he wasn't going to give up. Fear flooded her body. She was well acquainted with her husband's pathological jealousy, fits of paranoia, and ability to hold a grudge. She also knew the violence that these feelings triggered in him. He could read the fear in her eyes, she couldn't see anything anymore, was just trying to get away from him. And all he was doing was trying to get her to listen. He began to talk rapidly, to give her as much information as possible so she would understand how volatile the situation was, how it could turn nasty at any moment.

"Nora, for God's sake, calm down! I'm just trying to get you to understand. They're murderers, they've already killed once, they may even have killed Milo's parents too. That Tiphaine woman, she's . . ."

"Milo's parents?" she yelled, almost hysterical now. "They *are* Milo's parents. You're losing your mind, Gérard!"

"No! That's the whole point. You remember I told you about the guy who hanged himself? That was Milo's father, he committed suicide in the house next door."

"What absolute nonsense. You're scaring me. Please, Gérard, I want you to leave."

"You're not safe here, you don't know what she's capable of. Come with—"

Before he could finish his sentence, she managed to slip away from him and darted to the front door. Gérard let out a cry of frustration, then turned sharply and caught her in two strides. He wasn't in control of the situation, he didn't know what to do; he was flustered and losing precious time, and his inability to get her to see reason was maddening. He grabbed her by the arm and shook her.

"You have to understand you cannot stay here tonight. Not on your own. That woman is crazy. They lost a child eight years ago, and not long after they murdered Milo's godfather, I'm almost certain of it. And I strongly suspect they had something to do with his parents' double suicide as well."

Nora wasn't listening. Panicked, confused, scared stiff, she could only think of one thing: she had to get away from him. She pushed past Gérard and raced up the stairs. She heard his heavy, determined step following her; he was just a few steps behind, her heart was pounding harder and harder as he got closer and closer. Gérard kept shouting her name.

"Nora! Come back, goddammit! You should be afraid of them, not me!"

She was at the top of the stairs, out of breath from the climb and from fear. As Gérard got to the top of the stairs and put out an arm to her, Nora turned to him and saw she had lost. With an instinctive, desperate, defensive gesture, she pushed her husband with all her strength.

Gérard was standing at the top of the stairs. Nora's push destabilized him, he felt himself tipping backward, reacted too late, futilely waved his arms up and down . . . and lost his balance. He fell back, hard, and broke his neck. Shattered his spleen. Smashed several ribs, one of which perforated a lung. Rolling to one side, he hit his head against the banister, then cracked his skull on the tiled floor of the entryway.

From the top of the stairs Nora, trembling from head to foot, stared down at Gérard's lifeless body.

# CHAPTER
## 36

Time stopped. And so did Nora's heart.

The sound of someone's panting breath. Hers. She was hyperventilating. A ghastly silence. An impossible reality, like a vacuum, sucking her in, a fact she refused to process.

She had gone from being the victim to being the executioner.

And soon she would go from being free to being a prisoner—of guilt, grief, human justice.

"G . . . Gérard?"

More silence. Paralysis. Cold. Death.

Seconds ticked by, drawn out by fear, an almost unendurable horror that can only be understood with time, a great deal of time, maybe an entire life, when one knows that the life one is about to leave behind will echo forever across the arid plains of guilt.

Nora stared wide-eyed at Gérard's body. Just a few moments before, she had been terrified of his presence and his physicality; now she would have given anything for him to move, get to his feet. For him to be alive.

She forced herself to remain motionless; it was the only way to stop time. If she didn't move, there was still a tiny chance it hadn't happened. Maybe she could fix it somehow. Go back. Rewind. By wanting it badly enough, praying, believing.

"Gérard . . ."

Nora realized she wasn't even asking the question anymore. It was as if she already knew. As if she had capitulated to this reality that had descended upon her with such sudden, unimaginable, excruciating brutality. She felt her reason close to giving in to madness—the widest path, the least precipitous, the brightest.

But on the path of reason, horror-filled, dark and rocky, she saw two figures moving, two familiar, beloved shadows for whom she would do anything. Their voices echoed in the frigid silence, and the word they uttered pierced her heart with its cold, metallic teeth.

"Maman!"

Almost reluctantly, Nora turned away from the bright, tempting light of madness toward the harsh gloom of consciousness. Only then did she stagger down the stairs, clinging to the banister so as not to fall.

When she reached Gérard's unmoving body, she knelt. He had fallen onto his front so all she could see was his back, and the bald patch on his head. Covered in blood.

For a few moments, she didn't dare touch him, she didn't know how. By the arms? His left arm was bent at an unnatural angle. By the side he was bleeding from? By his head, which seemed to be cracked in several places?

She began to cry, little heaving sobs, feeling the panic return, the path of madness calling her again, flashing its psychedelic lights. Then she screamed. A shriek that came from deep within her, as if she were exorcizing the fear that had filled her moments—or centuries—ago. When at last she had shrieked herself out, when her lungs were empty, she began to breathe again, as if clinging to a tiny ledge on the edge of a precipice, trying to regain a foothold in reality.

She stood up and tried to gather her wits. The children! Where were the children? What time was it? 7:15! They would be at their father's house, of course.

She stared down at Gérard's lifeless body.

The children, on their own. This was an emergency. Trembling, she stumbled into the kitchen to find her phone. She grabbed it and began trying to tap out Inès's number, which she knew by heart, had called so many times, as confused, anarchic words raced through her mind.

What on earth was she going to say to her daughter?

She canceled the call with a moan. She needed help. She was too distraught to make the slightest decision. She looked for Mathilde's number in her contacts. Only she would be able to help her.

At the sound of her friend's voice, Nora burst into tears.

"Nora?" exclaimed Mathilde when she heard the jagged sobs. "Is that you?"

Unable to utter a word, Nora simply wept.

"Nora, what's the matter? Speak to me!"

"G . . . Gérard . . ."

"What about Gérard? What's he done this time?"

"He's dead."

There was a brief, stunned silence, then Mathilde said, "What are you talking about? Where are you?"

Nora whimpered. The only sound she could utter was one of sorrow.

"Nora, talk to me. Where are you?"

"At home."

"Don't move, I'm on my way."

Mathilde set off almost immediately, after telling Philippe she had to go out. "Yes, now. Straightaway. It's an emergency. Nora. No, I don't know what it is, and no, I don't have time to put the little one to bed."

For several interminable minutes, Nora remained motionless on the stairs, staring into space, eyes averted from the body. Its image was carved into her memory. There was no risk of her forgetting it.

Gérard. Dead. The father of her children. Her husband.

The man with whom, a long time ago, she had fallen in love. This was how it ended—with her sitting on the stairs, him lying at her feet bathed in his own blood, after a deadly fall. In a house she had rented in order to get away from him. After too many fights, shouting matches, recriminations, tears. And happy times, too, back when they had still loved each other, when the pleasure of seeing each other had outweighed the discontents of married life.

After two children.

The sound of a phone ringing tore Nora away from the waltz of fractured images spinning around in her head. Her heart quaked beneath an icy blade of terror; she felt her blood freezing in her veins, coursing through her limbs and turning them to stone. What was that sound? It wasn't her phone. It was coming from somewhere nearby, right by her. Gérard. It was his phone. Someone was trying to reach him. Petrified, Nora didn't dare move. She waited, her heart in her mouth, for the sound to stop. After five rings, it did.

The house was once more filled with silence. And Nora with dread.

What would she say to the children? How could she look them in the eye? Support them in their grief? How could she ever again claim any authority over them? How would they survive this?

Her thoughts led her to the edge of a horror-filled void. She still wasn't ready to face up to what had happened. She had to stop thinking and find a way to prevent the terrible images from unspooling in her mind's eye: Nassim's face, then Inès's, their expressions of suffering and incomprehension. What a ghastly tragedy, befalling them so young. She pictured patrol cars in front of the house, an ambulance, Gérard's body being carried out on a stretcher. She saw herself emerging from the house in handcuffs.

And after that?

Who would take care of the children?

The doorbell rang, ripping through the funereal silence that filled the house. Nora let out a cry of fright, before realizing it must be Mathilde. She leaped to her feet and rushed to the door.

When she opened it, her heart nearly stopped. There stood Milo, an awkward smile on his face.

# CHAPTER
## 37

After Gérard left, Milo went thoughtfully upstairs to his room, still holding the attorney's business card.

Downstairs, Tiphaine and Sylvain avoided each other's gaze, she out of disgust, he out of shame. Not so much for having cheated on her, but for the way she'd learned of his infidelity, which he now realized had been more of a fantasy than anything else: apart from some kisses and one torrid afternoon, their love affair had barely had time to exist.

Perhaps that was what he most regretted at that moment. So much damage for so little satisfaction.

Without a word, Tiphaine went into the kitchen to prepare dinner. Sylvain, who knew her so well, understood that now was not the time to try to explain himself. It would be better to let her digest the news. He walked through the living room into the dining room and out onto the deck, where he stood ruminating for half an hour. Then, with a heavy heart, he went back inside to face his wife, ready for a mauling. He might as well get it over with. He walked into the kitchen and leaned against the wall.

"Can we talk?"

She didn't respond immediately. She was concentrating on what she was doing as if her life depended on it. Which, in a way, it probably did. Sylvain sighed; he would have preferred her to scream, insult him, hit him, anything rather than this unbearable stony contempt.

He was just about to leave the room when she turned, her eyes lit up with a fierce gleam. "Don't think you can get away with it so easily."

"Of course not," he said, almost relieved. "I'd like to talk about it."

She burst out laughing. She sounded almost joyful.

"I don't give a damn who you sleep with, Sylvain. I really don't. How banal, to be screwing your neighbor. It's almost funny. The problem is you picked the wife of a man who could land us in deep, deep shit. Bury us in it. Destroy our lives. And that, Sylvain, isn't funny at all."

Sylvain couldn't hide his astonishment. It wasn't as if he'd been expecting her to fall to pieces, brokenhearted, but he felt a little wounded by this level of cynicism. Was there really nothing between them anymore? Not the tiniest crumb of attachment, the vaguest trace of affection?

"Stop looking like that, Sylvain," she said. "You weren't expecting me to collapse in tears and call you a bastard, were you?"

"Of course not," he said again. Now he knew there really was nothing left between them but the stain of misfortune, the stigma of suffering. Hostility born of solitude. Grief had turned out to be stronger than love. They had become toxic to each other. They reminded each other of everything they had lost.

When Maxime had died everything else had died with him, even the most infinitesimal recollections of joy.

"You can carry on screwing her, I don't care," Tiphaine said mockingly, as if she could read his thoughts. "But you'd better make sure she doesn't do us any harm." She looked at him. "Because if you don't, I will."

Sylvain raised his eyebrows and said nothing. Her words needed no elucidation.

He was utterly overwhelmed by the turn events had taken. How had they gotten to this point in less than a week? Seven days before, they'd been trundling along quite happily. No fear or sorrow. No emotions or surprises. No dreams either.

"No, Tiphaine," he said, his voice flat. "Not again."

In the heat of the moment, she failed to hide her surprise.

"I beg your pardon?" she said, sounding like a queen dressing down an insolent subject.

"You heard me," he said, his voice firm. "No more of that crazy stuff."

"I don't think you are in any position to discuss—"

"I'm in a position to do whatever I like, Tiphaine. And I am not going to do that."

"I've never needed you for anything," she sneered.

"I'm not going to be anyone's accomplice either," he said firmly.

Tiphaine looked at him, trying to assess his resolve.

And this time she understood that even the ghastly liability they shared wouldn't keep Sylvain from standing in her way.

As if to confirm her fears, he stepped a little closer to her and looked her in the eye, his face grim.

"Tiphaine, if anything happens to that attorney, I swear to God I will turn you in."

They were interrupted by the sound of footsteps on the stairs. They sprang apart to opposite sides of the kitchen, like two lovers surprised. Milo poked his head in and looked from one to the other without a word. Tiphaine turned to him and flashed him the fakest of B-movie smiles.

"Are you looking for something, mon chéri?"

Milo smiled distractedly. He hated it when she called him that.

"I have to go out for a bit, I won't be long."

Normally, Tiphaine would have asked him where he was going, who he was seeing, how long he'd be gone.

"Sure. Don't be late for dinner."

Milo mimed a look of thoughtful reflection, one eyebrow raised in mock surprise, then turned and left. He was still clutching the attorney's business card.

He walked out of the house and went to call at the house next door.

# CHAPTER
## 38

"Milo?" said Nora hoarsely, taking a step outside and pulling the door closed behind her to conceal from her unexpected visitor the sight of a body lying in the entryway.

The young man waved the business card awkwardly at her by way of explanation.

"Nora, I'm sorry to disturb you. I was wondering if Inès is around? I wanted to talk to her about something."

"Inès?" Nora seemed so taken aback by the question that Milo somehow felt foolish for asking. But surely it wasn't dumb to ring the doorbell of the home of the person he was looking for.

"She's at her father's," said Nora, looking like she'd seen a ghost.

"Actually, that's what I wanted to talk to her about. Her father was over at our place, about twenty minutes ago . . ." Milo noticed streaks of mascara on Nora's cheeks; there were dark rings around her eyes, and they were red from crying. She looked a wreck.

"Are you okay?"

Nora stared at him as if the question were absurd.

"Absolutely!" she said eventually, forcing herself to pull herself together. Then she fell silent again. Milo, shocked by his friend's mother's terrible appearance, felt increasingly uneasy. Here was an adult who clearly needed help, but he felt totally powerless to do anything.

There was the sound of a car slowing down and they both turned to see someone pulling into a parking spot a little farther up the road. To Nora's relief it was Mathilde, who eventually managed to maneuver the car into the tight space, then grabbed her purse, opened the door, climbed out of the car, and ran to Nora's house. Seeing Milo on the sidewalk, she tried to figure out her friend's frame of mind. The panic on Nora's face left her in no doubt: it was clearly not the boy's lucky day. Nora was looking at Mathilde with an imploring expression like a silent cry for help, as if she were begging.

Mathilde was caught off guard. She reached the house and smiled reassuringly at Nora and Milo. The young man stared in bewilderment from one to the other until Nora found the strength to give him a smile.

"I'll tell Inès you dropped by to see her. Have a nice evening, Milo."

Milo understood he was being dismissed and, in truth, was deeply relieved. He said goodbye, turned, and went back into his house.

Mathilde and Nora waited until the Geniots' front door swung closed, then Nora fell into her friend's arms as if she no longer had the strength to stand.

"What is going on, Nora?" Mathilde asked, holding her. "Where's Gérard?"

Nora nodded miserably at her house. Mathilde slowly pulled away from her friend and, with her hands on her shoulders, looked her in the eye.

"You mean . . . ?"

Nora could only nod feverishly.

Mathilde gulped. "He's dead?"

Nora lowered her eyes in response.

"Oh no!" whispered Mathilde with a horrified sigh. "What happened? No, wait, don't tell me here. Let's go inside."

"No!"

Nora instinctively stepped away from the house. Mathilde gave her an apprehensive look.

"Fine. Let's go sit in the car."

She put one arm around her friend's shoulders and guided her to the car. They got in, shut the doors, and Nora began to give Mathilde a rambling account of what had happened, her words tumbling over one another incoherently, forming sentences whose meaning was vague, obliging Mathilde to interrupt her every so often for clarification. After ten minutes or so, Mathilde had a sketchy outline of what had happened.

For several minutes the two women sat in silence, as if time had congealed into a sort of insipid purgatory. Before the descent into hell.

After a while Mathilde put an end to this strange, leaden state of penance.

"You have to call the police."

Nora looked horrified. "You don't really think that!" she exclaimed, bursting into loud sobs.

"It's your only hope," said Mathilde firmly. "You were defending yourself. Gérard had no reason to be in your house. He threatened you. All you did was protect yourself!"

"What if they don't believe me?"

"Why wouldn't they? It's the truth, no?"

Nora was staring straight ahead, lost in the appalling prospect of giving herself up to the police. Being interrogated. Revealing her crime to her children. Facing the consequences of her act, even if none of it had been intentional. She was seized with fear, engulfed in horror, unable to see the slightest glimmer of light at the end of the dark tunnel that seemed to have swallowed her up.

"Nora!" said Mathilde urgently. She sensed her friend spiraling into despair. "If you don't, it'll only be worse. They'll find out eventually. One way or another. And when they do, you'll have no way out."

"Unless I get rid of the body," Nora whispered.

"Stop!" Mathilde stared at Nora in shock. She had no idea how to get Nora to see reason. She was fully aware of the gravity of the situation, and terrified her friend was about to make a dreadful mistake that she would spend the rest of her life regretting.

"Nora, I beg you. Don't do that. Don't even think about it. Only the truth will save you."

"I'll just have to make it look like an accident," Nora went on, apparently unaware Mathilde had spoken. "It *was* an accident!" she cried, as if she were trying to rouse her friend. She was trembling. She turned slowly to look at Mathilde.

There was an ocean of despair in her eyes. She began speaking very rapidly, as if trying to articulate the thread of her thoughts, but the words weren't coming out quickly enough.

"An accident that had nothing to do with me! We can put him in the car and push it over a cliff . . . But there aren't any cliffs around here . . . What about the shopping mall, behind the hardware store? There's a new building going up. I was there just yesterday. They've dug a massive hole and there's only a barrier in front of it. We could put Gérard in the car, drive up there, sit him behind the steering wheel, and push the car into the hole."

"That's insane."

"No, it's simple. I'll block the brake with something, I don't know, a rock or something, turn on the engine, and when it starts to rev I'll shove the rock out of the way with a stick, an umbrella, I read something like this in a novel, it shouldn't be very hard . . ."

Mathilde groaned, aghast. "We're not in a novel," she said, horrified by her inability to get Nora to see reason. "That would never work!"

"Yes! It could work! But I'll need your help. I beg you, Mathilde, don't let me down."

Mathilde stared at her friend in consternation, alarmed by her distress. Myriad thoughts were rattling around inside her head; she had to figure out a way to bring Nora back down to earth.

"Think of the children," she begged, drawing on all her powers of persuasion.

The mention of the children seemed to achieve her objective: Nora shivered and seemed at last to come to her senses.

"They're all alone at Gérard's house," she exclaimed, appalled. "I have to go and fetch them. Pass me your phone."

Disconcerted by this precipitous change of tone, Mathilde hesitated.

"My phone? Why?"

"I need to call them, reassure them. Tell them I'm here. That I'm on my way over."

"Why would you do that? You're not meant to know they're on their own."

"Pass me your phone," Nora repeated coldly.

Mathilde was overcome by misgivings. She knew the situation was beyond her control and she wouldn't be able to prevent whatever it was from happening. Her mind was confused, she couldn't think straight anymore. Feeling panicky and helpless, she reached into her purse, took out her phone, and handed it to Nora, who grabbed it and dialed Gérard's landline. It rang three times before Inès answered. At the sound of her daughter's voice, her heart contracted.

"Hello, sweetheart, it's Maman."

Her voice sounded as if it came from beyond the grave.

Inès greeted her mother warmly. She told her all was well, her father wasn't home yet but they were with Mélanie. In the background Nora could hear the secretary asking who was on the line. Inès told her.

"Can I speak to her?" Nora heard Mélanie's voice distinctly; she must have moved closer to Inès so she could take the call.

Inès told her mother she was passing her to Mélanie, said she was looking forward to seeing her on Sunday, told her she loved her, and handed over the phone.

"Madame Dep— um . . . Madame Amrani?"

"Hello, Mélanie."

Nora was relieved to know that the children were not home alone. But she was terrified of the secretary's questions.

"I'm so sorry to get you involved, but Monsieur Depardieu promised he'd be back over an hour ago. I really can't stay all evening, I have plans. I've been trying to call, but he's not answering his phone. If I don't hear from him in the next half hour, can I call you and you can come and take over?"

Caught off guard, Nora turned in a panic to look at Mathilde. The urgent need for a response made her stammer.

"Of course . . . sure. . . . it's . . . er . . . fair enough."

Mathilde watched her with concern. "What's fair enough?" she whispered.

"Or I could bring them over to your place, if you prefer?" Mélanie suggested, a little embarrassed to be asking such a favor of her boss's estranged wife. But they were her children, too, after all.

"No!" Nora said, aghast. "I'll come and fetch them."

"Great! I'll get back to you if he's not home in half an hour."

Nora ended the call and turned to Mathilde looking totally panic-stricken.

"We have half an hour."

"Half an hour to do what?" asked Mathilde in panic.

"To get rid of the body!"

Mathilde froze. This refusal to accept reality triggered a wave of fury and revulsion. She had the feeling that when Nora had called her for help she was just trying to offload a problem she couldn't deal with on her own. She was using her as a crutch. Dragging her into the abyss of guilt. Rage pounded her stomach more violently than if she'd been kicked in the abdomen. She suppressed the desire to throw herself at Nora and tear out her eyes.

"If it's the two of us we can manage it," Nora went on, as if in a trance.

That was it. Mathilde turned and slapped her friend as hard as she could. If words weren't enough to persuade her, maybe physical pain would bring her to her senses.

Nora's head pivoted violently, and her hair whipped the window. For a few seconds the car was filled with stunned silence. Then Nora turned slowly to Mathilde, her eyes brimming with tears.

She began to sob. Floods of tears that bore away with them the illusion that she could escape punishment, devastating upheaval, and the agony of guilt. She crashed abruptly back to earth so hard that the shock reverberated through her body, her mind, and her soul. It would be an endless descent into hell. Branded forever with the stigma of guilt, that wicked sorceress who insinuates herself into everything, leaving a long trail of venom in her wake.

Mathilde heaved a deep sigh of despair and compassion. At last Nora seemed to have come to her senses. Crying would do her good: Mathilde allowed her to purge herself of her pain for several long minutes, before exclaiming, "Damn it, Nora, look at the mess you've gotten us into." She put her head in her hands. What was she going to do now? Could she turn around and go home, act as if she knew nothing, get on with her exhausting life as a working mother and wife? Was it too late?

She knew.

She knew that Gérard had died falling from the top of the stairs because Nora had pushed him as she tried to get away.

She was already complicit.

She was already guilty.

And now Nora seemed to have lost her mind. How could she trust her? How could she be sure that, in the event of her being interrogated by the police—which was bound to happen—Nora wouldn't crack, and tell them everything, dragging Mathilde in her wake?

She could think of only two options: either she helped Nora get rid of the body, leaving her in constant fear that once the body was discovered the autopsy would reveal the real cause of Gérard's death, and the police would open an investigation.

Or . . .

Or she managed to convince Nora to call the cops.

To explain what had happened. After all, Gérard had no reason to be at her house, much less upstairs. Her story was plausible, especially if she were the one to deliver it. If she didn't, though, if she tried to escape justice, she was signing her own death warrant. No one would ever believe her story later on.

Mathilde lifted her head and gave a deep sigh. "Nora," she began, in a voice so somber and lacking in vitality she didn't recognize it. "I really can't."

Nora's eyes widened.

"Don't look at me like that, I beg you," Mathilde said, avoiding her gaze. "I can't, Nora. For my kids, for Philippe . . ."

"Mathilde!"

"Damn it, Nora!" she snapped, feeling a thudding anxiety pervade her body. "You're asking me to be nothing more nor less than an accomplice to murder. You've completely lost your mind. I can't take the risk—"

"You can't just drop me like this," said Nora, her voice cracking. "Not now! I have to pick up my kids in twenty minutes and their father's corpse is lying in the entryway. Mathilde, I beg you." She stared at her beseechingly, trying to find the words to persuade her. "And you're forgetting Milo," she went on more assertively, as if she had found the decisive argument in her favor. "He saw you turn up at my house."

Mathilde looked at her, appalled. Nora was right, there was no getting out of it now. She was in it up to her neck. "Unless you call the cops and tell them what happened."

Nora was beside herself now. She was shaking uncontrollably. Her face was haggard, her eyes so tear-drenched she couldn't see. She hiccupped with sobs as she pleaded with her friend, stammering out endless prayers and excuses. Distraught, Mathilde put her arms around her and held her tight.

As she clasped Nora to her, she knew she would never get her to call the police. But she also knew she didn't have the strength to go any further. She was drained of all energy, and she felt as helpless as her friend. Ashamed, terrified, devastated. She loosened her embrace.

"I'm sorry, Nora. I can't. I won't say anything to anyone, but I can't help you either. It's too risky. You have to understand. I—" The words stuck in her throat, her mind was frozen with panic. If she spoke up now, she could still save her skin. She could tell the cops she'd tried to get her friend to call and tell them what had happened. That Nora had promised she would. After that, whatever Nora did, Mathilde would be protected: no one could accuse her of having shielded her friend. She clung to this logic: her responsibility to her family, the rightness of her decision. She fixed her gaze on the dashboard, where a photograph of her three children teased her with their beguiling grins, desperately focusing on avoiding Nora's reproachful expression. Her pleading eyes. Her trembling lips.

"Mathilde . . ." Nora begged in a barely audible gasp, with a moan of utter despair.

Mathilde stared at her lap, unable to confront her friend's desolation. "I'm sorry," she replied dully.

Faced with such a pathetic surrender, Nora stopped weeping. She looked at Mathilde with sadness infused with disappointment and slowly nodded her head.

"I understand."

That was all she said. Time seemed to stand still. A deathly silence filled the car. Two women, sitting side by side, each trying to break free from the other: Mathilde, bogged down by shame and confusion; Nora, caught between terror and bitterness. She was on her own now. There was no one else she could count on.

And so, drawing on an undreamed-of reserve of willpower, Nora wiped her eyes and breathed in deeply. Outside, a light rain was falling on the windscreen in unbroken, parallel rivulets. She stared at one of the drops that, unlike the others, seemed to be tracing its own path on the damp surface of the glass. A crazy thought, like this tiny glinting drop, began to glow as if from a great distance, from her dark future, like a cord appearing miraculously from who knew where, tumbling toward her. Into her mind burrowed a plan. An unbelievable image. A solution that could perhaps put everything right. A last exit. A dreadful, despicable, cruel, diabolical idea, so dastardly that she shuddered even to be considering it. Could she pull it off? And would her nerves prove solid enough to deal with her conscience?

The digital clock on the dashboard told her she had fifteen minutes left before Mélanie's call.

Fifteen minutes to make a decision.

To make a choice.

To save her skin.

# CHAPTER
## 39

In the house next door, the sun had set on the pitiless gleam of the shards of a long-moribund marriage, where two people who were once in love now saw in each other nothing more than a threat, an ordeal, danger.

They ate dinner in silence, for every single word Tiphaine or Sylvain uttered, brimming with shame, concealed in its syllables a potential wound. They were contaminated by a history that refused to remain in the past. That evening, the dead came, uninvited, to join their meal; the dead, whose absence filled their hearts and their minds.

A little boy with a broken body, whose empty eyes obstinately refused to meet those of his mother.

An elderly man, his features frozen by the violent ending of his life when he left behind the prison of his flesh.

A sallow young woman, eaten up from within by the poison of suspicion.

A man with a broken neck, garroted by the bonds of friendship.

All four took their places at the table, miming the act of

eating, bringing invisible forks laden with nonexistent food to their lips. Tiphaine watched them, lost in the transitory meanderings of her penitence, grief, and guilt.

"Well, you're a bundle of fun tonight," muttered six-year-old Maxime.

"That's enough, Milo, don't push it," said Sylvain, without looking up from his plate. Tiphaine looked up, shocked, to see the adolescent sitting opposite her, taken aback by the impossible metamorphosis. Maxime and Milo merged before her eyes, the smile of one, the expression of the other, the years that separated them, their voices echoing within her head in a demented chorus.

"Are you okay, Tiphaine?" asked Milo, looking at her with concern.

She shuddered. "Are you talking to me?"

"Um, yes," he replied, surprised by the question.

"Why are you calling me Tiphaine?"

Milo cast a startled glance at Sylvain, who was staring miserably at his wife.

"What do you want me to call you?" Milo asked.

"Maman. I want you to call me Maman."

"That's enough, Tiphaine," said Sylvain.

She gave him a look of profound sadness.

"What do you mean, that's enough? Every child calls their mother Maman."

"Yeah, they do," Milo said, on the defensive. "Except you're not my mother."

Tiphaine trembled at this strike, devastated by the cruelty he was raining down on her, these words, like daggers, spat out in a loathing born of unrelenting bitterness. Why did he hate her so much? She had done nothing wrong.

All she had done was forget to close a window.

As soon as the meal was over, Milo went up to his room, with no intention of coming back down again. The atmosphere in the house was so suffocating, it was making his life a constant misery. They'd obviously had another fight, but this time it looked serious. And there was the visit from that guy who was probably the last person to have seen his father alive. Inès's father. Life could be so strange sometimes. Milo drew out the attorney's business card from the back pocket of his jeans and thoughtfully spun it between his fingers. What an idiot he was to have gone to see Inès. What would she have been able to tell him? She wouldn't know anything. And he had promised himself not to have anything to do with her anymore, to protect her from his feelings, which put her in danger. A bit like he'd done with those two downstairs, who were clearly going to end up destroying themselves, consumed by their destructive relationship, the poison of passing time, the memory of Maxime.

The whole thing was toxic.

Milo gave a bitter laugh. He must never give in to the siren song of love. The happiness of love is a lure, a lie we tell our children so as not to scare them. Love breeds nothing but torment, sadness, and despair. Love causes devastating harm.

Downstairs, Sylvain cleared the table, put the dirty dishes and flatware in the dishwasher, and scrubbed the saucepans. Tiphaine sat at the table staring into space, while various devious solutions unspooled in her mind. She had to grab the sword of Damocles that hung over her head and decapitate the problem. Definitively. With a sharp blow, without any missteps. Shut up that despicable lawyer once and for all, in the most horrible way possible. And so find peace.

But first she would have a little fun. Something she hadn't experienced in a long time.

"I'm going up to bed," Sylvain said in a toneless voice. It was very early, but she didn't reply. Sylvain looked at her sadly for a few seconds, then left the room.

Tiphaine sat, caught up in her fantasies, soothing her misery by envisaging various ways of hurting the attorney. Glimpsing the end of this nightmare. He shouldn't have attacked her, threatened to tell Milo everything, stuck his obnoxious, lawyerly nose into her business. He shouldn't have done it.

She was going to make him suffer. He had no idea what she was capable of. What she was planning would destroy them both, him and his bitch of a wife.

In the middle of the night Sylvain woke with a start. He was soaked in sweat, his heart was beating abnormally fast, and he was struggling to breathe. He felt for the lamp switch and turned it on. The other side of the bed was empty. Tiphaine hadn't come up. He sighed, kicked off the covers, and went downstairs. She was lying on the sofa underneath a blanket. The message was clear: from now on they would be sleeping apart.

# CHAPTER
## 40

Saturday morning. Nora opened her eyes after a restless night. Her sleep had been peopled by malevolent specters. She was in pain, emotional and physical. Her neck hurt, her shoulders and back were stiff, the echo of a night filled with terrible dreams. She groaned, desperate to fall into the no-man's-land of sleep, to escape the throes of fear. She tried turning onto her side, curling up as if to protect herself from the abuses her memory was inflicting on her. Every movement triggered a dull pain and the memory of the ghastly events of the previous night.

The worst night of a life that now lay in ruins.

It took her several long minutes to gather the strength to get out of bed. From downstairs she could hear the muffled voices of her children, who were already up. She gave a sigh that seemed to vibrate with all the world's misery.

At last she managed to haul herself out of bed. Her arms ached; it felt as if she would dislocate her shoulders if she moved. Her muscles hurt from the effort of moving Gérard's body. Christ! Had she really done it?

She tiptoed to the bathroom and steadied herself on the edge of the basin. She felt like throwing up. She barely recognized the face in the mirror, cruel witness to the awful hours she'd been through.

Yes, she had done it.

She had seen it through to the bitter end.

She had climbed out of Mathilde's car like an automaton and walked back to the house without a backward glance, her expression vacant, finding from deep within her a determination she didn't recognize. She stopped outside the front door, perhaps giving herself one last chance to change her mind before she committed the irrevocable. Don't do *that*.

Braving her revulsion, she pushed open the door and went inside. Gérard lay at the foot of the stairs, blood pooling on the tiles around his body. The sight of the dark, sticky substance almost broke her resolve: *who would have thought he would have had so much blood in him.* She had to act quickly; cleaning up hadn't been part of the plan. Pulling herself together, she glanced at her watch and went down to the basement. She lost precious seconds looking for the tarpaulin she knew was in there somewhere, that must once have belonged to Madame Coustenoble, the previous owner. At last she found it, blue and crumpled, and dragged it up the stairs to wrap Gérard's body in. It wasn't easy to lay it out; the entryway wasn't very wide and the body was already taking up a fair amount of space. She had to keep starting again, forcing herself to control her shaking and her clumsiness, but she managed it eventually. Then she had to drag the corpse over to the tarp to roll it up inside. Touching the dead body repulsed her. Summoning all her courage, she seized Gérard by his jacket lapels and bumped him over to the plastic-coated canvas. Disgust. Don't think about it. Don't breathe. Focus on what has to be done and do it. Get to the end of this nightmare.

Once she'd rolled the body up inside the tarp, she dragged it by the feet to the kitchen, then turned right into the dining room. She hauled it out through the glass door and onto the deck, then dragged it along the back of the house to the bay that protruded at the corner, far enough from the outside light to be plunged into shadow.

It was almost nightfall. Gérard's body wasn't exactly hidden, but it couldn't be seen unless someone was really looking. It would do for the time being.

Wasting no time, Nora hurried back inside and into the kitchen, where she grabbed a pair of rubber gloves, a mop, a bottle of floor cleaner, and a bucket that she filled halfway up with hot water. She went back into the entryway. Just then her phone rang from inside her purse, which was sitting on the kitchen table. She started at the sound, her nerves on edge, swore under her breath, put down the cleaning equipment, and went back into the kitchen to rummage in her purse for the phone. It was Mélanie, of course. She answered, cutting short the secretary's apologies, and promised she would be over as soon as she could.

She had never scrubbed a floor so thoroughly in her life.

Suppressing her nausea, she wiped up the blood, rubbed down the tiles and the grout, soaped, rinsed, and polished until there was not the slightest trace left of Gérard's fall. Then she did the same on the stairs. When she had finished, she put away all the cleaning materials, took a quick look at herself in the mirror to check she was presentable, and hurried out of the house and into the car.

Ten minutes later she drew up outside her former home. She turned off the engine and took a few moments to compose herself. The hardest part was still to come. First, she was going to have to face her children without letting them see that anything was amiss, which, given her state, was going to be tricky. Then, after they went to bed, she was going to have to carry out the second part of her plan. She felt a wave of overwhelming weariness and had to force herself to control her despair. Now was not the moment to waver.

Mélanie greeted her with relief. It was already almost nine, and this unfortunate hiccup had made her late for dinner with some friends who had been expecting her an hour ago. The children were thrilled to see Nora, too. They bombarded her with questions about their father, asking her if she knew where he was or had heard from him.

Nora hugged them tight, feigning complete ignorance about everything, before shooing them off to pack their bags.

"We're going back to your house?" Nassim asked, surprised. "How will we know when Papa gets back?"

"We'll call him," said Nora.

As she spoke she felt a cold sweat running down her entire body. Gérard's phone! She'd left it in his jacket pocket. If it rang, it would draw attention to where his body lay like nothing else. How could she have forgotten about it? She tried to calm her rising panic, forced herself to think logically. If anyone called him before she got back, what was the risk if a neighbor heard it? Wasn't the sound of a cell phone ringing so utterly banal today that it would arouse zero curiosity?

She had to hurry home to sort out this bothersome detail.

"Get a move on, you two," she said, sounding flustered. "It's late."

"So?" said Inès with an insouciant shrug. "We don't have school tomorrow, it's Saturday."

Nora eyed her daughter with a mixture of consternation and sadness. "Maybe so, but if you don't mind, I'd like to get home," she said testily. "I haven't eaten yet, for one thing."

"Fine, no need to get mad about it."

Inès went up to her room to pack her stuff. Nora began pacing up and down, unable to stop thinking about the signal she'd left in Gérard's pocket. If she'd wanted to tell the whole world she had hidden a body in the garden she couldn't have done it better. She knew her husband: he was always getting calls, even in the evening, and if someone was trying to get ahold of him . . . her head began to fill with the most terrible scenarios: she imagined arriving back at her house and finding the street filled with police cars, blue lights flashing, a body being brought out on a stretcher, all the neighbors standing at their front doors observing the scene in horror.

And her driving up, the kids in the back seat with a barrage of questions, why are there cops outside our house, what are they doing, who's that on the stretcher?

"Are you ready?" she called up to hurry things along.

"Are we coming back here to spend the weekend with Papa?" asked Inès from the top of the stairs.

Nora was about to say no, but she caught herself in time.

"I think so, yes. I'll bring you back once he gets home. But it's late now, so tonight you'll stay with me."

"Should we bring our backpacks?" asked Nassim.

"You might as well, you never know," Nora replied, trying—not very well—to conceal her impatience.

At last they were ready to go.

"How will Papa know where we are?" Nassim asked as she opened the front door.

"Good point!" said Inès. "We should leave him a note so he doesn't worry."

"That's enough!" said Nora, losing her temper and at the same time wondering how she could be so cynical. "He's the one who's let you down, and now you're worrying about him?"

"Maman!" said Inès reproachfully. "He might have a very good excuse."

"Your father always has a good excuse," said Nora under her breath, thinking to herself that this time he'd surpassed himself.

She found a scrap of paper in her purse and scribbled a brief note telling Gérard where the children were. She put it on the table in the entryway.

Inès read the note. "That's not a very nice message," she said.

"Well, that's how it is," snapped Nora. "Let's go. I'd like to get home." Inès cast a dubious look at her mother and followed her out of the house, her purse dangling from her shoulder. She was tapping at her phone's screen.

"What are you doing?" asked Nora.

"I'm calling Papa, just in case."

"Stop that right now," her mother said curtly.

Ignoring her mother's command, Inès brought the phone to her ear. Nora snatched it out of her hands.

"Hey," her daughter blurted out. "How dare you do that? What's up with you?"

"Don't speak to me like that, Inès."

"Give me back my phone!"

"Learn to obey when someone tells you to."

"I'm allowed to call my father."

"I just told you, he won't answer."

"You could say it a little more pleasantly. What's up with you?"

At the end of her rope and not wanting the situation to deteriorate any further, Nora didn't reply. Inès glared at her and mumbled something, no doubt unpleasant, then the three of them got in the car and Nora sped off.

There was a gloomy atmosphere in the car the whole way back to the house. Nora drove fast, staring straight ahead. Inès glowered in the passenger seat beside her, while Nassim sat in the back and stared out the window. As she turned down rue Edmond-Petit, Nora let out a sigh of relief: everything was quiet, as usual.

Once inside, against all her basic principles, she gave the children permission to kill their brain cells in front of the screen of their choice. Surprised, Inès rewarded her mother with a triumphant smile, convinced that this magnanimous gesture resulted from her embarrassment at having been so unfair earlier. Nassim, who couldn't care less what the reason was, simply leaped on his PlayStation. Nora went out onto the deck to the body she'd hidden in the shadowy nook.

Recovering the phone from Gérard's jacket required her to be patient and rational: the body, rolled up in the tarpaulin, was bent double. She had to get it almost upright and then, using her shoulders and hips to keep it more or less straight, slip her arm beneath the tarpaulin. She couldn't bear having to touch the body. Turning her head away from Gérard, repulsed and appalled, she patted her ex-husband's torso. It gave out a waft of pungent air, adding to her revulsion. She groaned as she realized the phone wasn't in his breast pocket and she was going to have to explore lower down, obliging her to get even closer to the body. This time she almost touched his cheek. Her hand continued its blind exploration and eventually reached the left-hand pocket. Empty. If it wasn't in the one on the right, it was a catastrophe. Nauseated by this final proximity to Gérard, Nora could barely control her disgust. She stretched her arm as far as she could to reach the third pocket and felt, at last, the shape of the phone. She grabbed it and immediately pulled away from the corpse. Gérard collapsed in a heap. A dead weight.

Nora immediately switched off the phone. She didn't know what to do next. Taking it into the house seemed too big a risk; the children might find it and wonder what their father's phone was doing at her house. On the verge of a nervous breakdown, she shoved the object inside the tarpaulin alongside Gérard's head, and went back inside.

The evening seemed to go on forever. For the first time in a long while she couldn't wait for the children to go up to bed, but as Inès had already pointed out, given that it was Saturday the next day, there was no reason for them to go to bed early.

Midnight. At last, everyone was asleep. Nora was a nervous wreck. She went back outside to the corpse. She took the phone and slipped it into her pocket, then swiveled the body around so she could grab it by the feet, and began to pull it along the hedge that separated their property from the Geniots'. The dead weight of the corpse made progress difficult, but adrenaline gave her strength. Fear did too. Fear of losing everything. A survival instinct kicked in that was stronger than anything else—principles, morals, conscience. She would have killed to save what could still be saved. Actual murder.

When she reached the farthest end of the hedge, she let go of Gérard's legs, then gave herself a few seconds' rest to catch her breath. She was drenched in sweat, out of breath, terrified. She felt so tyrannized by this feeling of suffocation that she wished she could detach herself from her body.

In front of her rose the wall that marked the boundary of her property. On her right, the hedge that separated her from the neighboring yard. Tiphaine and Sylvain's yard.

This was where the operation grew complicated. Unfortunately for Nora, the final part of her plan was the riskiest: the hedge was almost as tall as she was, and hauling the body up in order to tip it over to the other side required more strength than she possessed.

# CHAPTER
# 41

Nora splashed her face with cold water and made herself go downstairs. The children had eaten lunch, and now Nassim was settled in front of the PlayStation and Inès was in the middle of one of her seemingly endless conversations with Léa—or was it Emma?—on her BlackBerry. The indifference with which they greeted Nora was salutary: the less they demanded of her, the better her mood. She gave each child a brief hug, which they barely acknowledged, then walked over to the door that led onto the deck. She stepped outside, squinting at the back of the yard to see if she could make out any traces of the previous night's activity. There were marks on the grass where she had dragged the body, and she knew she was going to have to spend the morning mowing. Farther back, the end of the hedge didn't seem to have suffered too badly, but Nora didn't dare go down there in case Tiphaine, Sylvain, or Milo spotted her from an upstairs window—she didn't want to draw the slightest attention to that end of the yard.

She turned back and went inside to make herself coffee. Then, knowing she had no time to lose, she went upstairs to get dressed. Ten minutes later she began mowing the grass with particular care. When she reached the end she peered at the gap between the hedge and the wall through which she had managed to push Gérard's body. There were a few broken branches on the ground, which she kicked into the pile of grass clippings.

The night before, once she had realized there was no way she was going to be able to hoist Gérard's body over the hedge, Nora had almost given in to despair. But as she felt blindly up and down the hedge, she noticed a gap between the end of it and the boundary wall. At first glance it looked too narrow for the body to pass through, but by pushing the branches aside perhaps she could do it. Once again, adrenaline, fear, and nervous tension gave her a surge of energy: she took hold of the corpse by the armpits and pulled it with all her strength as close as she could to the spot she'd identified, where she leaned it against the wall, facing away from the hedge. Then with a massive kick she pushed it through the branches. Gérard collapsed miserably in the middle of the hedge. Nora stifled a cry of victory. All she had to do now was step over the body into the next-door yard and pull it toward her. Gathering her courage, she grabbed the end of the tarpaulin and bumped it along slowly and haphazardly, almost falling backward with each tug. Utterly exhausted, Nora had to draw on all her strength not to give up and simply kill herself. Hang herself from the top of the stairs.

For a second, the image of a hanged man appeared in her mind, and Gérard's words came back to her: "The cops didn't really have any evidence against the guy, and he was released that evening. I drove him home. And it was here. The next day, he was found hanging in the stairwell."

A man had hanged himself here, or in the house next door, because he had been accused of a crime he said he hadn't committed. And now she, Nora, was thinking of hanging herself to atone for a crime of which she was well and truly guilty.

Life seemed so grimly ironic that she was tempted to abandon the whole thing. Let events follow their course. Stop fighting it. What was the point? It was all going to end badly. Again, it was the thought of her children that forced her to pull herself together. She was filled with the determination of a mother protecting her children. How could she give up now? The thought of Inès's and Nassim's lives falling apart because of the tragedy that was racing head-on toward them—their mother, who had killed their father then hanged herself, or been taken away by police, she didn't know which was worse—gave her a bit of energy, like a spell that can't be broken. She had to carry on. She had no choice. As long as she was able to breathe, she had to do everything to protect her children.

At last she got the body to the other side of the hedge and began to glimpse the end of the nightmare. It was only a few more meters to the compost bin. The row of bushes that Tiphaine had planted to protect the yard from the smell that rose from the compost hid her from the house. No one would be able to see her. She dragged the corpse over to it and then, using the last of her energy, began to empty the compost bin, first by fistfuls, then handfuls, then armfuls, paying no heed to the stink or the dirt. She moved frenetically, as if the physical contact with the rotting vegetables mixed with earth was a way of evacuating her soul of the shame contaminating her. As though by smearing herself with garbage she would not become garbage. It was

231

a pathetic attempt at appeasement. She felt dirty. Debased. A piece of garbage in the middle of all this shit.

She finished the grim job in a daze. Once the bin was empty, she unrolled the tarpaulin to free Gérard's body, then tipped it in, not before putting his phone back inside his jacket pocket. Then she repeated the operation in the opposite direction, blanketing the corpse in compost.

Buried under the scrap heap.

Buried in muck.

R.I.P.

"Maman, have you heard from Papa?"

Inès came out into the yard, having apparently run out of things to talk about with Emma (or Léa). Nora jumped, abruptly delivered from her horrific memories.

"No," she said.

"Have you called him?"

"Not yet."

Realizing how odd it was that she still hadn't tried to get ahold of Gérard, who was supposed to be looking after the children and had shown no sign of life since the previous day, she hurriedly tried to explain herself.

"To be honest, I don't want to call him. He should be the one calling me. I'm mad at him. I hope he has a very good explanation for his behavior."

"But, Maman, this is weird. Maybe something's happened to him."

"What are you talking about? He was busy at work, didn't notice the time, and when he realized how late it was, he rushed home. But then he saw my message and decided he'd rather get a good night's sleep before he had to face me."

Inès looked skeptically at her mother.

"Okay," said Nora. "I'll finish mowing the grass and then I'll call him."

"Do it now," her daughter begged.

"When I've finished mowing the grass," replied her mother.

Inès pursed her lips and glared at her. Then she turned on her heel. "I'll call him myself," she muttered as she went inside.

Nora frowned as she watched her daughter disappear into the house, then hurried to finish the mowing.

A few minutes later, Inès came back outside. "It's still going straight to voice mail. Something's not right."

"Call Mélanie and ask if she's heard from him."

"What's wrong with you? Why would Mélanie have heard from him and not us? We don't need to call Mélanie, we need to call the cops. Papa's disappeared, and we have no idea where he is." Inès looked both furious and bewildered at her mother's lack of concern about what had happened to her father. Nora had to admit she had a point. And their recent separation in no way justified her blatant lack of interest.

"Last night, before Mélanie called me to complain that your father hadn't arrived, Milo rang at the door," said Nora, as if suddenly recalling something that might be important. "Apparently, your father paid a visit to the neighbors yesterday afternoon."

"Papa went to see the Geniots?" Inès looked astonished. "Why?"

"I have no idea," Nora lied.

"And you're telling me that just now? We have to go see them, find out what time he left!"

Go to see the Geniots? Find herself face-to-face with Tiphaine? Out of the question! And yet, if she hadn't told Inès this valuable information, her daughter would begin to ask serious questions about her mother's refusal to act.

"All right, I'll call him," she said in a grave tone of voice.

The two of them went inside and Nora called Sylvain. It rang three times before going to voice mail. Clearly Sylvain didn't want to answer her call. Nora felt a touch of regret: obviously her ex-lover didn't want to take the risk of having any contact with her.

"It's gone to voice mail," she said to Inès, sounding disappointed.

"I'm going to call Milo," Inès declared.

She took her BlackBerry, dialed Milo's number, and held it up to her ear. She heard it ring once, twice . . . and then the voice mail clicked on before the third ring.

"He's declined the call!" she exclaimed, shocked.

"Like father, like son," thought Nora to herself, mortified for her daughter. Had Tiphaine told Milo, and now he was furious with her, and consequently with Inès? She knew that her daughter had a crush on the boy and was annoyed with her for interfering—even without meaning to—in her love life. She looked at Inès, perplexed, even as she realized she wasn't going to be able to put off the inevitable hostilities for much longer.

"All right, I'll call the police," she said.

# CHAPTER
## 42

After explaining the reasons for her call and briefly describing their family situation, Nora was told by the duty officer that if she considered this lack of news to be worrying or unusual, she should go down to the local police station to report Gérard's disappearance. She put down the phone and told her daughter what she was going to do. Inès's opinion was that they'd wasted quite enough time already and needed to get moving right away.

"Stay here with Nassim, I'll go on my own," Nora said.

Inès tried to protest but her mother cut her off: she didn't want to worry her son by telling him of their concerns. Inès agreed. So Nora went alone down to the police station. As she drove, she practiced out loud what she was going to say. What she would tell the police and what she would keep quiet about. What she supposedly did know and what she couldn't possibly know. The interview was going to be very stressful, and she already felt a deep anxiety that put her nerves on edge. After the night she'd had, she had been hoping for a few hours of respite. On the other hand, she was relieved she had managed to persuade Inès to stay behind with Nassim: she'd have been even more terrified at lying in front of her children.

When she drew up to the police station she made a super-human effort to control her nerves. She couldn't put a foot wrong. Her statement had to be watertight, and she had to make it with the confidence of someone whose conscience was clear. Which was absolutely not the case. She glanced in the rearview mirror to check her appearance, arranging her features into a mask of concern about her husband's disappearance, but erasing all other traces of anxiety. She climbed out of the car and walked the short distance to the station with a quick, nervous step. She entered the building and went straight to the reception desk, where she was asked why she had come.

"I haven't heard anything from my husband since yesterday" was all she said.

She was told to take a seat and wait, and that someone would be along to speak with her very soon. Some twenty minutes later she was led into a large room furnished with three desks. She sat down opposite a police officer who invited her to speak and took down her statement.

The facts were straightforward: Gérard Depardieu, her husband, from whom she had recently separated, had shown no sign of life since the previous day, even though it was his week to have the children. According to his secretary, Mélanie, he'd left the office around five thirty in the afternoon. Mélanie had agreed to fetch their son from school and to stay with him and his older sister at the house until he returned. Just before 8 p.m., Nora had received a visit from her neighbors' son, who told her that Gérard Depardieu had called in on them in the late afternoon, which surprised her, since she couldn't imagine what reason he might have to want to see them. It wasn't until she phoned the children to wish them good night, as she did every evening, that she learned that her husband hadn't returned home. He wasn't answering his cell phone, and no one had seen or heard from him since.

The officer asked her a few questions about Gérard's routine and their relationship since they had split up. Was this a familiar pattern of behavior? Nora said that he often came home late from work, but that vanishing for an entire night wasn't like him at all.

"Do you consider this disappearance to be of an alarming nature and that an offense may have been committed that might have put him in harm's way?" the man asked, as if he were reciting a text by heart, which in fact he was.

Nora looked at the officer with a confused expression. She had the terrifying sensation that he could see right into her soul. Had an offense been committed that might have put Gérard Depardieu in harm's way? The image of his body buried under three feet of compost flashed into her mind and she could do nothing to chase the memory away. For goodness' sake, not now! She felt her heart beating faster and faster, her mouth grew dry, her stomach was in knots. She swallowed hard and the image faded.

"I have no idea," she said at last. "All I know is that my husband hasn't been seen since yesterday, which is very unusual."

"Your husband or your ex-husband?"

"We don't live together anymore, but we're still married."

The agent looked at her for a moment, as if trying to assess the level of enmity she felt for Gérard. Nora couldn't hold his gaze. As she turned her head to the window, she was already cursing herself for her weakness.

"Well, we'd better get going with the search. I'll need three recent photos of Monsieur"—he glanced down at the statement he had just taken—"Gérard Depardieu, his address and yours, and the details of anyone who might have been in contact with him: friends, colleagues, family. And I'll also need the name and address of your neighbors, the ones he went to see yesterday."

Nora nodded. She gave him what she could, apart from the photographs—she'd removed the picture of Gérard from her wallet weeks ago. The officer dictated the email address so she could send the pictures from her computer at home and they could begin their inquiry as soon as possible. She also gave him Tiphaine and Sylvain Geniot's details. As she uttered their names, Nora felt a squirm of remorse. An insistent twinge in her gut that, she already knew, would never leave her.

She clung to the memory of her phone call to Sylvain, which he'd declined to answer. This was his way of imposing distance, of not even doing her the favor of bestowing a few words on her. Their story had died almost before it had even been born, before it had had time to blossom. Had anything actually happened between them? Or had Nora—so eager for romance and passion that she had believed that what was actually no more than a fling was real love, love at first sight—imagined the whole thing? How on earth had she been dumb enough to believe in such a mirage at the age of forty-four, when even teenagers didn't believe in such a thing anymore? Oh, Nora, you fool! What were you thinking?

Filled with anger and resentment, ashamed of having let herself be fooled, and no less ashamed of having found in revenge the only alibi to justify what she was doing, she hung her head.

# CHAPTER
## 43

Inès didn't understand what was going on. Her heart sank as she kept tapping away on Facebook, trying to find some trace of Milo. He hadn't posted anything for three days or reacted to anything she'd posted. What was going on? Whenever they saw each other there was such ease in their interaction that it felt completely natural and right. She felt good in his company and she knew—yes, she knew!—that he felt the same. And then, for no reason at all, he had become conspicuous by his absence and indifference. *Conspicuous* was the word—he was always there in her thoughts, her dreams, and her aspirations. Since the first evening they had spent together, and even more so since their first kiss, her heart beat faster whenever she thought of him, with an airy cadence that gave rhythm to her days, the gallop of emotional excitement that so intoxicated her, she found herself constantly dreaming of distant and unfamiliar places.

Though she refused to admit it, Inès was falling in love.

Why was he not answering her calls or responding to her messages? What was wrong? She hadn't dreamed it—the way he looked at her, their complicity, their closeness, the kiss . . . It had all happened!

Was it possible he'd just been polite, he couldn't do otherwise for fear of upsetting her, and she, carried away by desire, had been imagining something that existed only in her head? Inès felt completely lost. Angry and upset. She missed him. She had a vague but constant burning in her chest, as if her lungs were on fire. She didn't know what to think. She wanted to flood him with messages on Facebook and email, but she didn't let herself, knowing it would only trigger the opposite reaction to the one she was hoping for.

"Where are you, Milo?" she whispered, as she scrolled down her Facebook page trying to find him.

Everything was falling apart. Fate was against her. Even her father wasn't answering her calls. Absolutely no sign of life. He was playing dead. The same question was going around and around in her head, the same word repeating itself indefatigably, like a nagging echo rattling around in her skull: *why?*

What had happened? Was each of the men behaving by choice, or under pressure? She wanted to pour out her heart to one of them . . . Milo . . . She wanted to snuggle up to him, lie in his arms, knowing that he would never hurt her, that she could always depend on him.

But no. It was impossible. He wasn't there, when she so desperately needed him. Filled with apprehension, more questions began to waltz around her head, ringing out like a cackle: *Are you sure you didn't imagine it all? The way you get along? You've hung out with him twice! Your closeness? A few giggles about some dumb memes that everyone's talking about at the moment. That kiss? You were the one who made the first move!* None of it was proof he felt anything for her. *Open your eyes, you stupid girl. This guy doesn't give a damn about you. You bore him.*

She had seen that glimmer of annoyance, that tiny twinge of irritation on his face when, on two occasions, she had rung at the door. She hadn't been welcome either time. The first time he had managed to get rid of her. The second, he hadn't had time to come up with an excuse, and she'd marched in like she owned the place. *Get down off your high horse, you idiot! Not every guy is going to throw himself at your feet. And this is the proof!*

Inès's eyes welled up, and two heaving sobs caught in her throat, pressing against each other, trying to break through the dam of pride to escape. She began to cry, desperate to pour out the overwhelming desolation that was consuming her from within. For several long minutes, she wept with sorrow.

# CHAPTER
## 44

The two police officers who showed up on the Geniots' door-step were dead ringers for Laurel and Hardy. One was portly, with a superficially open and friendly expression that belied the dangerous gleam in his dark eyes. His colleague was tall and thin, with gentle features that contrasted with a bearing that was clearly meant to be intimidating.

Sylvain opened the door and frowned, despite their comical resemblance to Laurel and Hardy, when he saw their uniforms. His throat tightened with apprehension. What now?

"Monsieur Geniot?" Laurel asked.

He paused before nodding his head in assent: at that moment, he would have given anything not to be Monsieur Geniot.

"We'd like to ask you a few questions about this person," Hardy went on, thrusting a photo of Nora's husband under his nose. "Gérard Depardieu. Do you know him?"

Sylvain's heart seemed to stop beating. As he looked at the picture, he tried to figure out why they were there; he had no idea how to respond or what attitude to adopt.

"I know him by sight," he said, cautiously. "He's my neigh-bor's estranged husband."

"Indeed he is," Laurel confirmed. "Might we come in for a few minutes?"

Reluctantly, Sylvain stepped aside to let the two officers into the house, and gestured them toward the living room. Then he went into the kitchen, where Tiphaine and Milo were finishing their lunch.

"Could you come here for a moment, Tiphaine?"

She gave him a questioning look, which he answered with an imperious glance. She put her sandwich on her plate and stood up. Her face was drawn, betraying the sleepless night she had just spent. When she saw the two men in the living room, she frowned and turned to Sylvain for an explanation.

"They want to ask us some questions about Nora's husband," he said, looking for a reaction from Tiphaine. She looked genuinely surprised.

"Nora's husband?"

"Monsieur Gérard Depardieu," Laurel clarified.

"What do you want to know?" she asked, slightly too aggressively for Sylvain's taste.

It was Hardy who spoke this time. "Did he come to see you yesterday afternoon?"

Tiphaine and Sylvain glanced at each other.

"Yes," Sylvain said before Tiphaine could respond.

"Why do you want to know?" asked Tiphaine.

"What time did he leave?" said Hardy, ignoring Tiphaine's question.

"About six thirty, six forty-five maybe," replied Sylvain, a little disconcerted by his wife's reaction.

"What was the reason for his visit?" said Laurel.

"I'd like to know the reason for your visit," said Tiphaine angrily.

"Tiphaine, please," said Sylvain.

"No one has seen or heard from Monsieur Depardieu since he left your house," explained Laurel in a deadpan tone of voice. "You are, until proved otherwise, the last people to have had any contact with him."

Sylvain felt the earth open up beneath his feet. He turned to his wife with an expression of shock and incredulity. Tiphaine stood there in stunned silence, looking at the police officers as if she were trying to see through a joke, or dismantle a hoax. But her oversincere expression only increased Sylvain's alarm: she'd actually done it! That was why she hadn't come up to bed last night. He'd thought she was sending him a message, telling him she was ending their relationship, both physical and emotional—if there was anything left to end. But there had been no message! The reason she hadn't come to bed was simply that she'd been busy with something else. Sylvain had an inkling of what she might have done. He could barely contain his anger, and still less keep from letting it show. He was seething.

Laurel asked again, "What was the reason for his visit?"

Again, Tiphaine and Sylvain looked at each other, this time with a kind of artificial politeness, each clearly wanting to leave the other one to speak. Seeing that neither was going to answer, Hardy chose for them:

"Madame Geniot, can you tell us?"

Tiphaine looked thoughtfully at Hardy for a few seconds. Then she said, in a voice that managed to sound both outraged and dignified, "Gérard Depardieu came to beat the shit out of my husband because he's been sleeping with his wife. His ex-wife, whatever. Our neighbor."

Laurel and Hardy were speechless. Sylvain felt like he had just taken a deep breath into his lungs after having held his breath for several minutes. There was an embarrassed silence, which Laurel eventually broke with a change of subject, a kind of diversionary tactic to try to fix the situation. Instead he made it worse.

"Did he seem to be in any particular frame of mind?"

"Why, yes, he did!" said Tiphaine with an ironic laugh, as if he had put his finger on an important element of the mystery. "He was nervous. That would be one way of putting it."

"I mean . . . apart from the situation with your husband," said Laurel, only making things worse.

"That was all he wanted to talk about, officer. His entire being seemed to be focused on his loathing of my husband. I have to say I was tempted to give him a helping hand. But rest assured, he left our house in perfect health."

Hardy interrupted her. "You have a son, I believe," he said.

"We do."

"Was he at home when Monsieur Depardieu came to the house?"

"He arrived home just as he was leaving."

"Would it be all right if we asked him a few questions?"

"Ask him as many questions as you like. But I would ask you not to mention the reason for his visit. Our son knows nothing about the affair. I'll ask him to come down."

Without waiting for them to respond, she called up to Milo, who was in his room. The boy came down to the living room.

He cast a doleful look at the police officers, then smirked as he took in their startling resemblance to Laurel and Hardy.

Hardy asked him three questions: had he ever seen the man in the photograph he showed him; had he seen him here the previous evening; and, if so, what time had the man left. Milo's honest answers were fluent and natural. His testimony corroborated that of his parents. Moreover, the absence of emotion with which he evoked the facts added to the overall credibility of their collective version. Tiphaine stood there, arms crossed, with an almost victorious smile on her face, her eyes fixed on the two men.

As soon as Milo finished talking, she took them to task.

"I have a question for you, if I may. If we are indeed the last people to have been in contact with Gérard Depardieu, how come you know he was here?"

"Why don't you ask your son?" Hardy replied.

Tiphaine and Sylvain both turned to Milo, who, finding himself the center of attention but with no idea why, instinctively adopted a defensive attitude.

"I didn't do anything wrong! I just went over to Nora's!"

"Why?"

"I wanted to see Inès. She told me Inès was at her father's house, and I said he'd just been at ours."

"Why did you want to see Inès?" Tiphaine asked, fully aware she wouldn't get a straight answer.

"What does it have to do with you?"

"Watch your mouth, Milo!" said Sylvain.

"Well," said Hardy, as he and his colleague, hot on his heels, turned to go. "We'll leave you to settle this among yourselves."

"We may be in touch with you again," said Laurel as the two men took their leave. "And if you do hear any news about Monsieur Depardieu, you can contact us at this number." He handed his card to Tiphaine and the two men left.

As soon as the front door closed behind them, Milo demanded an explanation.

"What's going on? Why are they asking questions about Inès's dad?"

"He's disappeared," said Sylvain darkly, giving Tiphaine an accusatory glare. "No one's heard from him since he left here last night."

The implication, if she got it, didn't get a rise out of Tiphaine, who contented herself with a glower directed at Sylvain. Milo, however, looked stunned.

"What do you mean, disappeared?"

"Disappeared!" Sylvain repeated with a touch of irritation. "He didn't go home last night. Vanished into thin air! No more Inès's daddy."

"What? How's that possible?"

"Well, that's the six-million-dollar question," Sylvain said, giving Tiphaine a meaningful look.

"Why did you go to see Inès?" Tiphaine repeated, ignoring Sylvain's insinuation.

"It's none of your business," he said, turning heel and going back up to his room, taking the stairs three at a time. Tiphaine and Sylvain didn't move. Sylvain turned to his wife, who didn't give him time to open his mouth.

"I know what you're thinking. And I don't give a damn. Whatever's happened to that piece-of-shit attorney, it's nothing to do with me. But don't think I'm going to waste a second of my time trying to prove that to you."

And she turned and went back into the kitchen, leaving him standing there, open-mouthed. After a minute or two he sat down on the sofa and put his head in his hands.

Did Tiphaine have anything to do with Gérard Depardieu's disappearance? She had seemed genuinely surprised when she'd heard there had been no news of him since he'd left their house the previous day. But he knew his wife. He knew what she was capable of.

# CHAPTER
## 45

The weather turned foul that afternoon, lasting through the weekend. The Geniots spent Sunday with Tiphaine's family, pretending to be a regular couple. For the last eight years they had never shown any affection in public, which meant that no one noticed the chill between them.

Tiphaine seemed to have perked up again. She had abandoned the listless air she'd maintained throughout Friday evening, and over the course of Saturday she grew gradually more cheerful, more so after the police officers' visit. By Sunday she was up and about again, though that didn't allay Sylvain's concerns. There was something hard about her. Cold. Determined. To do what? It was impossible to know. She was a warrior about to go on the offensive—he was sure of that. From time to time he caught her staring at him, and the gleam he saw in her eyes sent a shiver down his spine. He knew her by heart. He knew she was up to something.

That afternoon he took her aside and spoke to her frankly.

"You have something up your sleeve. I know you do. Be careful, Tiphaine: we may have gotten away with it once, but we won't have such luck next time. Tell me the truth: did you have anything to do with Depardieu's disappearance?"

By way of an answer she simply threw him a contemptuous look, then turned and went back to join the others in the living room.

Nora, meanwhile, spent Sunday holed up inside, alone, her nose glued to the upstairs windows that looked out onto the two neighboring backyards. Her stomach was in knots. There was a lump of anxiety stuck in her throat, keeping her from breathing freely. She dragged herself from one room to another, short of breath, tortured by this forced stillness, this unbearable apathy. If one of the Geniots were to discover the body before the police did, what would happen? Why hadn't the police searched the house, the basement, the attic? The garden?

Not to mention the children's growing anxiety about Gérard's radio silence. The atmosphere at home had become electric. Several arguments had broken out between them, which Nora, already at her wit's end, could barely deal with. The children were able to express their suppressed anxiety about their father only with bursts of aggression toward each other, which was torture for Nora. All three were jittery with the endless waiting. Inès and Nassim were waiting for their father's return, or at least some sign of life, an answer, an explanation. She, powerless to offer them the least comfort, unable to reassure them, was waiting for the tragic news to break, and all the sorrow and pain that would come in its wake. Her unbearable responsibility. The weight of a secret she could never admit.

To make matters worse, she hadn't heard anything more from Mathilde. Her friend's silence filled her with resentment, regret, and guilt. Disappointed and uncomprehending, Nora felt caught in the trap of solitude. She had no one to share the burden of her guilt, to alleviate the horror that was flooding her mind in great waves. As she began to realize that the only person who had the strength, love, and composure to help her through this terrible ordeal was Gérard himself, she almost collapsed in despair.

The only thing that helped her to bear the torture of her conscience was the total absence of any sign of life from Sylvain. Not a word, not an email, not even a brief text message to tell her that he'd be in touch as soon as things had calmed down. She was furious with him, though she blamed herself even more for having believed in fairy tales; for having killed Gérard, even unintentionally; and for having hidden his corpse in the Geniots' yard. But there was no way back.

Lost in thought, her forehead pressed against the glass of her bedroom window, Nora was drawn from her lethargy by the shouts of her children downstairs: they were fighting again. She closed her eyes, tempted to stay there without moving, to sink into a stupor that lacked any emotion or pain.

With a sigh she forced herself to move, put one step in front of another, leave her observation post and move away from the window.

To leave the room.

Downstairs in the entryway, Nassim was accusing his sister of stealing his pencil case.

"Why do you think I care about your dumb pencil case?" she yelled at him in the most jeering tone she could muster.

"It was in my backpack, and now it's not there!" the boy yelled back, shaking his open backpack under Inès's nose, as if it were irrefutable proof of her guilt.

"It's not my fault if you don't know where you put your things!"

"I didn't touch it," said Nassim furiously.

"Nor did I!" Inès said, even more furious. She was mad at being bugged by her younger brother for something she hadn't done.

"What's going on?" said Nora, coming down the stairs.

"She's taken my pencil case," said Nassim, pointing an accusatory finger at his sister.

"Yeah, right!"

Nora reached the bottom of the stairs, took her son's schoolbag from his hands, and felt about inside.

"It's not in there," Nassim insisted.

"I'm just checking, am I allowed?"

Once she had ascertained that it wasn't there, she put the bag down on the floor.

"It wasn't you, Inès?"

"Goddamn it!" Inès barked angrily. "What on earth would I want with his stupid pencil case?"

"Please don't speak to me like that," said Nora, raising her voice. But her heart wasn't in it. Nora wanted to say to Nassim that no one cared about his pencil case, and he should go and play somewhere else.

"Maybe you left it at your father's house."

"No, I brought it here, I know I did. I put it in my backpack."

"Maybe it's fallen out. Are you sure you've looked everywhere?"

"Yes."

Nora looked around the entryway, peering under the coatrack, the shoe cupboard, the chest of drawers . . . where she saw Gérard's folder that had slid underneath when she had slapped him. Her blood froze. It was a bright green, plasticized file folder, just like the ones he used for work. Nora stood up, trying to control the fear that gripped her, to hide the sudden panic she was sure could be read on her face.

"Have you searched your room?" she asked, trying hard not to sound flustered. Luckily Nassim was so focused on his pencil case that he didn't notice anything. Inès had already gone back into the kitchen.

"I haven't taken it out of my bag since we got back."

"It has to be somewhere. Go check your room while I keep searching down here."

"But I told you—"

"That's enough, Nassim! Can't you see it's not here? Go and do what I said."

Nassim, looking mutinous, grudgingly obeyed his mother and went upstairs. The moment she was alone in the entryway, Nora crouched down to pick up the folder. She opened it, cast a brief glance at its contents, and saw that the name Geniot was repeated several times. With a shaking hand, she snapped it closed and looked around for a place to conceal it. The sound of footsteps coming from the kitchen forced her to come up with a hasty hiding place; just as Inès appeared, she shoved it above the coatrack, on the shelf where they put their scarves and hats in the winter.

"Found it?" the girl asked.

"What?"

"The pencil case!"

"No . . . no, not yet."

"I'm sure it's at Papa's."

Nora was so distracted by the discovery of the folder and its startling contents that she didn't react. It was only when Nassim came back downstairs, increasingly frustrated by the disappearance of his pencil case, that she was forced to interrupt her muddled contemplations and continue the search. After a good twenty minutes of doggedly hunting, they finally located it where no one had thought to look—in the front pocket of Nassim's schoolbag.

The incident over, everyone returned to what they'd been doing, and Nora was finally able to satisfy the curiosity that had been gnawing at her since she'd happened upon the folder. She grabbed it from the shelf and, heart thudding, went and locked herself in the bathroom.

The folder wasn't very full, but what she learned from a cursory glance threw her into deep dismay. She read the account of the Brunelle affair that had been written up eight years previously, in which the attorney had meticulously detailed the charges against his client, the manner in which his detention had unfolded, and the suspicions of the accused regarding his neighbor. The file folder also contained a copy of the family court's decision about Milo Brunelle's guardianship, including

Tiphaine and Sylvain Geniot's address at the time—her house, the house that Nora had been living in now for several weeks.

Which meant that Tiphaine had been David Brunelle's neighbor when the events had taken place—the neighbor David Brunelle accused of being responsible for the death of Ernest Wilmot. Sylvain, however, seemed to have avoided any suspicion. Why?

And why had her neighbors never mentioned that they used to live in this house?

The next document made her shudder in horror. It was a printout of an article from the internet about the death of six-year-old Maxime Geniot. The child had died after a fall from his bedroom window. The kind of domestic tragedy that happens far too frequently. The implication of the article was that his mother had been responsible, for it was due to her carelessness that the child had been left alone in his room with the window open.

Nora stopped reading for several seconds.

Tiphaine and Sylvain had lost a child! The most terrible thing that can happen to a parent. They had never talked about it. Never even mentioned it. As if it had never happened. As if Maxime had never lived.

As if . . .

As if Milo had taken Maxime's place.

Nora swallowed, and a retrospective terror seized her, squeezing her chest to the point that for several long minutes she could hardly breathe. Was it possible to recover from the death of a child? Into what abyss of grief and pain had Tiphaine and Sylvain collapsed? What had they gone through, enduring a suffering like no other, the kind of suffering that knows no respite or redemption, that drags you to the very edge of vacillation, the only refuge for surviving the present, for continuing to live, or at least trying to?

When you've lost all reason for living, what other choice do you have but to live without reason? To give yourself up, body and soul, to the euphoria of madness? To let go. She, Nora, had just taken a life by accident, and she felt like she was losing her mind. And that was an adult man whom she no longer loved. How was it possible to survive the loss of a child more beloved than anything else in the world?

It was unimaginable.

Nora understood now that the only link still connecting Tiphaine to reason was Milo. There were almost no limits to what she might do. Her moral conscience had been shattered when Maxime fell onto the deck. And that made her very dangerous.

And now the woman had become her enemy. By falling under Sylvain's spell, Nora had disturbed the fragile mental equilibrium of a vulnerable soul, damaging the veneer of normality that prevented that great leap toward other psychic realms. Where consequences do not exist—or are so very insignificant compared with the death of a child. Where there was no point anymore in holding back.

And she, Nora, had entrusted her son to this woman.

She had let her into her house. She had even given her a front-door key. The key!

Tiphaine still had the key to Nora's house. She had to get it back. But maybe Tiphaine had already made a copy. Nora decided to have the lock changed rather than take the slightest risk. Today was Sunday. She weighed the risks of waiting until the next day. It would cost her a fortune. She hardly had any money in the bank. But safety was more important. She would do it first thing tomorrow morning. To reassure herself, she put her own key into the lock on the inside to block anyone if they tried to come in from outside.

She went through the notes, questions, and deductions written in Gérard's scrawl, everything he had tried to warn her about before he died: the Geniots' responsibility for Ernest Wilmot's death, and even the possibility that they were in some way involved in the deaths of Milo's parents, a double suicide whose motive remained unclear.

What had happened the night David Brunelle was in police custody? Apart from a few official documents and with no material evidence to support his suspicions, Gérard had relied mostly on hypotheses.

"Maman!"

Inès was standing outside the bathroom door, whining that she needed to pee. Nora hurriedly closed the folder and looked around for a place to conceal it. There was nowhere discreet enough to evade her daughter's curiosity.

"Maman! Let me in. What are you doing in there?"

"Nearly done," Nora answered, flushing the toilet. She was out of ideas. She pushed the folder under her T-shirt and buttoned up her cardigan over it. She glanced in the mirror to check it wasn't visible. "No need to get worked up."

She unlocked the bathroom door. Her daughter glared at her and went inside like a queen entering her boudoir. For once, Nora was thankful for teenage self-absorption.

She went back downstairs. She had to get rid of the folder. If anyone were to find it in her house, that would be the end of everything.

But at the same time she knew it was the perfect weapon with which to control Tiphaine, to calm her desire for vengeance, or even to feed suspicions about her, if those cretinous police officers were ever to find Gérard's body.

Perhaps she shouldn't get rid of it too soon. Thinking about it, the documents were her only protection against the machinations of a woman who seemed prepared to stop at nothing. The folder was the only thing that would allow her to play on the ultimate weak point of a woman who had nothing left to lose. It might be better to keep hold of it a little longer. Just in case.

Trying to convince herself this was the right decision, Nora looked around for a place to conceal it. She went into the kitchen, thinking she might hide it in a drawer, before giving up on this idea; Inès was always rooting around the cabinets and drawers, looking for food or some utensil or other that Nora had no idea how to use. It was the same in the bathroom. Nora went into the dining room. It was too sparsely furnished to offer any options. She went into the living room; looking around, her eyes were drawn to the bookshelf. What better hiding place for a book, or something resembling one, than tucked in among a lot of other books? She looked along the shelves, then pushed Gérard's file folder between two hard-cover novels.

# CHAPTER
## 46

The weekend drew to a close without any further incident. The rain rinsed both yards of all trace of Nora's presence, which reassured her somewhat. At last the children went up to bed, leaving her alone with her distress and anxiety.

She had a terrible night, her sleep broken by images of dismembered bodies, shattered bones, and splashes of blood. And the tears of her children, their eyes, filled with accusation and hatred, fixed upon her, projecting her into a despair from which she knew she would never recover. She awoke at dawn with a start, bathed in a cold sweat, more exhausted than when she had gone to bed. She forced herself to get up and tried to drown her misery under a long shower.

Wasted effort.

The seconds went by with unbearable slowness, as though time itself were frozen in the treacly mass that hobbled her movements, her emotions, and her thoughts. She went downstairs to make breakfast, hoping to lose herself in the reassuring routine of ordinary life. The before times. But there was no such thing as ordinary life anymore. Anything she did that just a couple of days before had been utterly banal was now suffused with intolerable gravity, dragging her into a slow, painful descent into hell. An endless demise.

She had to do something.

Force the hand of fate.

Put an end to this nightmare.

The children were up at last. She focused on the tasks at hand: preparing their lunchboxes, making sure they got dressed and ready for school, cheering them up, promising that as soon as she heard from their father she'd let them know. She took them to school and hugged them tightly as she said goodbye. Then she went to work.

The morning was not as tough as she'd been expecting; the endless demands of her small charges kept her busy enough to take her mind off everything and soothe her nerves. She left the building at noon sharp and headed down to the police station, thinking she would point the police officers toward Tiphaine and Sylvain's garden. She'd tell them she'd witnessed some strange goings-on the night of Friday to Saturday, the night Gérard had disappeared—that his disappearance had kept her awake for part of the night and when she got up to get a glass of water from the kitchen, she'd seen a figure in the adjoining garden, dragging a long, dark mass toward the back wall.

But as she got closer to the police station, she grew increasingly unsure. Perhaps she'd divert suspicion from the Geniots to her? If what she'd seen through her bedroom window that night had so intrigued her, why had she failed to mention it when she'd reported Gérard's disappearance to the police on Saturday?

By the time the station came into view, Nora didn't know

what to do. She had a desperate urge to phone Mathilde, which she had to fight with all her strength: she couldn't count on her anymore. Her friend's radio silence was proof she no longer wanted to have anything to do with this ghastly saga.

She decided to wait a little longer, hold on until the next day, and then she'd decide. Best not tempt the devil. Better to let things take their course. She had already done enough damage as it was.

She spent the afternoon in a daze. She was comfortable nowhere, dreaming of being alone when she was surrounded by people, and longing for company when she was alone. She waited patiently until 4:30 to pick up Nassim from school.

At 4:20, she was already standing at the school gate. When the school bell rang, she went inside and straight to her son's classroom. At the end of a corridor she spotted a line of children heading to the cafeteria where the children staying behind after school went for their afternoon snack. She went up to Nassim's teacher, who looked at her in surprise. Nora greeted her politely.

"Madame Depardieu!" the teacher said, seeming confused. "What are you doing here?"

Surprised by the odd question, Nora raised her eyebrows to signal her incomprehension. "I've come to fetch Nassim."

"But Nassim's not here. He left half an hour ago."

Nora was struck dumb, as though she didn't understand what the teacher was saying.

"He's left?" she said after a second or two, already feeling the noose of panic. "Where? Who with?"

"I don't know," replied the poor teacher, who was beginning to realize that she'd let the child go with someone the mother knew nothing about. "Someone came to pick him up, she said you weren't able to come yourself. She said she was sorry she was early, but she had to run an errand. The person who runs the after-school program said she's been to fetch him from school before, with your permission. She's your neighbor, apparently?"

# CHAPTER
## 47

"Where's my mom?" asked Nassim, as he and Tiphaine entered the house. "Why didn't she come to fetch me?"

"Something came up. But don't you worry, she'll be back soon."

Without taking off her jacket, she went into the kitchen and put her purse down on the table along with a bag of groceries. Then she began opening the drawers one by one. It didn't take long to find the drawer with the kitchen utensils, out of which she took several knives. A bread knife, a carving knife, long knives, paring knives, serrated, not serrated. She lined them up on the counter and looked at them. At last she picked out one that had a twenty-centimeter blade, nice and sharp, as fine as a cigarette paper, long and thin and pointed. Perfect. She put it in her purse, replaced the others, and shut the drawer.

"Nassim, would you like a snack?"

The child appeared in the doorway, with a surly yet uncertain expression on his face.

"Don't look like that. What's wrong?"

"I want my mom."

Tiphaine smiled sympathetically. She went over to the child and crouched down to his height.

"How about we play a game while we wait for her to get back?"

"What kind of game?"

"You want your mom, and I want my little boy. So let's pretend I'm your mom and you're my little boy. What do you think?"

Nassim frowned. He looked at Tiphaine with a grave expression, observing the strange smile that wreathed her features in a mask of feigned kindness, lacking any real warmth. Even though she was trying to look friendly, there was something scary about her, like the reflection of a broken gate that leads to a bottomless pit in which terrifying things lurk.

"I don't want to play," he declared warily.

"You'll see, it'll be fun. Look, I bought lots of delicious things to eat."

She straightened up and pointed at the bag of food on the kitchen table. She took out a packet of cookies, a container of vanilla yogurt, and a bottle of fruit juice, all of which she'd bought with him in mind.

"Ta-daaa! Are you hungry?"

She was behaving with an enthusiasm that was slightly grotesque, like a bad actor. There was something ridiculous about the look of elation on her face.

Still frowning, Nassim squinted at the container of yogurt, then looked back at Tiphaine.

"I'll have some yogurt."

"What's the magic word?"

"Please."

"Please who?"

"Please, Tiphaine."

Tiphaine rolled her eyes, overplaying an indulgent protest.

"No, Nassim! We're playing a mom and her little boy, have you already forgotten? Please, who?"

The child felt a knot in his stomach. He knew what Tiphaine wanted to hear, but some instinct told him not to play this strange game.

"Come along!" Tiphaine insisted, sounding like an overexcited teacher. "Please, who?"

"I don't know."

"Of course you do!"

Nassim didn't answer. He looked at her timidly, the knot in his stomach growing bigger and bigger, until he felt like he couldn't breathe anymore. Tiphaine, meanwhile, was fidgeting with the yogurt with the same fake smile on her face.

Nassim was obstinately refusing to answer, so she decided to help him.

"Please, M . . . Ma . . ."

Silence. Tiphaine's smile began to fade into an altogether more alarming expression.

"Ma . . ." she said again, trying to encourage Nassim with little nods of the head that were almost parodic.

". . . man," he responded eventually.

"There you go," she exclaimed, as though the child had managed to complete a complicated exercise. "That wasn't so hard, was it? Now, say the whole sentence."

Another silence. Nassim was feeling more and more uncomfortable. The knot in his stomach had reached his throat, and he was genuinely finding it hard to breathe.

"Please, Maman . . ." he said at last in a little trembling voice.

"Coming right up, my darling!" she answered, and began preparing his snack. When she was done she told the child to come and sit at the table.

"Not there," she said, sitting at the chair facing the window, "there!" She pointed at a chair with its back to the window.

"That's not my chair," he protested. "That's where Inès sits."

"We're playing a game, sweetheart, remember?" Tiphaine explained in the patient tone of a teacher. "Be good, do what I said."

Nassim sat where she told him to without further protest. Tiphaine's ridiculous behavior was increasing his unease; he had the feeling that even the slightest opposition would set off an extreme reaction that could be very scary. Tiphaine served him a big bowl of yogurt, a glass of orange juice, and several cookies in a beautiful bowl. A snack fit for a king.

"So come on, tell me," she said, sitting down alongside him.

"What?"

"About your day. What you did, who you played with, what your teacher's like, your best friends, the kids you don't like so much . . ."

She was interrupted by a call on her cell phone. She stood up, rummaged in her purse, and drew it out. She squinted at it with a satisfied smile.

"Nora's on her way."

She canceled the call, pressing her thumb on the screen with an imperious gesture, then turned and faced the child.

"I'm listening!" she said, as if she were taking a lesson.

"I—I worked . . ."

"I'm sure you did. You worked, you played, you ate, I'll bet you even went to the bathroom. Tell me everything, but don't forget to eat your snack."

Nassim's throat was so tight he could barely swallow. He plunged his spoon into the yogurt and brought it to his mouth. Never had he struggled to swallow like this.

"I played with Jonathan."

"Who's Jonathan?"

"My friend."

"Your best friend?"

"No."

"Who's your best friend?"

"Alexandre."

"Why didn't you play with Alexandre, if he's your best friend?"

"He was out sick today."

"Okay. Go on. What did you play with Jonathan?"

"Hide-and-seek."

Tiphaine waited in vain for him to carry on. She gave a disappointed sigh that still managed to sound magnanimous, almost kindly.

"Honestly, Maxime, this is like pulling teeth."

"My name isn't Maxime."

She grimaced at his words. Her jaw clenched, her lips pursed, and her eyes filled with a nasty gleam that didn't escape the child's notice.

"It's for the game," she explained, not quite able to conceal her annoyance. Then she corrected herself, like a bad actress whose attention had wandered trying awkwardly to get back into character. Nassim started to cry. He had a lump in his throat and a great weight in his stomach.

"What's the matter, sweetheart?" she said, genuinely taken aback to see the child in tears. "Why are you crying?"

"I want my maman," he said again, clinging to Tiphaine's exaggerated kindness.

"I'm right here, my darling. Come sit on my lap."

Her voice flowed like a nauseating liquid, a foul syrup that sticks to everything and leaves its tacky mark everywhere. She held out her arms to him, convinced he was going to throw himself into them and snuggle up. Nassim wiped his damp cheeks and managed a feeble smile.

"No, I'm okay now."

"Hey, don't make me beg. Come give me a hug."

"I'd rather read a comic," he said, remembering she'd wanted to do that the last time she'd babysat. Tiphaine's face lit up with surprise and satisfaction. She beamed at him.

"Great idea!" she said. "Go find the one you want to read and we'll sit together in the living room."

He shot off like an arrow.

Tiphaine went into the living room and sat down to wait for him on the sofa facing the bookshelves. She looked around the room, as if not really seeing the shapes and colors of the room, lost in thought, recalling all the different periods of her life. Vanished realms. She was diving into the past to escape the present. Her eyes focused on the shelves, and without thinking she began to decipher the titles on the spines as if they were a coded message, an initiatory, subliminal path ironically recalling the defining events of her life. *Stranger Than Truth* by Vera Caspary. *The Woman Next Door* by Barbara Delinsky. *The Stranger* by Albert Camus. *The Great Secret* by René Barjavel. *Regrets* by Joachim du Bellay. *Lost Illusions* by Honoré de Balzac. *Journey to the End of the Night* by Louis-Ferdinand Céline. Her eye fell on an unmarked spine, a book that stood out because of its unusual dimensions. It was bright green, sandwiched between *The Pleasures of Crime* by Jacqueline Harpman and *"J" Is for Judgment* by Sue Grafton. Tiphaine frowned. A flash. The glimmer of a memory. An indistinct image. A feeling of suffocation. Intrigued, she stood up and bounded over in two steps to the bookshelf, took hold of the book, and pulled it out. It was a folder. Strangely familiar. Where had she seen one that looked exactly like this one?

She opened it and began flicking through the documents inside.

# CHAPTER 48

The moment she heard that her neighbor had taken her son, Nora called the police, who took the report of a missing child very seriously. Two investigators were at the school gate within ten minutes, one bald, the other bearded. In the meantime, Nora tried to reach Tiphaine on her cell phone, without success: her call was declined before it went to voice mail. She was in a state of panic bordering on hysteria.

There was no time for discretion. She summed up the situation to the two officers, leaving nothing out: the amicable relationship she'd established with her neighbors; the favors Tiphaine had done for her when she'd needed someone to fetch her son from school; her brief dalliance with Sylvain. Her husband's jealousy and its consequences; Tiphaine discovering what had happened, and now undoubtedly filled with resentment toward Nora and her family, which was why Nora was so distraught to discover her son was with her. And, finally, the fact that Gérard had not been seen since the previous Friday, after his visit to the Geniots.

After listening to the distraught mother's account, the officers were in no doubt that the situation was sufficiently serious to launch a search operation. They asked for details about the child—photos, what he was wearing, and so on—which Nora gave them with the help of the school principal, who was quite mortified by the turn of events.

The information was transmitted to the central police station. The two officers then headed straight for rue Edmond-Petit, following Nora in her car. As soon as she turned into the street she saw Tiphaine's car. She parked on the opposite sidewalk, where parking was prohibited, then ran to the Geniots' front door, heart thumping, ready to fling herself at her neighbor and tear out her eyes.

The two officers told her to stay calm and let them deal with it. They rang the doorbell . . . No answer. Nora began pounding on the door with all her might, yelling Tiphaine's name and pleading with her to open up. Beardy admonished her sharply and Baldy tugged her arm to get her away from the house.

"You have to break down the door!" she screamed at them.

"You have to remain calm, madame," Baldy said. "We'll do exactly what is required. It doesn't help for you to get all worked up like this. We'll get a search warrant and—"

"Are you insane? We don't have time for paperwork. I want my son back!"

"That is precisely what we are trying to accomplish, madame. But there is a procedure to follow," Beardy replied, as his colleague tapped on his phone's screen and put it to his ear. Nora thought she was going to lose her mind. Her son was inside, just a few feet away from her, grappling with a crazy woman out for revenge for her husband's infidelity. God knows what she was capable of, what she might tell him or do to him, how she might hurt him.

"How long is this going to take?" she wailed, stamping her foot impatiently.

"The case file is already on the examining magistrate's desk. We've asked for it to be dealt with as a matter of urgency, so we can go in right away. It won't take long."

Nora covered her face with her hands, feeling desperate and powerless. Through her fingers she saw Tiphaine's car parked a little farther up the road. An idea struck her.

"Hang on a moment." She ran over to her own house, rummaged in her purse for the key, and inserted it hurriedly into the lock. As she went inside, immediately followed by the two officers, she called out her son's name. When they heard Nassim answer his mother in a tiny voice, all three froze. A moment later Nora burst into the living room like a Fury, Baldy and Beardy at her heels.

The moment Nassim saw his mother he ran over and jumped into her arms. She held him as if they had been apart for years.

"Nassim!" she cried, patting him anxiously, as if to check that nothing was missing. Then she turned to Tiphaine. "Are you out of your fucking mind? The next time you get anywhere near my son, I'll tear your guts out."

Tiphaine opened her eyes wide, apparently bewildered by Nora's unexpected and irate entrance.

"Nora, what is wrong with you?" Only then did she seem to become aware of the presence of the two police officers. "But . . . what on earth is going on?"

"Madame Tiphaine Geniot?" asked Beardy.

"Yes, that's me . . ."

"I gather you were not authorized to fetch Nassim from school today . . ."

"What are you talking about?" She turned to Nora. "Really, Nora, we agreed—"

"We never agreed anything," Nora shrieked, almost hysterical.

"That's not true," said Tiphaine, feigning outraged surprise. "Nassim, didn't we agree I would pick you up today?"

Still huddled in his mother's arms, the little boy began to sob.

"What has she done to you, my darling?" Nora said, furious and fearful at the same time.

"I haven't done anything to him," Tiphaine said, appearing more and more appalled by the turn events were taking. "You're the one scaring him with your screaming." She knelt down in front of Nassim. "Wasn't it agreed I would get you from school today?"

She looked into his eyes: cold, hard, implacable. A look filled with loathing and menace; a barely veiled threat. For the first time in his life, Nassim sensed he was in danger. Terrified, the child simply nodded, hiccupping with sobs.

"Don't cry, Nassim," said Tiphaine in a voice so gentle it was like a caress. "It's just a misunderstanding between your mommy and me. Everything is going to be fine, I promise."

"Liar!" roared Nora. Now it was her turn to kneel down in front of her son. "What's gotten into you, Nassim? You know perfectly well I was coming to fetch you."

The boy stared at his mother in distress, his eyes filled with tears.

"Calm down, madame," said Baldy. "You're frightening your son."

"Nassim, answer me, please," Nora said, ignoring the officer. "There was never any question that Tiphaine was picking you up from school, was there?"

"Nora, this is absurd!" exclaimed Tiphaine, before the boy had a chance to answer. "What's gotten into you?"

"Let him speak," Nora barked back at her. She turned to her son and held him by the shoulders, as if about to shake him like a plum tree. "Say it, for heaven's sake, say that it was me who was coming to fetch you. Have you lost your tongue?"

"Madame!" interrupted Beardy. "There's no point in getting all worked up like this. Your son's been found, safe and sound. We'll call off the search."

All of a sudden it dawned on Nora that in under five minutes the situation had turned against her. She was losing all credibility. It was as if she were actively furnishing evidence of Tiphaine's trustworthiness. Now she was the monster. Nassim was standing in front of her, clearly terrified by her behavior, when she was the one who was meant to be protecting and reassuring him. She froze, seeming to become aware of her son's ordeal, and felt her anger melt away. She stood up and hugged him tightly to her again.

"Forgive me, my darling . . . I was so worried. You weren't in school, and I never agreed anything with anyone about picking you up. And certainly not Tiphaine! It was me picking you up today, do you understand?"

Nassim hugged his mother like a drowning man clinging to a life buoy, his body racked with huge sobs.

"Nassim, are you all right?" The boy continued to cry, his face buried in his mother's neck. "Nassim, darling, answer me."

Baldy nodded and pursed his lips. "Well, I think we can leave you now."

Nora whipped around as though she'd heard a shot. "What about her?" she asked, gesturing at Tiphaine with a scornful nod. Baldy lifted his shoulders as though to express his impotence.

"There's nothing we can charge her with. We found the child safe at home. I don't see what she could be guilty of."

Nora flinched as though she'd received an electric shock. She put Nassim down with awkward haste and strode over to the two police officers.

"You're not going to do anything? You're just going to let her go?"

"My colleague has just explained to you that we have nothing to hold against Madame Geniot," said Beardy, sounding a great deal firmer than his colleague. Nora felt like an insect caught in a spider's web: the more she struggled, the more she found herself tangled in a psychological trap.

She turned to Tiphaine and said, "Don't ever come near me or my children again."

"That will be tricky, I only live next door," said Tiphaine with a wry smile, not missing a beat.

"That's not my problem," replied Nora, with an assertiveness that surprised her. "And incidentally, I'd like my front-door key back."

Tiphaine raised a disdainful eyebrow. Without saying a word, she went to the dining room, where she had left her jacket, plunged her hand into one of the pockets, and pulled out a set of keys. She removed one and held it out to Nora, who grabbed it, her eyes lit up with a glint of hatred.

"Stay away from me, Tiphaine. It'll be better for everyone."

"You're saying that to me? That's rich coming from you."

"Calm down, ladies," said Baldy. "Sometimes people say things they later regret." The two women eyed each other for a few more seconds, each prepared to force their enemy to be the first to look away. And then, unexpectedly, it was Tiphaine who gave up and turned away. Nora was surprised and relieved. What Gérard had told her just before he died, and what she'd seen in the file folder, filled her with dread. Her neighbor scared her. She didn't feel safe here anymore.

Her relief didn't last long. Suddenly, the presence of Tiphaine in her house and the feelings she inspired in her made her think of Gérard's file. The possibility that her neighbor might have found the precious document—thus providing clear evidence that Gérard had come over to Nora's house after leaving the Geniots, not to mention everything that had happened after—petrified her. Panic blurred her clarity of thought. She had to make sure the file folder was still in its place. But she also had to avoid drawing Tiphaine's and the cops' attention to the living room, and especially the bookshelf.

It was time for everyone to leave. Her nerves on edge, she turned to the officers and thanked them for their help. They inquired solicitously as to how she was feeling, wanting to be sure that she was okay before they left. Nora reassured them she was fine. Tiphaine got up to go as well. She put her jacket on and headed for the front door with the police officers. All three left the house at the same time. As Nora pushed the door closed behind them, Tiphaine nodded goodbye to the police officers. She was about to go into her own house when she turned around to them and said, "I have no idea what she told you, but the woman's lost her grip on reality. I'm not sure she's capable of looking after her own children. You saw what a state she put her son in."

The two men nodded in agreement and got into the car.

Nora shut the front door and went into the living room, where she saw, with relief, that the folder was still in its place. She felt herself flush with a kind of retrospective horror—she had not even realized she had left such damning evidence in plain sight. What incredible luck Tiphaine hadn't seen it. She had to be more careful in the future, find a more discreet hiding place.

Nora reached for the folder to put it somewhere safer. But as she took it down she realized immediately that it was unusually light, and there was no sound of rustling pages inside. Another shock, much worse this time, because there was no getting away from it. She knew what had happened. She felt it in her hands, the emptiness, the nothingness, the absence.

Even so, the physical evidence didn't correlate in her mind, like a theory so absurd it can't be proved. Shaking from head to foot, Nora practically ripped it open to check the contents.

Her body felt as empty as the folder she was holding in her hands.

# CHAPTER
## 49

It was Inès who saw Milo first. Her heart pounded in her chest. She recognized him from a distance, his height, the way he moved, like someone who had shot up too fast and still hadn't come to terms with his new physique. The way he walked, too. Slow but sure. Poised. Thoughtful, almost. She hesitated for a moment, wondering whether to turn around and pretend not to have seen him. It seemed prudent to let him be the one to see her first. To wait for his reaction. If he didn't want to see her he could just keep walking, and at least she would know where she stood. And if he did decide to greet her, she would feign surprise.

She continued walking in the opposite direction to Milo. She could feel the cardiac muscle in her chest beating harder and harder, like it was out of control. He couldn't possibly avoid seeing her, it was a matter of seconds now. If he didn't react, it meant he wasn't interested in her. She kept walking, forcing herself to slow down. She felt the blood pulse in her temples, her breathing growing shorter and faster; she almost had to force herself to put one foot in front of the other. She wished she could disappear because he hadn't called out to her, he was going to pretend not to see her.

"Hi, Inès."

She thought she was going to faint. She was still facing away from him; she closed her eyes and forced herself to breathe. She turned to him with a glorious smile.

"Hey! Milo! I didn't see you."

She stood on tiptoes and gave him a kiss on each cheek. Two anonymous kisses, as indifferent as she could be. He seemed disappointed, looked at her circumspectly, trying to work out how to interpret this chilly greeting.

"How are things?" he asked in a friendly manner.

"Not too bad, thanks," she lied, with far more composure than she really felt.

"Have you had any news from your dad?"

Inès looked at him in surprise. "Who told you he'd disappeared?"

"The cops came by our place. Asked us a few questions, told us you hadn't heard from him."

"So you knew," she murmured, more to herself than to Milo.

It felt like her guts were gaping open, leaving an aching emptiness in her belly.

"Er, yeah, I knew," said Milo with disheartening honesty.

"And you didn't call me? You didn't even answer when I called you."

"I . . . I didn't want to disturb you."

"But I called you, so you weren't disturbing me," exclaimed Inès. Her fury swept away her sadness all at once.

Inès's anger left Milo lost for words. He took in her distress with a crushing sense of guilt.

"I just thought—"

He stopped. He didn't know what to say. He didn't know how to explain his fears without her thinking he was crazy.

"Forget it," said Inès bitterly. She turned and began to walk away. She quickened her pace to keep ahead of him. Milo bit his lower lip, torn between his desire to pursue a relationship and the nagging feeling in his gut that his attraction to her put her in mortal danger. He wanted to catch up with her, to apologize, confess his anxiety, explain. Explain what exactly? "If I show my love for you, you'll die"? Absurd! His rational self mocked his fear. He understood how ridiculous he would sound, how irrational his conviction was, and yet he was incapable of letting go of it.

As he watched her walking ahead, he knew he would lose her if he didn't do something. It was probably better that way, but God, it hurt! He felt a great weight of regret and gnawing sadness. He despised himself for his weakness.

"Inès!"

He caught up with her and tried to find words to allay her bitter indignation. He found nothing to say that sounded sane, hated himself for being so useless. He vacillated between doubt and conviction, lacerated by this inner struggle that was unfolding, that was damaging his heart, scorching his lungs, tearing his guts apart.

"What's your problem?" she hissed at him furiously. "Are you or are you not my boyfriend?"

"Um, yes . . ."

"Or are you just a friend?"

"Um, no . . ."

"'Um yes, um no.' Is that the best you can do?"

"It's not that . . ."

"What is it, then?"

She stopped and turned to face him with her arms crossed, waiting for an explanation. Milo held her accusing gaze.

"Look, it's complicated. You don't know anything about my life, and—"

"You're with someone else?" she burst out, her eyes widening with anger and horror.

"No!"

"Because if that's what it is, you might have been decent enough to tell me right away," she screeched. She wasn't going to be able to hold back her tears much longer. To hide how sad she was, she dumped him right there and then, on the sidewalk, and ran off.

Devastated by the turn of events, Milo stood rooted to the spot and watched her go. It seemed as if the more he tried to put things right and smooth things over, the more he tried somehow to appease both his superstitions and his sweetheart, the worse everything got. And now, at the thought that Inès was suffering because of him, he was devastated.

"Inès!" he called after her and began to run. He caught up with her and, grabbing one of her arms, forced her to stop. She was in tears. His last line of emotional defense was utterly destroyed by the heartrending sight. He drew her to him and held her tight in his arms, as if trying to crush her grief. Inès began to sob even harder as she clung to him. Milo closed his eyes, buried his face in her hair, and banished all thought of the danger his feelings might pose to her.

"Forgive me," he whispered in her ear. "It's all my fault. Please don't cry. I feel so many things for you. I like you! I really, really like you."

Inès lifted her head and looked at Milo in surprise. The tears made her dark eyes seem even deeper; misery made her even more beautiful.

"Is that true?" she asked in a slightly wobbly voice.

"Yes," he said unhesitatingly.

"But then . . . why did you . . . ?"

"Never mind. Because I'm an idiot. But all that's over now. I promise you from now on, nothing will take me away from you ever again."

She looked at him a little skeptically, trying to make out if he was telling the truth. She could see in the way he looked at her that his promise was absolutely sincere. And then she gave him a smile that, despite the trace of sadness that still marked her features, lit up her entire face.

# CHAPTER
# 50

Back at home, Tiphaine was both satisfied and perplexed. Satisfied with the way things had gone: Nora had been perfect, beyond expectation, running headlong into the trap, transforming herself from victim to executioner. Perplexed, because she didn't know what Gérard Depardieu's file was doing at her neighbor's house—the one which, she checked, contained enough compromising information about her and Sylvain for the case of Ernest Wilmot's death and Milo's parents' double suicide to be reopened.

The file that must under no circumstances fall into Milo's hands.

She had to think quickly and clearly. Nora now posed a real threat. Even if she didn't have the documents in her possession anymore, she knew too much. And she was bound to exploit that knowledge now that Tiphaine had used the child to weaken the mother. Did this change her plans? Not really, except now she didn't have much time: she couldn't let her rival act before the trap closed on her.

She couldn't give her the slightest chance to escape.

She had to get her out of the way.

The second stage of reflection: what was Depardieu's file doing in Nora's house anyway? Tiphaine remembered that when the attorney had left her house, he'd had the file folder under his arm. The fact that she'd found it in Nora's house seemed proof that, contrary to what the police had said, she and Sylvain were not the last people to have seen the attorney before he vanished without a trace. It was becoming clear that Nora knew a lot more than she was ready to admit. And whatever she was keeping to herself was an asset to be reckoned with. Never underestimate your adversary. The border between suspicion and certainty was sometimes tenuous, and it only took a slight misstep for the situation to tip from one extreme to another. Nora had some highly incriminating information about her neighbors, but the very fact that she had it in her possession put her in a tricky position.

Time was running out. There was no room for risk. Improvisation was out of the question. She had to act quickly. That evening. Presumably Nora hadn't mentioned the file folder and its contents to the cops because she had something else in mind. Attack or defense? Tiphaine tried to consider the situation from every angle, but she couldn't work out what her neighbor might be up to. And this inability to predict her response set her nerves on edge.

Milo's return home put an end to her pondering. The young man dropped his backpack at the foot of the stairs, called his usual "Hi!" to Tiphaine, and headed for the kitchen, where he contemplated the contents of the refrigerator.

"Do you want me to make you something to eat?" she asked, as she always did.

"No, thanks."

"How was your day?"

"Fine."

"Do you have any homework?"

"I don't know."

There was something reassuring about the monotony of their dialogue. Tiphaine looked mournfully at the teenager's gangly figure and felt a powerful urge to take him in her arms, to hold him close to her and rock him tenderly. To cover him with kisses. To tell him how much she loved him. To ask his forgiveness.

After hesitating for what seemed like forever, Milo took a container of yogurt and a bottle of milk from the refrigerator, opened the cupboard above the sink, grabbed a bowl, opened the next cupboard and took out a box of cereal and the sugar, and finally took a spoon from another drawer. He sat down at the kitchen table and prepared himself a hearty snack. She sat down beside him and watched him eat. She wanted the moment to last, for time to stop, so she could hold on to this perfectly ordinary moment that was suddenly so precious. To share a moment of intimacy with him, the memory of which filled her with burning regret, eternal guilt. It was a life sentence, she knew, she had always known it, but until now, the tiny glimmer of possible redemption had kept alive in her a flicker of hope. Could she expect any affection from anyone ever again? A friendly look, a gentle smile? A caress, however fleeting, even just a kind word? The generosity of a compliment? The tenderness of an emotion? It had been such a long time since anyone had shown any warmth toward her.

"Milo . . ." she began tentatively.

"Mmmh?"

"Do you . . . do you ever think about your parents?"

If he was surprised by the question he didn't show it. He kept munching his cereal, staring vacantly ahead. He didn't answer straightaway.

"No," he said eventually, without any emotion.

"Never?"

"Never."

"Why not?"

Another silence. He finished his cereal and slowly peeled off the cover of the yogurt, sprinkled some sugar on top, and mixed it all together.

"Were they thinking about me when they killed themselves?"

Tiphaine closed her eyes on the tsunami that broke over her soul, laid waste to her heart, and drowned her in the bitter waters of perfidy. Spume gnawed at her from within, drawing her soul down to the bottomless depths of the shipwreck of her life.

As the elements raged inside her she opened her eyes. A single tear rolled down one cheek. A single, tiny tear that held all her grief. The final tear. Her very last.

And that was it. Her eyes were dry again. Dry as a stone. Dry as the eyes of those who never weep.

It was time for the confrontation.

# CHAPTER
## 51

On Monday Sylvain came back early from work as usual for Milo's basketball training. He made himself a quick sandwich, just to keep himself going until he and Milo finally got to enjoy the dish of the day at the Ranch restaurant.

Moments later, Tiphaine walked into the kitchen. She stood, arms crossed and leaning against the counter, and looked him up and down without a word. There was a softness and weariness in her eyes, a slightly lost expression. A kind of disillusioned affection. A touching vulnerability.

Sylvain stopped chewing, surprised and curious.

"Are you all right?"

Instead of replying, she shrugged, and asked him if he wanted a cup of coffee. Increasingly taken aback, Sylvain nodded. "Is everything okay?"

"Why?" she asked, in a tone that managed to sound friendly and irritated at the same time.

"No reason. It's just been a while since you've looked at me without seeming to hate me."

"Are you surprised?"

"No," he conceded, almost in a whisper.

They caught each other's eye briefly, then Tiphaine turned away and focused her attention on making the coffee.

"Is Milo ready?" asked Sylvain as he finished his sandwich.

"He's getting his stuff together."

Sylvain looked at his watch and began to clear away the elements of his sandwich-making. He washed up his plate. The atmosphere was unusually calm, serene even; there was no tension or wariness at all. Even the silence didn't feel pernicious.

Tiphaine took two cups out of a cabinet and poured the coffee. She handed a cup to Sylvain.

"Thank you."

She nodded as though to say "no worries" and took a sip. The two of them sat there, sipping their coffee, deep in thought. It was an astonishingly peaceable moment, like a parenthesis in the midst of the raging chaos of their lives.

Milo broke the fragile charm of this momentary truce.

He clattered down the stairs with all the grace of a galloping horse and burst into the kitchen with his basketball stuff in a bag slung over his shoulder.

"I'm ready!"

"Me too," said Sylvain, putting his cup in the sink.

"Let's go."

Milo turned and went into the hall to put on his jacket.

Sylvain followed and did the same, then they both headed for the front door. Tiphaine came out of the kitchen.

"Aren't you going to say goodbye, Milo?"

"I'll see you later, won't I?"

"Maybe not. I'm tired, I think I'll turn in early."

Milo leaned toward her and gave her a quick kiss on the

cheek. As he turned to leave she grabbed his arm and pulled him to her. Taken by surprise, he didn't have the reflex to dodge the embrace, and stiffened imperceptibly.

Tiphaine hugged him tight for a long moment, ignoring his obvious embarrassment, an embarrassment that was all the more visible because he wasn't hugging her back.

"Tiphaine!" said Sylvain. "We're going to be late."

With regret, she loosened the embrace but kept hold of Milo's arm. He started to leave, but she held him back and looked straight into his eyes with an expression of infinite sadness.

"Play well, my boy. Be strong."

"You can count on me," he said automatically.

"Can we go now?" Sylvain said impatiently.

At last she let Milo go. He marched out the front door ahead of Sylvain. As Sylvain was about to follow she said, "Goodbye, Sylvain."

He turned and looked at her for a moment, frowning as if asking her a question. "I'll see you later, Tiphaine."

She didn't reply, and the door swung closed.

# CHAPTER
## 52

"What exactly did she say to you?"

Nora sat gently stroking Nassim's hair and trying to get him to tell her precisely what had happened with Tiphaine. She needed to figure out the threat. The child had calmed down now and was trying to tell his mother about the horrible experience he'd been through.

"She wanted to play. She said she was my mom and I was her little boy."

Nora looked at her son with concern.

"How did she want to play?"

"She told me to call her Maman."

Nora closed her eyes and sighed. Tiphaine was crazy. Her little boy had been spending time on his own with a crazy person. She decided to file a complaint against her neighbor, in no doubt that Nassim's account of what had happened would be enough to prove what a danger Tiphaine posed to her and her children.

"Then what did she do?"

"She made me a snack."

"And then?"

"She wanted to give me a hug."

"A hug? What kind of a hug?"

"A hug, in her arms."

"And did you?"

"No. I didn't want to."

Nora pondered this. The fact that Tiphaine had played with Nassim, made him a snack, and asked for a hug wasn't proof that she posed any kind of danger.

"Was she mean to you?"

"Not really."

"So why were you scared of her?"

"Because I don't like her."

She sighed. She had no evidence at all against Tiphaine. If she filed a complaint that claimed the woman had mistreated her son and had said the things he'd just told her, the cops would laugh her out of town. And now she didn't have the incriminating documents either. Her only defense was held in the enemy camp—Tiphaine had the documents, which meant she must have realized that Gérard had been to see Nora before he disappeared. Basically, the file was as much of a double-edged sword for Tiphaine as for her. No one would think it had been in Nora's house until Gérard's visit to the Geniots: why would her estranged husband's work have ended up in her living room?

But if Nora couldn't provide proof of the danger posed by her neighbors without betraying the fact that Gérard Depardieu had been in her house after he visited the Geniots, nor could Tiphaine accuse Nora of having seen the lawyer after she had without presenting documents that incriminated her.

The documents were the pin in a hand grenade ready to explode. It was much better to be the one to decide when the time was right to set it off. The only problem was that right now it was Tiphaine keeping the pin in place.

# CHAPTER
## 53

For a few seconds Tiphaine enjoyed the echoing silence of the house after Sylvain and Milo's departure. The sound of solitude, with fear her only companion—a fear she had never felt before, not even eight years earlier. Now the risk had turned from a threat to a nightmare.

She sat for a while staring at the front door, through which the two people she loved most in the world had just disappeared. The house creaked, making strange sounds, almost crystalline, as if she were in a palace. It was a warm evening, and she felt a film of sultry heat spreading over her, damp and slightly sticky, heady too, a faintly rank, cloying smell. She had a nasty taste in her mouth, like reflux.

And just above her head the shadow of a man swinging from the end of a cord.

How had she ever thought she could escape the demons of her conscience?

All of a sudden she stood up. She walked into the living room and over to the bookshelf with a determined step, and drew out Gérard Depardieu's documents, which she had concealed in a row of books. The documents basically accused her and Sylvain of having been, if not the instigators, at the very least implicated in three deaths, one disguised as a heart attack and the other two as suicides. She went out into the entryway, absentmindedly caressing the documents' smooth surface, and up the stairs to Milo's bedroom, where she glanced around before eventually deciding on the bed.

She carefully placed the pile of documents on Milo's pillow, in plain sight. She felt as if a vise gripping her throat had miraculously loosened, or a deep gulp of oxygen were being drawn into the lungs of a drowning man. It was like shuffling off a great weight that couldn't be supported any longer. Tiphaine took a step back, then another, turned around and lost her balance from this strange lightness of being. She staggered out the door and into the hallway almost as though she were fleeing, and clung to the banister so as not to fall.

When she got downstairs she gave herself a few moments to pull herself together. This was not the time to fall apart. She focused all her attention on the next step, how events were going to unfold, the order in which everything needed to happen. The next step.

The telephone.

Tiphaine selected Nora's name from her contacts and called the number. It rang five times before her neighbor answered. The first and second were the time it took Nora to locate her cell phone, the third to digest that it was Tiphaine who was calling, the fourth to hesitate, the fifth to decide to answer.

"Tiphaine?" Nora's voice sounded crisp, hostile, assured.

"We need to talk."

"I'm listening."

"Not on the phone. We need to see each other. Face-to-face. We can't live next door to each other in a permanent state of hostility. We need to talk things through once and for all."

"What do you mean by 'once and for all'?" Nora asked sarcastically.

Tiphaine sighed. "Listen, Nora . . . I don't know what was going on in your husband's mind, but what's in those documents is a web of lies."

Nora's response was a skeptical silence.

"If you look closely, if you analyze everything he says, none of it holds up," Tiphaine went on, sounding a little weary.

"And Maxime?"

This time it was Tiphaine who didn't respond.

"That's Sylvain's and my business," she said after a pause. "So, shall we get on with it?"

There was silence at the other end of the line. Nora seemed to be considering Tiphaine's proposal. She weighed up the pros and cons, torn between the desire to deal with an untenable situation and her genuine fear of her neighbor.

"There's no way you're setting foot in my place."

"I wasn't planning to," Tiphaine retorted. "You come to me."

Nora couldn't stop herself from a scornful exclamation. "Do you think I'd be dumb enough to go over to you on my own?"

"What are you afraid of, Nora? That I'll kill you?" Tiphaine let out a wry laugh. "That's absurd! If anything were to happen to you, don't you think after our love scene the other night in front of the two cops I'd be the principal suspect?"

At the other end of the line, Nora's dismay was palpable: the argument had hit home. Tiphaine said, "In fact, I'd better make damn sure nothing happens to you in the next few days."

Another silence. Tiphaine was waiting. Savoring her victory, no doubt. Reveling in Nora's hesitation and confusion.

"Sylvain isn't here," she said. "Nor Milo. We'll be on our own."

"I can't come right away. I have to put Nassim to bed."

"I'll see you at eight thirty."

Another brief silence.

"Great. See you then." Tiphaine ended the call with a satisfied smile and looked at her watch. It was a quarter to eight.

She put her phone in her pocket, went back into the kitchen, opened the cupboard beneath the sink where she stored her cleaning products, and pulled out a plastic bag hidden behind a bottle of detergent that held a long, thin object, which she removed carefully and put on the kitchen table. It was Nora's knife. The one Tiphaine had picked out from the others in the drawer in her neighbor's kitchen. She picked up a knife sharpener and carefully moved the already honed blade back and forth on the hard, rough surface. She felt the blade several times, stroking it carefully with the tip of her thumb. When she was satisfied with the result she carefully laid it back on the table.

That done, she walked through the dining room and opened the door onto the deck, then went upstairs to put on her pajamas. Her footsteps echoed through the house like a heart beating out the ineluctable rhythm of fate. She put her phone on her bedside table, went to the bathroom to wash her face and brush her teeth, then climbed into bed. She felt time dripping, drop by drop, into the well of memory, onto each stone, each level, tears splashing on each floor of her life, flooding it with images long banished from her mind. She closed her eyes and immersed herself entirely in the warm waters of memory.

At 8:40, the doorbell rang.

Tiphaine jerked awake as if being roused from a bad dream. She was bathed in sweat. She sat up in bed, heart pounding.

Back to reality . . .

The next step.

She picked up her phone and dialed the police. Before it had even finished the first ring, Didier Parmentier, the duty officer, picked up.

"You've reached the police. How may I help?"

# CHAPTER
## 54

Tiphaine opened the door to find Nora standing on the front step in a wool jacket, her arms crossed and her eyes dark. If she was surprised to see Tiphaine in pajamas, she didn't show it—that was the least of her worries. She nodded a brief greeting and came inside. Tiphaine stepped back to let her pass and closed the door.

Inside the entryway, Nora turned to Tiphaine to ask her the one thing she was desperate to know. "What are you planning to do with Gérard's file?" she said, unable to conceal her gnawing anxiety. As far as Tiphaine was concerned, the case was closed, and she had no desire for it to be reopened. It was a detail that had no part to play in the next steps of her revenge. But Nora's concern amused her.

"What was it doing in your house?" she said with a sardonic smile.

"It's not the original file," Nora lied with aplomb. "It's a copy. One of several, as far as I know. Gérard came by to give it to me before he saw you. Just in case."

"Is that so!" Tiphaine laughed mockingly. She didn't believe a word of it. "So did Gérard always keep multiple copies of his files?"

"Of course," said Nora.

"But no one knows where Gérard is."

"Maybe so. But his secretary is at the office. And she knows all about his cases."

If the situation hadn't been so critical, Tiphaine would have burst out laughing out of pity for Nora. But even in the face of such naïveté she felt hollow, ravaged by the emptiness that had swallowed up the very last crumbs of forgotten emotion. Her heart was beating abnormally slowly. As if, with each beat, it was hesitating to generate the next. As if it were going to come slowly to a stop. Emotional torpor. Sensory lethargy.

Tiphaine shook herself. There wasn't much time, she'd already lost precious seconds, and the police would be there any minute.

"Shall we go into the kitchen?" she suggested, cutting short the pointless debate. Walking ahead of her neighbor, she made her way down the corridor. Nora followed, feeling uncomfortable: Tiphaine didn't seem convinced by her story of multiple copies of the documents.

Tiphaine walked to the kitchen table, on which sat Nora's knife, gleaming and sharp. She stopped and turned to her neighbor, who took a couple of seconds to notice the knife, then frowned when she recognized it as hers, and looked at Tiphaine, confused.

"That's my knife."

"I borrowed it from you the other day when I was babysitting Nassim. I've been meaning to give it back to you."

She sounded slightly bored, as if she were reciting a text she'd learned by heart. By heart but without soul. She felt like she no longer had a heart or a soul. The two women stood on either side of the knife. Tiphaine didn't take her eyes off it. There was no menace in her eyes, just a faint dislike. She seemed bloodless, as if she had been emptied, almost absent, already gone.

"Here you go, take it," she said, pushing the knife toward Nora.

Nora felt the grip of fear tightening. She stepped back, drawing a grimace from Tiphaine, a baleful smile, a grin that was half absurd, half comical. As Nora watched her with growing distrust, Tiphaine stepped back to reassure her neighbor about her intentions.

"Take it, for heaven's sake!" she said angrily. "We're not going to spend the evening staring at a knife. I'm just giving it back to you."

Nora tried to take control of the situation, to avoid making a mistake or a misstep. A few moments before, she'd been terrified of seeing her knife in Tiphaine's hand, and now that Tiphaine said she wanted to give it back to her, it seemed that picking it up was the last thing she ought to do. What was Tiphaine planning? Why would she give her rival a weapon that could injure her?

Bright blue lights from out on the street blinked through the transom above the front door. Nora wouldn't have paid any attention if Tiphaine hadn't shot a glance in their direction. Her eyes suddenly lit up with a gleam of alarm. She looked fiercely at Nora, then back to the knife. Something unusual was going on. The situation was becoming absurd. Tiphaine was trying to get Nora to pick up the knife, but it was this very persistence that kept her from doing so.

The lights in the street were growing brighter. The two women heard car doors slamming, voices coming closer. Tiphaine was growing nervous and agitated, as if her body had suddenly received an electric charge of unpleasant emotions.

Aggressive.

"Are you going to take it or not, yes or no?"

Suddenly Nora understood. Tiphaine was planning to get rid of her by claiming legitimate self-defense. She was trying to get her to pick up the knife so she could prove that. It would appear Nora was threatening her. It all made sense now. Here she was in Tiphaine's kitchen, which was proof that she had instigated the meeting, not the other way around. It was her knife, so it would seem as if she had brought it with her. Here was Tiphaine in pajamas, a clear sign she wasn't expecting a visitor. She was the intruder, the danger, the threat. Nora had walked straight into the lion's den. Done precisely what Tiphaine had wanted her to.

Except she hadn't picked up the knife.

Nora took a step back, which seemed to trigger a swift change of mood in Tiphaine. Everything happened very fast after that. She barely had time to take it in.

The doorbell rang, shattering the silence, like a signal to escape.

Tiphaine glared at her for a split second.

There was a fleeting moment when everything began to spin out of control. The next moment, Tiphaine moved to the table, grabbed the knife by the handle, and ran toward Nora, the weapon pointing straight at her heart. Nora held her arms in front of her chest in an instinct for survival.

Voices called out from behind the front door. Instructions. Orders. Then loud, repeated knocks.

Nora anticipated the pain of the blade sinking savagely into her flesh. She held back a cry of panic, wanted to move, to get away, but found both her body and her mind paralyzed by terror. There stood Tiphaine, knife in hand, the blade a few centimeters away from her chest . . .

There were noises, policemen's voices on the other side of the door, so close, but they couldn't intervene to save her. There was the light turning, blue, bright, cold . . . a blinking light giving rhythm to the impulses of an obsessive delirium.

Nora saw herself lost, felt her body being emptied of its life-blood, about to suffer, to die.

"Police, open up!"

And then . . .

And then nothing. No pain. No terrifying sensations except those provoked by a mind ravaged by fear. Nothing unpleasant, except Tiphaine's cold fingers gripping her wrists, forcing her to open her hands . . . What was she doing? Why didn't she just kill her?

Outside, cops were banging on the door, as if they were hammering her thoughts with stupid questions. Tiphaine was so close now that Nora could feel her breath on her cheeks.

"Open the door or we're going to break it down!"

Now Nora could feel the touch of the knife. But instead of the icy shock of the blade on her skin, it was the handle that she felt slipping into her hand, and Tiphaine forcing her to close her fingers around it. She couldn't react, paralyzed by the noises, the knocking, the flashing lights, her rival's face, Tiphaine's eyes staring into hers, holding her attention for as long as she could. As though trying to divert her mind from her hand. From the knife that was now pointing at Tiphaine's heart.

The front door rattled and there was a loud crash, at the same moment that Nora, standing there with the knife in her hand, realized that Tiphaine was about to throw herself at her. She felt a resistance, like an awkward obstacle between their two bodies, then her neighbor coming at her and throwing herself at her with all her weight. Something hot and slightly sticky was spreading over her hands.

A second crash, more violent still, made the foundations of the house tremble.

Tiphaine was leaning against Nora and moaning. Her eyes were rolled back yet somehow she still held Nora's terrified, uncomprehending gaze. She gave her a beatific smile, and as she parted her lips, blood trickled out.

The front door burst open with a resounding crash.

Nora turned to the source of the noise and saw two policemen rushing into the house; she looked back at Tiphaine, who was slowly slipping to the ground, held upright only by the knife, whose handle Nora was clutching in her hands, planted deep into her chest. It had gone right through her rib cage. As life leached out of her in ragged gasps, Tiphaine clung to Nora's gaze, drawing from her neighbor's horror the strength to smile, despite the blood and the almost unbearable pain.

"At last," she murmured with a smile twisted by a sort of appalling ecstasy.

"Put your hands in the air," yelled a policeman, pointing his gun at Nora.

Horrified, she dropped the knife and obeyed.

Tiphaine collapsed to the ground at her feet.

The policemen ran to Nora, grabbed her, yanked her hands behind her back, handcuffed her, and then pulled her away from the body sprawled on the ground. Just before she was led out of the kitchen, Nora threw one last glance at Tiphaine. As she lay there, eyes open but unseeing, the mask of hatred slipped from her face and, at last, she looked at peace.

# EPILOGUE

A neighborhood in a Parisian suburb. A calm street lined with houses, havens of peace where families come together in the evening after work and school. A place of safety, where life is good. Few passersby, little noise, no drama. A refuge.

A window onto happiness.

And then, sometimes, in one of these outwardly tranquil houses, a drama bursts out, shattering the facade of serenity. Fate, uninvited, knocks at the door, disrupting the quietude of the place, which the day before had seemed immutable. A blow of fate so unreal that its suddenness leaves everyone stunned.

Impossible.

Alerted by the unusual sound of police sirens and the ominous glow of blue flashing lights, the residents of the street open their front doors and post themselves in front of their houses as if to protect them from the spreading stench of misfortune. It's as though they want to forbid access, as if adversity is contagious. They observe, curiously trying to figure out what's happened.

Reassured by the presence of police officers, they cautiously walk over to the house and gather around the site of the disaster. They have plenty of things to say about the scourge of society, and plenty of judgments to make about the guilty party, who is now no longer a part of their world.

Details of the drama seep out of numbers 26 and 28, rue Edmond-Petit. Open doors, forensics officers coming in and out, police tape. Residents rubbernecking outside the two houses, trying to disentangle the arcana of this dark story. In the first house, the bloody corpse of a woman lies on the cold tiles of the kitchen floor. In the second, another woman, hands covered in blood, is protesting her innocence at the top of her voice. Between the victim and the guilty, a wall of silence, unhappiness, and lies. Of betrayal.

Outside, the neighbors form a crowd, everyone trying to glean information, pass on rumors.

"It's that new woman from number twenty-six, she's stabbed Madame Geniot!"

People shout and exclaim. No one can believe it. They hold their hands to their mouths in shock. Their eyes widen. Their features freeze in expressions of horror.

"It can't be true!"

"My God!"

Some make the sign of the cross.

And then people start to talk. First in brief sentences. To explain. Because they know, of course. They've figured it all out already.

"Those people. It's in their blood. It's part of their nature."

The echo swells to become a rumor that can only grow. "I never liked that woman. Fancied she was the Queen of Sheba, she did."

"You can say what you like, but it's always the same people causing all the trouble."

And off the words fly, taking with them the scandal whose crumbs they will scatter on streets farther and farther away.

Before long a car pulls up and the driver hurriedly double-parks. It's Mathilde. She gets out, looking utterly stunned, and runs straight into the officer guarding Nora's house.

"Let me in. I am Nora Amrani's friend. I've come to get her children."

"Ah yes, I was told you were coming," he says and steps aside to allow her in. She enters the house, walks through the entryway, is stopped by another policeman, shows her identity card. She is led into the living room. Inès and Nassim are sitting on the sofa, their cheeks shiny with tears. Alongside them is a woman trying to comfort them. Mathilde rushes over and puts an arm around each child. She whispers soft, soothing, reassuring words. The woman stands up and introduces herself: she's a police investigator. She tells Mathilde to take the children away.

"What about Nora, where is she?"

"She's in the kitchen right now. But she'll be going down to the station pretty soon."

Out in the street, more neighbors have joined the crowd. Madame Appleblossom is sitting on her folding chair; she has been there from the beginning. She has seen it all. And she has a great deal to tell.

Suddenly the buzz of speculation dies away, like the volume on a radio being turned down. Heads turn, throats tighten, people move aside. Sylvain and Milo make their way slowly through the crowd, following a path that opens up almost naturally. Silence precedes them. They see all these familiar faces, eyes lowered as they pass. Milo twists his head to look over the crowd, torn by the desire to know and the fear of finding out. His front door is wide open, there's a policeman guarding the entrance. The same with the house next door . . .

Out of which emerge Mathilde and Nassim, with Inès just behind them, her eyes red with crying, her body shaking with sobs. Their eyes meet. And what Milo sees in her expression crushes him into a thousand pieces. Shatters him. Rips him apart. She looks at him with such desperation that he feels hammered by her suffering. He does not know what's happened, all he knows is that disaster has struck again. Something indescribably terrible. He had been warned against love. He shudders, cannot take his eyes off Inès. He wants to run to her, take her in his arms, hold her tight. But it's as if the ground has opened up, revealing between the two houses a bottomless chasm enclosing an impassable mire.

Night is falling on the neighborhood, plunging its inhabitants into darkness. Sylvain follows Milo, his heart clenching as he, too, tries to understand: the crowd of onlookers, the police guarding his house. They reach the front door, tell the police who they are. And just as they are about to go inside, a great clamor arises from the midst of the onlookers. Out of the house next door, framed by two policemen, Nora emerges in handcuffs and is led to one of the unmarked cars. She walks unsteadily, keeping her head down. Sylvain is rooted to the spot, his eyes fixed on her. Blinded by terror, crushed under the weight of the calumny, she doesn't see him. She passes right in front of him. He wants to reach his hand out to her, say her name, pull her out of this unfathomable nightmare. But he is paralyzed by fear, unable to move or produce the slightest sound. Nora walks past him, following the police officer without resistance, allowing herself to be drawn toward the darkness of her improbable future, her life in tatters, devoured by the inevitable.

"Monsieur Geniot?"

Sylvain winces. He stops staring at Nora, who is now only a silhouette in the distance, about to be swallowed up by the crowd, and turns to the police investigator, who invites him to follow her. Her expression is filled with compassion. He complies, looking haggard, already knowing that whatever he is about to find out will cast him once again into the depths of horror.

Gradually the street empties. Tiphaine's body is taken away. The police leave the scene of the crime. The neighbors disperse in clusters, anonymous figures returning to the comfort of their humdrum lives. Calm returns to this peaceful street in a residential neighborhood lined with family houses; havens of tranquility where people return in the evening after a day at work or school. A good place to live. Not much traffic, quiet, uneventful. A place of safety.

Milo and Sylvain are alone now, drowning in the silence of the house. Stunned by what has happened. Milo is lying curled up on the sofa staring at an imaginary point in front of him. Sylvain is standing at the window that looks out onto the yard. Probing the darkness outside, eaten up with misery and bewilderment. His eyes skim the shadows of the night, he stares at the outlines of the trees and the bushes, follows the indentations of leaves faintly lit up by a ray of moonlight. He has no idea that at the bottom of the garden, behind the row of bushes, Gérard Depardieu's corpse is slowly decomposing beneath a pile of compost.

"I'm cold," says Milo suddenly. He gets to his feet and takes a few steps toward the entryway.

"Where are you going?" asks Sylvain in a tight voice.

"To fetch a sweater."

"Let me, I'll go."

Milo doesn't need persuading. He slumps back on the sofa and curls up in a fetal position, and it is Sylvain who goes up to the young man's bedroom.

Here ends Barbara Abel's
*After the End.*

The first edition of this book was printed
and bound at Lakeside Book Company
in Harrisonburg, Virgina, in November 2025.

A NOTE ON THE TYPE

The text of this novel was set in Sabon, an old-style serif typeface created by Jan Tschichold between 1964 and 1967. Drawing inspiration from the elegant and highly legible designs of the famed sixteenth-century Parisian typographer and publisher Claude Garamond, the font's name honors Jacques Sabon, one of Garamond's close collaborators. Sabon has remained a popular typeface in print, and it is admired for its smooth and tidy appearance.

HARPERVIA

An imprint dedicated to publishing international voices, offering readers a chance to encounter other lives and other points of view via the language of the imagination.